He stared   er
bottom lip. "I   te
like. You asked ... . your mouth resembled a rose
petal, and I have decided I must know the answer."

Her lips parted in anticipation, and she dared not
breathe for fear the spell would break.

He leaned close, blocking the moonlight above her
as his warm lips covered hers. Afterward, she would
always equate the scent of magnolias with her first kiss,
for they surrounded her along with the duke's heat
beneath the magical night sky.

He slid his firm mouth over hers, searching and
applying gentle pressure while his hands caressed her
face. She could not believe this was happening and
leaned against him, wrapping her arms high around his
neck. His embrace comforted her as no one else had, and
for the first time since Nathan dragged her to London,
she felt safe.

With a groan, he tipped her head to the side. "Open
for me."

She opened her mouth to ask what he meant but
never got the chance, for his tongue slid between her lips
and stroked along hers, sending shivers of delight
through her body.

She trembled against him, wanting each moment to
last for an eternity. The taste of him in her mouth
intoxicated her, and she could not get enough. Her blood
sang, and heat filled her belly.

Praise for Virginia Barlow

"If you're a historical western romance reader, you're going to love Wylder Bachelor. If you're a fan of feisty, independent heroines, pick up Wylder Bachelor. Highly recommend!"

~ N. N. Light's Book Heaven

"I loved this book! Lots of twists and turns, with all the characters getting exactly what they deserved at the final denouement. The chemistry between the main characters was very believable and I loved Emma's grandmother's ghost stepping in to help her. This is a great story and I couldn't put it down."

~ Coconut Macaroon Scandal Net Galley Review

"Fans of both historical romance and paranormal romance will love The Witch of Rathborne Castle. Reminiscent of Jude Deveraux's historicals, The Witch of Rathborne Castle will sweep the reader away. Highly recommend!"

~ N.N. Light's book Heaven

Gamble of Hearts

by

Virginia Barlow

Gamble of Hearts

Cover Art by *Jennifer Greeff*

The Wild Rose Press, Inc.
PO Box 708
Adams Basin, NY 14410-0708
Visit us at www.thewildrosepress.com

Publishing History
First Edition, 2023
Trade Paperback ISBN 978-1-5092-4794-3
Digital ISBN 978-1-5092-4795-0

Published in the United States of America

Dedication

For Cora. You kept me going when I was young and got me interested in romance…

Best Wishes Chrissy!

Virginia Barlow

Chapter One

London, England
March 1812
Gambling is a trick of the devil designed to lead men to hell. Nothing good can ever come of it.

Lady Amora Hargrove believed her mother's statement true until the first Sunday in March when her older brother, Nathan, commanded she rise at the ungodly hour of three in the morning and come to the sitting room for instructions.

Dressing hurriedly, she reported with trepidation, concerned the trio of lecherous friends her brother invited over the previous evening might still be about.

Her older sibling inherited the title of Earl of Hargrove at age twenty-two, five years earlier, upon their father's death. Preferring London, his friends, and drinking to any responsibility their father wished him to accept, he ignored her existence and left her for the servants to care for at their country estate.

Everything changed the year she turned eighteen. Nathan arrived unannounced and dragged her to London to live with him in his townhouse outside Mayfair. Confused over his sudden interest in her well-being, she assumed her brother missed her.

Her first indication things were not as she thought came when he tossed a deck of cards at her the first night and demanded she play with one of the men he brought home. His choice of friends haled from the dregs of society, and his insistence she remain in the room with such filth shocked her.

When she refused, Nathan struck her, sending her sprawling face-first onto the parlor floor, followed by the first beating of many.

Papa taught her to play cards as a maid when Mama left to go calling. Mathematically inclined, she ran the odds of potential hands in her head following each round of betting and studied her opponent's mannerisms to determine who held a prospective win. Papa's gentlemen friends thought the matter a grand lark and tossed in their advice, as well. When she grew so skilled they could no longer beat her, they taught her to play Brag and any other new games they picked up. Papa would smile, call her a "natural," and give her sweets when she won.

She had no idea the games were evil until Mama returned home early one teatime and discovered their secret. She promptly put an end to the situation, saying if Amora played again, she would end up in hell or worse, a spinster, for no good man would offer for her. She did not touch a card again, at least not in front of either parent but kept her games for the privacy of her chamber or a clandestine late-night row down in the servants' hall when her parents were out.

Amora believed her days of playing in the open were over until her brother requested she play her first night in London. Not wanting to die a spinster or go to hell, she refused, and his violent treatment afterward came as quite a shock following her sheltered country life. For not only did he drag her out to seedy, smoke-filled taverns twice a week thereafter and force her to play cards, he also required her to wait on him and his friends or suffer his wrath. After two weeks, she revisited her decision. Hell seemed a welcome retreat to the life she lived with Nathan.

This Sunday morning, when she arrived in the sitting room, peeking with caution around the door to determine if she should bring the fire poker for protection, Nathan commanded she collect everything of value in their little townhouse.

"Stack it beside the kitchen door in the servants' quarters, and hurry, or you will wish you had." His growl sent shivers down her spine. Her brother outweighed her by a least ten stones and stood a head taller than her five foot five. Dark skinned with black hair, his once athletic form grew bulky with excessive drink, rich food, and lack of exercise. Dull black eyes stared at her until she nodded and hurried away to collect candlesticks and snuff boxes.

"Are we leaving?" Amora lifted her gaze to his flushed face when she passed him in the corridor, wincing when he caught her arm and twisted it behind her back.

"Never you mind. Keep gathering everything you see and do as you are told for once." He threw her from him as he stalked away, yelling for his valet, John.

Amora rose from the floor, righting her woolen skirt and tugging her long sleeves over the bruises on her wrists. After a year and a half of living with Nathan and his black, alcohol-induced temper, she picked her battles with careful consideration. This battle she would not win, so after setting her burden beside the kitchen door, she retraced her steps to the sitting room and removed paintings from the walls.

The sharp knock on their front door took her by surprise. Who in their right mind visited in the wee hours of the morning? Half-expecting her brother's newest trollop, she sucked in a breath of dismay at the elegant gentleman in the black cape and tall hat standing outside on the stoop. Dropping her chin to hide her features as best she could in the circumstances, she stepped back to allow him entrance.

The stranger's presence could only be described as magnificent, from the top of his windswept black hair, past the glittering blue of his eyes, to the intricate knot of his snowy white cravat, and down the immaculate tailoring of his evening clothes and ending with the high shine of his boots. The scent of lemon, bay leaf, and musk clung to his clothes and filled her senses.

Amora swallowed and dipped a curtsy. "Good morning, sir." This caliber of gentleman never crossed their threshold.

The ice-blue eyes swept over her, dismissing her. "Is the earl at home?"

"Of course. Please come in, and I will tell him you are here. Who may I say is calling?"

The man's gaze rested on the stacks of portraits against the wall and swept to the pile of tapestries laying on the red velvet settee. His full lips twisted. "Tell him the Duke of Ravencroft is here to collect his winnings." Stepping into the little sitting room, he unclasped his cloak and handed it to her as he inspected the interior of the room.

She closed the door and stared, ignoring her shaking knees. *Winnings? Please tell me Nathan was not so foolish as to place a bet with the duke.* Her brother had no feel for the game and cheated to make up for his lack of skill.

Hanging the cloak on the hook beside the door, she risked a glance at their caller's impassive face, careful to keep her own averted. She had no wish to see the disgust in his eyes the first glimpse of her face created in people unused to her reflection.

Her heart thundered like a runaway horse as she peeked at him beneath her lashes.

Everyone knew of the duke with his wealth and power. The most sought-after bachelor in England had the king's ear and many a lady's heart. Her mother's friends used to gossip about him as a young man when they called for tea before her mother's illness made it difficult for her to leave her bed. Mama would stir in her grave if she knew who called so early in the morning.

Amora stiffened her spine and turned away, anxious to escape the duke's notice. "I shall fetch him." With her chin down, she rounded the corner of the corridor and collided with her brother. "Nathan, I did not see—"

"Out of my way! John informed me a strange phaeton tooled up our street moments ago. Grab the rest of the things and take them downstairs. I do not have time—" Her bother shoved past her and stopped cold when he entered the sitting room.

The tension in the air crackled with animosity. "Good morning, Hargrove. Are you leaving on an unexpected trip?" The duke's cold voice challenged her brother.

Amora shivered to the soles of her leather shoes, where she stood behind her sibling.

"Your grace, what are you doing here? I told you I would meet you at my lawyers at ten." Her brother's voice held a tinge of fear, and she stared at his back in surprise.

A bully since the day his wet nurse weaned him, Nathan never backed down. Why would he be frightened unless….?

Her brother left for his gentleman's club, White's, to gamble not long after she retired every evening. His horse's hooves clattered on the cobblestone road as he rode away, and she breathed a sigh of relief, thankful to be spared more loud, raucous laughter and lewd jokes.

A frown wrinkled her brow as she studied the men. Nathan must have lost, and the duke come to collect. Shaking her head over the situation, she sighed. No matter how often she recited the rules of the games and practiced with him, her brother had not the natural talent she possessed.

Amora clasped her hands together, uncertain if she should go or stay. Whatever her brother lost involved her, too. Curious, she wanted to hear this conversation, but then she could do without the attention her presence might draw.

The duke must have strolled forward, his footsteps silent as he approached. Only his cologne and the nearness of his voice gave away his change in position. "I suspected you might try to run, and by the looks of things, I am right. You are a liar and a cheat, Hargrove, and will be banned from every club in London once word of your cowardice and thievery becomes known."

Amora gasped and peeked around her brother.

Satisfaction gleamed in their visitor's eyes as he spoke.

A band tightened around her chest as she considered her brother's reckless behavior of late. "What did you lose, Nathan?" Her quiet voice filled the silence.

Trepidation filled her belly, and a dark foreboding blanketed her in a sense of unreality.

"Everything." The duke's deep voice rumbled in the silence. "The earl lost it all to me last night. He is ruined." Blue eyes studied her brother's face. "How does it feel to know you have nothing? To know you risked it all on the turn of a card and lost? No one will extend you credit or lend a hand after the way you cheated and lost. They all know about the extra cards in your vest and your weighted dice. You have nowhere to go, Hargrove, and nowhere to run." He indicated the pile of portraits and tapestries. "The constables surrounding the house will be interested in these."

The duke's revelations dropped her to her knees. *Everything? He lost the family's entire fortune? What of Hargrove Manor? What of their country estate and this townhouse? What of the land?* Her brother's insistence she teach him tricks when they played now made sense. "Surely, we have something of value to pay your grace for what he lost."

"Be silent." Nathan's roar sent shivers down her spine. He did not spare her a glance but kept his gaze on their visitor. "You misjudge me, your grace. I thought to collect the wealth and make it easier for you to catalog. I have no plans to leave, and if you give me a little time, I shall have everything in order for you."

The ingratiating tone of Nathan's voice set her teeth on edge. His demeanor told her he planned to leave the country and abandon her to face his mess.

She knew the earl's fascination at the tables would bring them more harm than good and told him so one evening when he left with his foul-mouthed friends for the seventh night in a row. She received a split lip and a black eye for her trouble.

"Then you will not mind if I invite the constables in, and we go over the list together." The soft-spoken words chilled her to the bone as the duke swung the door open, and the sitting room filled with police.

Amora took advantage of the duke's turned back and whispered to her brother. "What about my dowry?" Before their father passed, he drew up a document setting aside a sizable amount of gold for her dowry. "Perhaps I could play…"

The earl turned in fury. "You will be silent. Even if the duke condescended to play a woman, which he will not, we have nothing of value to play with. And for God's sake, keep your mouth shut about Pudding Lane, or I will take a lash to you."

She sucked in a breath at the threat in his glare and snapped her mouth shut. Amora slipped past him into the sitting room and sank onto a settee, keeping her chin down. A sinking feeling filled her belly. The way Nathan avoided the question about her dowry meant he no longer had it.

"Shall we begin?" The duke cleared his throat and withdrew a paper from his jacket pocket. "We start with the titles to Hargrove Manor, your country estate, and London townhouse."

Anger and fear took turns twisting the knot in her belly. How could Nathan be such a fool as to lose everything? Amora listened as the duke read items on his list, and the constables collected what they could. A lot of the wealth remained at Hargrove Manor and the country estate, places she would never see again. Uncertainty formed a knot in her throat. She had no relatives other than Nathan and no money to go anywhere on her own. Freedom and terror tugged at her heart. No longer would she be subject to her brother's violent outbursts or crude friends. But then, neither would she have a warm bed or food to eat. Disquiet dropped her head until a noise behind her caught her attention.

She turned as three more police escorted her brother's valet into the sitting room in handcuffs. "We found this man loading valuables into a cart and brought him in."

The duke nodded. "Good work."

They arrested her brother a minute later. Five constables held him down while two more applied handcuffs. Only the threat of a longer prison time kept him quiet.

When they finished, the duke continued with his list.

Amora took in the whole scene with a sense of surreal fascination, wondering how her life came to this. Her mother's sudden illness and death came weeks after her father's accident, leaving her at the mercy of her violent older sibling at the tender age of fourteen. Thank goodness, Nurse demanded she stay in the country when her brother left for the cesspools of London. Then her quiet life ended when he forced her here. All the drunken nights of debauchery and extravagance, followed by moments of quiet when her brother spent the weekend or a fortnight at some unknown lord's country estate over the last few years, flittered through her mind. These occasions preceded a flurry of dinner parties, nights at the theater, and a new mistress.

Even though she witnessed the gaudy jewels and luxurious gifts her brother showered on these women, she had a hard time grasping how he could have lost their entire family's wealth.

"You are no better than me, Ravencroft. I know how you followed me around and lured me to the tables or the races for one more bet. You kept dangling a golden prize before my eyes, and all of it led to this moment. You planned my downfall and set out to ruin me. Admit your part in this charade. Do not accuse me of lying and cheating when you have done the same. I demand the duke be arrested, too."

Silence followed Nathan's outburst until the duke lowered the paper he held and stared at the earl. "I did plan your downfall and ruin with meticulous care. I spent months studying your card games and following you from one race or table to another. How do you think I know about the weights in your dice, the card holder up your sleeve, or the extra cards in your vest? I allowed you into my inner circle to feed your thirst to win and drew you in one throw of the dice and deck of cards at a time until our final match last evening. You could not admit defeat, although I offered a way out several times. The culmination of months of effort teetered on the turn of a card. Your card. And now I have everything I came for, except the one item you threw on the pile to even the ante for the last draw. Your pride and greed made you desperate, and so I allowed you to wager this item without checking for value or accuracy for this very moment."

Her brother glanced around at the waiting constables. "He is as guilty as I am. You heard his confession. Arrest him."

"His grace has not broken any laws." The lead bobby glowered from his position beside the duke. "He charges you with attempted robbery of his possessions."

"The items you speak of belong to my family, not to me; therefore, they cannot be claimed." The earl roared in fury.

"Lost in a wager signed by your hand and witnessed by several lords at White's. As the current earl, your signature is all the requirement needed to make my claim legitimate." The duke's bored tone of voice angered her brother further.

"They have been part of Hargrove for generations."

"Then you should not wager them away." The duke withdrew a folded sheet of paper from his jacket pocket.

"You have not even opened my last ante or read what is inside?" Disbelief crossed Nathan's face, followed by a sneer of contempt. "You are rich beyond reason. What is one man's fortune and ruin to you?" The words echoed in the silent room.

"Everything, while to you, nothing. Do you remember Lord Edward Baxter?" The duke's silky voice spoke volumes. Fury flashed from his brilliant blue eyes as he glared at Nathan.

The hair on the back of Amora's neck stood on end. She stared at the folded note in the duke's hand. Foreboding filled her stomach with butterflies and the need to be sick. Every item they possessed had been listed except her dowry.

"Lord Baxter?" Her brother shook his head and then stopped. "Oh yes. The stupid young man with the dark curly hair." Nathan laughed aloud. "What a gullible fool he turned out to be. A man so young has no business with so much money. The law of equality begged me to set matters right and relieve him of his wealth. Poor sod. He believed everything I told him and filled my pockets on several occasions."

"Do you know anything about him other than his bank balance?" the duke asked.

"The word among the Ton is he jumped from London bridge with a rope around his neck. Is he what this is all about? Because if it is, he had it coming. If I did not take his wealth, someone else would."

Amora sucked in a breath at the raw fury in the duke's eyes.

"Lord Edward Baxter was *my nephew*, only son to my widowed older sister, the Marchioness Esme Baxter." His statement hung in the air, pinning Amora to her seat.

Her blood froze. *Oh God! What had Nathan done?* Lightheaded, she dropped her gaze to the floor. A heavy stone filled her belly, and a lump formed in her throat.

Her brother recognized his mistake too late. "Oh, uh, I did not know. Look, there is no need for all of this." He waved his hand at the piles around the room. "I will apologize to your sister, and we can discuss this whole affair man to man—"

"No." A wealth of anger and contempt accompanied the single word. "My sister has not been the same since the day her son confessed how much he owed you. Frantic, alone, and without the means to pay, she sent for me. After listening to the tale of his downfall, I met his debt with the condition he never gamble again. But then, you persuaded him to come to Bath, where you crucified him with guilt and set him up to take the blame for your cheating, making him responsible for the debts you accumulated there. The boy could not hold his head up in polite society for the tales you told of him, and his pride would not let him ask me for more. He gave his word and took the only way out he could see. His death

12

nearly killed my sister, and with his death, she lost her home to her dead husband's second cousin, who succeeded my nephew to the title. She now resides with me and cares for my aging mother. Her eyes are dulled with the pain of loss, and my mother has not left the house since the boy's death. I am here for one reason, to avenge my sister and her son. I will show you the same mercy you showed them."

Amora gasped as the sharp pain of empathy twisted her heart in two. She had no idea things were so bad and rose to her feet so she could slip away to her chamber where she could think.

The duke glanced at her. "I will not tolerate trollops on my property. Gather your things and get out. This house belongs to me, now."

She swallowed. "But I am not—"

"Out."

Gulping, she turned on her heel and crept from the room. Now what? Where could she go?

Behind her, the duke asked. "So, tell me about your last wager. We have everything accounted for but the last item. My men are taking possession of the other properties as we speak and cataloging them. You bragged the value of this wager more than any on the table." The crisp sound of paper being unfolded followed. "What is Amora? Have you a ship?"

Disbelief, terror, and then anger raced through her. Turning on her heel, she stomped back into the sitting room, where she rounded on her brother, forgetting her bruised and broken features. Glaring, she faced him with her head high and her hands fisted at her side. "You bet *me* on a game of cards?"

Nathan's gaze narrowed on the duke as he peered over her head. "Your grace," he sneered. "Meet my sister, Amora."

Chapter Two

The duke stiffened. Disbelief and fury raced through him. The private investigators he employed made no mention of a sister. They came highly recommended but failed to deliver the thoroughness he required. Making a mental note to address the issue on the morrow, he glared at the Earl of Hargrove. Only the lowest reprobate alive would barter his blood to even an ante. "Get him out of my sight!" *The earl had a sister! How could they miss this important piece of information?*

Amora's ramrod-straight spine and furious voice echoed his own thoughts. "How could you?"

The constables dragged the earl to the front door, ignoring his eerie laugh. "Do not worry, sister dear, I have plans for you. The duke shall not have you for long."

"What do you mean?" She turned to stare after her brother, and the duke got a good look at her face for the first time.

Her features were puffy and twisted, with one eye swollen shut. Bruises and cuts covered her face, some old, some new, making it difficult to determine how the girl looked. Rage roared in his veins. Who could hurt a woman to this extent? He itched to administer the same wounds to the scoundrel she called brother.

The top of the girl's head came to his shoulder. Thin and frail, she wilted when she turned to face him.

"My lady, I admit, this piece of information took me off guard. I had no report of your existence and thought you to be a ship or some such item. Allow me to start anew. I am Alexander Xavier Remington, Duke of Ravencroft, at your service. I do apologize for this unseemly mess. Please have a seat and give me a moment to speak to the constable on what should be done for you."

The girl gave a little dip, staring at him with uncertainty and suspicion. "Lady Amora Elizabeth Hargrove, your grace." Her musical voice, cultured words, and gentle manners were the only indication her deportment gave of her noble birth. As her hand brushed the hair from her eyes, he caught sight of the bruising on her wrists.

Anger hummed through him as he cast his gaze over her again.

When she called the earl by his first name, he mistook her for a trollop. Coarse woolen gown with multiple patches, curly dark hair plaited down her back, big blues eyes, and worn-out slippers added to the picture, justifying his impression.

Disgusted with the whole affair, the duke stepped out the door, stopping beside the constable. "What do I do with the sister? It cannot be legal to transfer a lady as if she were property on the tables."

The constable shrugged. "She has no relative and no place to go. Both ye and the earl signed the paper, making ye the legal owner. Ye might want to speak to your legal man, but for now, I would say she is your responsibility."

His rage simmered. "I will take her back to my townhouse and speak with my legal advisor tomorrow."

He planned to spend what remained of the night with a glass of port in memory of his nephew, but the addition of Lady Amora to the mix threw him off. Why did he not know Hargrove had a sister? Employing the best investigators in the business should eradicate errors such as this. Tonight's events were meticulously planned and calculated, and somehow, she slipped through the cracks.

Striding back into the little sitting room, he found the lady sitting where he left her.

"I can take care of myself." Her quiet words drifted up to him.

He shook his head. "Not here. This townhouse is not situated in a good neighborhood, and by now, the neighbors all know the earl has been arrested."

He may not like the situation, but at the same time, he could not leave her defenseless.

Lady Amora winced as she rose to her feet, favoring her left side.

God, did not the earl give a damn about anything or anybody? Compassion twisted his insides. If anyone hurt his sister this way, he would kill them. The more he knew about the Earl of Hargrove, the more unpleasant he found him. "Is there anywhere the bastard did not beat you?"

****

Could her brother bet her in a game of chance and transfer ownership like a racehorse or acre of land? The thought swirled in her belly, making her nauseated. If Nathan paid attention to her instructions instead of cheating, they would not be in this mess. The duke beat Nathan at his own game. So, did she trade one guardian for a worse one?

His voice startled her from her thoughts, and she lifted her gaze to his. For a second, she thought she

17

recognized compassion on his face, and uncertainty made her pause. She could not reply. There was not an inch on her body unmarked by her brother's hands or boots. So, she ignored his question and asked one of her own. "What did the constable say?"

"You are my responsibility until I speak with legal counsel and learn otherwise." His lids dropped over his eyes, shielding his thoughts, but she heard his reluctance nonetheless.

Pride held her head high. "I shall remain here until such time as your legal man gives his advice. I am not as weak as I appear."

His left eyebrow rose. "Your bruises say otherwise. Without a man's protection, you will fall prey to the ruffians who frequent the dark alleys of London. I may not have known of your existence, but your brother's lewd friends do. What do you think they will do when they learn he is in Newgate?"

Amora shivered. She knew, and so did he. Many of Nathan's acquaintances would not doubt come for her.

"I have a spare room at my townhouse and lady's maids to see to your comfort. You shall be safe there. Come. We will sort this out later in the day after you have had some rest and food."

His tone gentled, and he held his arm out to her.

Fear held her still as she considered his proposal.

"Ye have no choice, m'lady. The duke will see no harm comes to ye, and I will check on ye later in the day." The constable nodded from his position inside the front door.

Amora had not realized he entered until he spoke. If the officer knew of her plight and location, the duke could not murder or rape her without consequence. With a heavy heart, she left to pack her few belongings in a battered valise once the property of her mother. Her hand hovered over the heavy, red velvet dress and domino mask Nathan required her to wear on their visits to Pudding Lane. The velvet gown made her appear as a woman of the world, and the mask hid her bruises. She left this life behind when she walked out the door with the duke and would have no further use for the beautiful gown. On impulse, she set the black mask in the middle of the dress and rolled them up before stuffing them in the bottom of her valise. One never knew when a red velvet gown would be required, and since the dress constituted her entire collection of evening wear, she would bring it with her.

The duke waited in the salon for her and upon her return, led her outside to his carriage waiting on the cobblestone road in front of the townhouse. Liveried servants opened the door of the duke's shiny black carriage bearing the gold and red emblem of Remington House and set the foot stool on the ground at her feet. His footman relieved her of her valise and set it on the floor of the conveyance.

Amora paused as this chapter of her existence folded. Surveying the scene, she whispered a quick word of gratitude to the stars for watching over her. Light from the street lanterns flickered over the scene, and a cool breeze blew against her hot cheeks, smelling of coal, smoke, and horses. Silver slices of moon danced across the rooftops and chimneys of the nearby homes. Silence filled the night until the black beasts drawing the duke's magnificent carriage snorted and tossed their heads.

Ready to play the new hand she had been dealt, Amora took the liveried servant's arm and stepped up into the shiny black carriage, sinking back against the red velvet seats with a sigh. She had not enjoyed such luxury since Papa died.

The duke climbed in after her, and his servant closed the door.

"I will stop by later. Good night, your grace." The constable tapped the carriage door and stepped back.

The horses moved off, filling the empty street with the clop of their hooves on the cobblestones, and Amora squirmed inside at the unwelcome intimacy of the closed carriage. The scent of the duke's cologne teased her senses. Dropping her chin, she stared at the floor, uncertain of what to say. The events of the night ran through her mind and stopped. "Does your sister live with you here in London?"

"No. She prefers the quiet of the country since the death of my nephew."

Amora nodded. Well, there perished the thought of having another female close at hand. She knew nothing about the silent man opposite her other than the gossip she heard while in her mother's chamber. What if he turned out to be a scoundrel?

"No harm shall come to you while you are in my home."

She glanced up. "How do you know my thoughts?" Amora took pride in her ability to hide her thoughts and frowned when he guessed the direction her mind took.

His lips twisted in a wry smile. "Your eyes are very expressive." And after a moment. "Not all men treat women as poorly as your brother. My sister and I are quite close. I would kill anyone who threatened her."

"Or her son."

"Yes." Silence filled the carriage. "But in this

instance, I consider revenge a better punishment. If a man never lives with consequence, how does he learn? Death is too quick and merciful an end to compensate for the lives your brother has ruined."

"Are there more?" She did not know if she wanted to hear the answer.

"Three more I know by name, all with the same result. Lord Danby used his father's pistol to end his life, the new Earl of Westgate drowned in the Thames, and Lord Peters rots in prison, unable to pay the exorbitant sum levied against him by men your brother made agreements with using his name and seal."

Their unfamiliar names drifted through her mind. She never played with them on Pudding Lane, so she was not responsible for their downfall, unlike her brother. Nathan must have drawn them in at his club, one of his numerous outings to the country, or the races. Amora closed her eyes as a weight settled in her stomach. "Do the families seek retribution as you have?" Without relatives, a home, or a name, how could she hope to survive or make any of this right?

"They will not seek it from you. They will come to the court to make their claims, and the magistrate will decide what it so be done."

She sat in silence, digesting the sudden turn in her world. Never again would she venture onto Pudding Lane and the smoky tavern of shame. Resolve and relief burned in equal parts in her stomach as her future stretched before her. "Papa set aside a dowry in my name. I do not know if Nathan used the funds, but perhaps you will allow me to access them for my keep if they still exist. I could rent a small place, and the remainder can be dispersed to the families of these other young men."

"I know of no dowry, but if one exists, I shall make it available for you."

For the first time since her parents' death and her sojourn to London, hope of a different life fluttered in her chest.

An hour later, she lay between freshly laundered silk sheets, staring through the large window at the lingering shadows of the night. A fire blazed on the hearth, filling the elegant blue and white chamber with welcome heat. Her night rail enveloped her body in silken delight, and a warm, hearty soup brought by a pretty, little scullery maid warmed her insides.

Amora wiggled and tugged the embroidered coverlet to her chin, warm and full for the first time in a long while.

Her thoughts wandered to the duke. Handsome, masculine, and arrogant, he embodied the essence of wealth and influence. His home reeked of gilded portraits, expensive furnishings, etched gold ceilings, Italian marble floors, and Persian rugs. What could such a man want with more possessions? She realized three things as she evaluated the events of the night.

The first being the duke ruined her brother to gain satisfaction for his sister, proving he cared for his family. Such a man might grant her a small cottage to live in. With her dowry, she would never have to rely on anyone again. The surge of hope she experienced earlier grew and danced through her.

The second being not once the previous night did the duke express disgust or revulsion for her disfigurement. A wrinkle furrowed her brow as she contemplated the novelty of such an idea.

The third one being she could never tell the duke her part in this or where her true skill lie. He would not understand she won on instinct, not by cheating, the way her brother had.

A shiver ran down her spine. Lord, deliver her from being the recipient of the same look of disgust, anger, and hatred he bestowed upon Nathan.

****

"Such a situation has never crossed my path in all my years of practicing law. As the lady's only male relative, the earl signed her over to you. With your signature, you accepted. Without any experience in like circumstances, I recommend you see the magistrate. He will decide what happens with the girl." Sir Reginald straightened in his chair. "I shall send a note over and get you an audience if one can be had. I will let you know one way or the other before the day is through."

"One other thing. Will you investigate a sum of money the late Earl set aside for Lady Amora? She claims he left a dowry for her. I should like to make the money available for her. God knows I have no need of her or her dowry."

"Very good, your grace."

Alexander shook hands with his advisor and returned home.

An hour later, he received a note informing him the magistrate would see them as soon as they could gather at his chambers.

The duke collected Amora and helped her into his carriage, giving the address to his driver.

The girl said nothing and kept her head bowed the entire drive, leaving him to his thoughts.

Alexander stared out the little window as they

passed Hyde Park. The scent of recent rain in fresh cut grass teased his nose. Gentlemen cantered their horses, dressed in immaculate riding breeches, high polished boots, embroidered jackets, and tall hats. Ladies strolled past swirling pastel sunshades and showing off their newest walking gowns while gossiping about the latest scandal. Carriages rumbled along the cobblestone road, filled with fashionable nobility, waving and smiling at those they passed. The women wore elaborate hats adorned with feathers, flowers, jewels, and ribbon. The men wore top hats and mustaches, puffing on their pipes as they inched along Rotten Row. Society put her well-dressed foot forward as if gambling, whoring, cheating, and murder never sullied their lives or the streets of London.

The duke frowned as he glanced at his silent companion, having no idea what to do for her. With no male relative or close family, her plight grew quite tragic. He planned revenge, pure and simple, and not to be saddled with some innocent blue-eyed victim. If things had gone as ordered, he would be on the street showing off Adonis, his new stallion, not on his way to the magistrate to discuss his responsibility to a villain's sister.

The clerk ushered them into the judge's chamber as soon as they arrived.

The magistrate questioned Amora quite extensively on her life in London and the visitors at their townhouse.

Wearing one of his sister Esme's gowns altered to fit her slender form, with her dark curly hair piled high on her head, the girl presented a better picture than she had earlier. Though she answered each question in her soft melodious voice, she stared at the floor, refusing to look up until the magistrate asked her to do so.

Alexander felt her reluctance from his position two feet to the side of her and waited.

The magistrate had the same reaction he did when gazing upon her bruised and broken countenance for the first time. Anger flashed in his eyes, and his mouth tightened.

"Who hit you?"

Amora hesitated for a second. "My brother."

Silence filled the chamber as the judge's eyes assessed her from head to toe.

Leaning forward, the magistrate pinned the duke to the floor with his keen gaze. "You are hereby named legal guardian and custodian of Lady Amora Elizabeth Hargrove and all her effects." He pounded his gavel and rose. "I shall set the trial for the Earl of Hargrove one month from now, giving the other victims' families time to gather evidence and testimony. You will be in attendance with information on his dealings with his sister."

The duke stared at the judge. "Is there no other avenue for Lady Amora?"

His Honor shook his head. "Not unless the lady marries, at which time she becomes her husband's responsibility."

The duke nodded, and the magistrate dismissed them both.

"And if my brother serves his time and is released? What happens then? Do I go back to him?" Amora's soft voice spoke beside the duke as they turned to go.

"He shall never set a hand on you again. I swear it." Alexander promised as he led her from the magistrate's chambers.

He thought on the subject all the way home. With marriage, she would be out of her brother's orbit and off his conscience. But how to make her enticing to the noble men of London would require some thought.

After depositing the girl outside her chamber door, Alexander strode to his study and rang the bell for his man, William, both confidante, and valet. The two had been inseparable since they were in knee breeches. Together they spent the afternoon organizing the whole procedure down to the day. Offering an unheard-of amount of coin as dowry to ease the pain of looking at the poor girl and dressing her in the latest fashion should do the trick. Most men would be drawn to her money rather than the grotesque frail creature in the wedding gown. The duke figured one London season should be sufficient time to see the plan through and retired to change for dinner.

****

Amora awoke the next morning to the gentle pat of a brown-haired woman with kind eyes wearing a stern navy dress. "I am Mrs. Brown, the housekeeper. His grace would like to speak to you in his study after breakfast." She waved a hand at the little housemaid who helped her into her silk night rail and the pretty borrowed gown the day before. "This is Mary. She will be your lady's maid while you are here, in the duke's home. If you need anything, ring the bell." Waving a hand at the silken cord dangling beside the bed, she smiled and left the room, closing the door behind her.

Thinking the duke must have found another way out for them both, other than a position among his possessions, Amora slid from the bed with a smile. "I am ready to begin." She knew his grace did not relish the task of caring for her any more than she did.

The little maid curtsied. "I brought ye a clean gown and undergarments. Mrs. Brown ordered a bath carried up to ye, and the menservants are here. Stay here where ye are until they leave, and I will help ye." Mary drew the curtains around the bed as she spoke, and men's footsteps filled the room.

The warm water and luxurious lavender soap eased the ache in her limbs.

Mary exclaimed over her injuries when she lifted the night rail. "Does his grace know how bad ye are injured?"

Amora nodded. "He knows enough. I do not think my condition important enough to elaborate."

"His grace should be told the extend of yer wounds." Mary helped her into the tub and worked the heavenly soap into a lather.

"I disagree. He knows about my arms and face. The rest is not important."

The maid pinched her lips and said nothing more.

Chapter Three

One hour later, Amora stood outside an enormous oak door, freshly bathed and dressed in a rose-colored gown with a darker wine-colored sash about her waist. Her clean hair, though still damp, clung to her cheeks and hung down her back, tied at her nape with a matching wine-colored bow.

She lifted her hand and knocked, shifting her feet as she waited. Years passed since she wore anything so fine or slippers so soft and pretty.

"Come." The duke's deep voice rang out.

The door opened, and she entered a masculine study in navy and wine tones. Dark walnut bookshelves filled the walls, and a hearty fire blazed in the stone hearth, keeping the early spring chill from the room. The Duke of Ravencroft sat behind a massive walnut desk facing her.

Dressed in a navy topcoat with white embroidery around the sleeves, neck, and hem, he studied her from the top of her head to the bottom of her rose silk slippers.

"Good, you are here, so we can start." He waved his right hand to a leather armchair behind her. "Lady Amora, meet Sir Reginald Taffet, my closest advisor and overseer of my estates."

She turned, meeting the green-eyed gaze of a man, well into his fifties, with gray peppered hair and a fit soldier's body, clothed in black, who rose to his feet when she turned.

"My lady." He bowed from the waist, removing his cap.

She dipped a curtsy. "It is nice to meet you, sir."

The duke waved at an armchair behind her. "Please sit. We have much to go over."

With trepidation, she sat and listened as he recited his plans to find her a husband.

"I should like to remain on my own. I have no need for a guardian or a husband."

The duke sat back in his leather armchair. One eyebrow rose as he waved a hand at her wrist.

"Obviously not. Without either, you will be the target of ruffians and villains, and I cannot allow this to happen. So, we will proceed with plans for a marriage."

He named an exorbitant sum as dowry.

Amora's jaw dropped. "So, you found the money my father left me?"

His blue eyes pierced her heart. "No. I offer this sum, and my help in procuring an advantageous marriage, to atone for my role in squashing your hopes for the future. My revenge on your brother did not take an innocent into account. Therefore, I alone am responsible. The men I hired to investigate the earl knew nothing of you, or my retribution would have taken you into account."

She sat in silence. What if she were not innocent? He must be desperate to rid his life of her presence to offer such a sum as dowry. "You owe me nothing,"

"On the contrary, I am your one hope for a future."

The truth of his statement weighed heavy. "If I am to wed, dare I hope I have some say in the final choice?" No way would she be tied to another man who used his fists on her.

The duke studied her face and then turned to Sir Reginald. "Add the condition to the bottom, and we shall both sign."

Sir Reginald turned to a table at his side and dipped a pen into an inkwell standing there. He scratched on parchment for a minute and then rose to his feet. "Will there be any other conditions?"

"No." The duke handed the parchment to her, and she took it with trembling fingers.

The wording on the document stated the Duke of Ravencroft would provide for Lady Amora Hargrove until the day she wed, and on such day, no further claims would be made against him for crimes, real or imagined. On the joyous day of matrimony, they would part ways, and the commitment entered into by the Duke of Ravencroft with the Earl of Hargrove in relation to Lady Amora Hargrove would be considered null and void. The document ended with the statement Lady Amora Hargrove would be given final say in choice of partner within reasonable limits.

She glanced at the duke. "Within reasonable limits? Are you afraid I want to stay among your possessions forever?"

He shrugged. "I am a careful man, my lady."

They both signed, and Sir Reginald rolled the document up, sealing it with wax.

"Now, my lady, I leave you in Mrs. Brown's capable hands while I journey to my country estate to appraise my mother and sister of the events of the last few days. And check on their wellbeing. When I return, I shall petition the king for an audience to present you at court, and then the real work will begin." He studied her face.

"If you need anything, Mrs. Brown will send a courier. I shall return in a fortnight."

He bowed and signaled their meeting over.

Sir Reginald offered his arm. "I will see you out."

Rising, Amora glanced from one to the other. "I have no clothes and no money to purchase something fitting for court without relying upon your good nature."

The duke did not look up. "All has been accounted for. Please explain the details to her, will you, Sir Reginald? I have not the time."

She did not know what to make of his curt reply and allowed Sir Reginald to escort her from the room, closing the door behind him.

"An account has been set up for your success in procuring a match. Mrs. Brown has instructions to purchase the things required. If you find she has forgotten some trifle, you may contact me at my office." He handed her a card with his name and address and bowed. "Good day, my lady." Whereupon, he turned on his heel and walked away.

Amora stared after him. She had no intention of getting married any time soon but could see no way out of her present predicament. The duke had one thing correct, without a guardian and a proper place to sleep, London would eat her alive. So, for now, she would allow the duke his way.

****

Bond Street turned out to be every bit as delectable as she envisioned. Too young to be taken on such an adventure by her mother while alive, Amora would sit on her little cushioned chair, listening to her discuss her most recent visit to London and the shops on Bond Street.

Today, silk, satins, chiffon, lace, ribbon, ruffles, tucks, and pleats were discussed with the dressmakers as Mrs. Brown worked out every detail of her new wardrobe. She would have new slippers, silk stockings, petticoats, night rails, stays, corsets, day gowns, tea gowns, evening gowns, walking gowns, traveling gowns, and riding habits. Hats, hair bows, capes, and sashes for every occasion were ordered and discussed until Amora's head whirled. The bill at the dressmaker and cobbler shops must be astronomical. She could not believe all this happened so fast and *so big!*

Biting her lip, she studied her reflection in the looking glass. Pale blue silk covered her from head to toe, drawing attention to her eyes and the faint blush on her cheeks. Seamstresses at the tailors altered the gown to fit her slender frame while they waited. The low square neck and the tight bodice molded her figure to society's standards. Rubbing the silk between her thumb and forefinger, she calculated the dress to be worth a hundred quid. Accepting the duke's generosity would give her a head start should the necessity of selling them arise. Making mental calculations on how long such an exquisite wardrobe would keep her as they traveled back to the duke's townhouse, she jumped when the door to the carriage opened and the footman held his hand out to aid her disembarkment. She would hate selling the beautiful garments, but neither could she eat them or use them for shelter, and prayed such a situation never occurred.

The first gowns arrived the next day and every day the same week. Mrs. Brown lifted them from the tissue, inspecting each one before instructing Mary to air them out and hang them in the wardrobe in Amora's chamber.

Without the constant beatings, her face began to heal. Mrs. Brown ordered a special cream saying it aided the healing process, and instructed Mary to apply some every day. First the swelling went down, then the older bruises turned yellow and brown before disappearing altogether. Soon her face rounded out, and she gazed once more upon her true reflection in the mirror. Without the bruises, swollen eye, and cuts, she resembled her mother, as her father often told her, and she smiled at the face in the mirror. "I have missed you."

When she walked into the morning room for breakfast, Mrs. Brown exclaimed over her appearance. "My, but you are a fine-looking lady. Wait until his grace gets a good look at you. He may wish to keep you." With a chuckle at some private joke, she shook her head and left the girl to her meal.

Lifting the silver teaspoon to her mouth, Amora blew on her food. She doubted the duke planned to "keep" her one second longer than he had to.

A fortnight passed, and still, the duke did not return.

Mrs. Brown hired dance and music tutors to teach her the latest dances and songs for their departure into the many drawing rooms of London's elite.

Three weeks after the duke left for the country, Amora strolled into the red parlor located to the left of the grand staircase and sat at the pianoforte. She plucked at the keys before her, thinking of her time in the townhouse since her brother's arrest. No one hit her, yelled at her, or tied her hands to her bed. No one demanded she scour dishes or scrub clothes. With proper food and rest, her body grew strong, and her energy returned. No longer afraid of being compromised, she fell asleep with ease and slept the sleep of the dead.

Everyone treated her with respect and kindness, both sorely lacking in her brother's home. The older servants told her tales of the young duke, and she felt like she knew him more and more as the days slipped past.

With the return of her health came the return of her sense of humor and confidence. She did not want her time here to end, although she knew it must.

Remembering a tune from the past, she picked out notes of a song her mother taught her to play before her death. One keystroke followed the next as the melody flowed through her mind and fingers to the musical instrument before her. Finding comfort in the familiar song, she lent her heart and voice until her elegant surroundings disappeared, and she sat once more beside her mother in their parlor at Hargrove Manor, playing for her father, who listened from his seat beside the magnificent fireplace smoking his pipe.

****

Alexander took the front steps of his London townhouse two at a time and handed Major Domo his cape and hat. God, he enjoyed being home. During his sojourn to the country, he found his mother and sister in good health, and although his mother strove to meet his standards of excellence, the country estate did not compare with Ravencroft Manner or this townhouse.

They listened to his account of his dealings with the Earl of Hargrove without expression until he related the part about Amora.

His sister Esme, a handsome figure of a woman in her forties, raised an eyebrow as she poured tea and handed it across the small table. Bereft of grief since the death of her son, she came to Ravencroft Estate to care for their aged mother. The arrest of the Earl of Hargrove soothed her spirits. "You ruined him as he ruined Edward, and he *gambled* his sister?"

Straightening in her chair, his mother asked question after question about Amora. "You must allow this girl to visit. I would like to get to know her."

Surprised at the request, he agreed. His mother never expressed such interest in anyone since the death of her grandson. If the truth were known, she spoke to no one on a regular basis except his sister, the servants, and an old gypsy woman she allowed to stay on estate property.

If Amora could draw his mother from her melancholy for a few minutes, the drive would be worth the effort.

"I would like to meet this girl, also. She suffered at her brother's hands as we did, and we must care for her." His sister commented as she kissed him goodbye before his return to London.

Now, striding through the elegant entry hall of the townhouse with its gilded mirrors, Italian marble, and gold etched plaster, he made a mental list of the items he must attend to until a sound stopped him mid-stride. The most beautiful, feminine voice drifted toward him from the red parlor.

Frowning, he strode toward the door. He thought he instructed Mrs. Brown to wait for his return before having guests over for entertainment. Lady Amora Hargrove's debut into society must be handled with extreme care.

Stepping through the open door, he stilled. He recognized this song. His mother often sang it as she worked her needlepoint. The haunting melody of "The True Lover's Farewell" drifted around him and teased his senses with pure delight. The slight figure of a woman sat at his pianoforte, playing the tune dressed in lavender silk. Her black, curly hair rose high from her head, threaded with a string of amethysts.

He stood enthralled, letting the music and angelic voice wash over him while he took note of the woman's tiny waist and delicate wrist bones.

When the last note died away, he stared, unable to breathe, as the beautiful, delicate creature rose to her feet and turned toward him.

Her blue eyes lit up when she caught sight of him, and a smile widened her pink lips. "Your grace has returned."

Her voice seemed familiar, as did her manner, and the duke searched his mind on where he could have met this entrancing lady before. He drank in the sight of her flushed cheeks and perfect shape, unable to remember where they crossed paths before. He knew every beauty of note in London, and yet this one eluded him.

When he did not respond, the lady flushed. "Do you not recognize me?"

He searched her face and figure for a clue, unable to tear his gaze away. God, she enticed and excited him. Then he stilled.

Amora. The earl's sister. When she smiled, a dimple appeared beside her lips on the left side, and his blood heated. The lavender gown complimented her coloring and drew attention to her blue eyes. Who would have thought the beaten, bruised waif of a girl would become the vision of loveliness walking toward him?

"Lady Amora." Mrs. Brown entered the parlor and stopped short. "Your Grace! I did not realize you returned. Welcome home."

He nodded in the housekeeper's direction, unable to tear his eyes away from the girl. "Thank you, Mrs. Brown."

Amora stopped a few feet from him and dipped an elegant curtsy. "Welcome home, your grace."

He stared at the tops of her white breasts and the valley between them. Naked, she would fill a man's hands while he stroked her swelling nipples with his thumbs. She would cry out with pleasure, arcing against him, while he swooped down to pull her into his mouth and suckle. His manhood stiffened at the thought.

Mrs. Brown coughed, and Alexander shook his head to rid it of the lustful, carnal thoughts cavorting there.

He had a responsibility to see to it no harm came to her and tamped his interest down to his heel, where it would remain.

Clearing his throat, he took a step back. "Thank you, Amora. I am delighted your wounds healed in my absence. Finding a husband for you shall be much easier than I anticipated." With those curt words, he strode from the room to put as much distance between them as he could. How could he lust after the Earl of Hargrove's sister when he vowed to keep her safe and through no fault of her own, relied upon his goodwill for survival? Disgusted with the way his body responded to her, he strode for the stables and Adonis. A good run in the park would dissipate any lingering ardor and allow him to think with clarity.

****

Amora stared at the closed door. The duke's curt words hung suspended in mid-air. *I am delighted your wounds healed in my absence. Finding a husband for you shall be much easier than I anticipated...*

Used to being in the way and taken for granted, she should not care the duke wanted her out of his home and life. But she did. How could he be so curt with her when she knew him to be kind?

With a sigh, she turned to Mrs. Brown. "Did you need me for something?"

The housekeeper stared after the duke with a wide smile, turning when Amora spoke to her. "Yes, my lady. Your dance instructor waits in the ballroom."

She practiced the minuet until time to change for dinner. A few more lessons and she would know all the popular dances and be able to perform them with ease and precision. Allowing Mary to help her into a new navy gown, with white lace at the squared neck and sleeves, Amora had a stern talk with her feelings. As soon as she got the chance, she would leave. The duke owed her nothing. The responsibility for her plight lay with her brother. Her future, however, depended on her, and she intended to make a good one.

Lifting her chin and straightening her spine, she lifted the hem of her satin skirt and descended the stairs.

The duke stood at the bottom, watching her with an unreadable expression. When she neared, he bowed, murmured, "Good evening," and extended his arm. Dressed in evening clothes tailored to fit his athletic body, they accentuated his broad shoulders, narrow waist, and lean hips. Never had she been allowed near a man such as he.

Dipping a curtsy, she responded to his greeting and placed her arm in his. The heat of his body enveloped her, and the scent of lemon, bay leaf, and musk assaulted her senses. Conscious of the hard length of his body next to hers, she stared straight ahead, ignoring her shaking legs, and focusing on putting one slipper in front of the other.

They spoke in monosyllables during dinner, the conversation stilted and awkward, until Amora set her napkin in her lap and faced him. "How are your mother and sister?"

He glanced at her and took a sip of wine. "They are in good health and ask to make your acquaintance."

Surprised, Amora, studied his face. Did he jest? "They know of me, then? Who I am, and how I came to be in your home?"

"Yes. My mother expressed little interest in my news until I spoke of you. If things go well over the next few weeks, I may decide to host a house party in the country to introduce you to her."

Not to appease his mother but more as a dual-purpose event. "Meaning if a lord expresses interest in me and you deem him appropriate, the house party in the country will be scheduled to create a more intimate setting in the hopes of encouraging a proposal. Am I correct?"

"Of course. How are your lessons coming?"

His nearness created flutters in her stomach, and he stared at her with bored eyes or ignored her altogether until mention of her fate, then he wanted to discuss the matter. His cold, distant manner irritated her.

The devil took hold of her tongue before she could stop him. "I dance all the popular dances, sing all the popular songs, play the pianoforte, and know how to serve tea. My clothes are appropriate, and so is my manner. You have nothing to fear. I shall marry straightaway except for one small flaw. Something I find most grievous, and yet, I have found no one to instruct me in."

She had his attention.

"What is this grievous flaw?" Frowning, he set his silver fork down and studied her face.

"You might consider it a trifle, but to me, it is of the greatest import, and I wondered if you would find a tutor for me."

"Of course." He waved a hand around the room. "Anything you require, you need only to ask."

"I understand men judge a woman on her ability to perform the proper technique, and I am afraid I have no knowledge on the subject."

"Amora. Tell me what this lack of training and technique is, and I will find a tutor for you."

She studied his face with a serious expression. "I have your word?"

"You have my word." Sincerity shone from his blue eyes.

She dropped her head to hide her smile. "I worry you will make jests when you learn of this flaw."

"Amora."

Swallowing her chuckle, she lifted her head, looked him in the eyes, and said, "Kissing. I know not how to kiss a man, and it is most important I make the right impression on my future husband. If you could find a preferably handsome man to teach me the proper technique, I would be most grateful."

He stared at her as if she had gone crazy. His gaze dropped to her mouth, and heat flared in his eyes for a second before his lids dropped over them, shielding his expression. "You want me to find a tutor to teach you how to kiss?" His voice sounded strangled.

Amora giggled. She shocked him out of his cold,

stuffy manner, and her success delighted her soul. "I think I shall enjoy his lessons the most."

The duke's eye twitched, and his hands fell flat to the tabletop. "There will be no tutor. Your husband shall teach you the proper way to kiss, and...other things. This discussion is over."

Amora gave him her sweetest smile. "But, your grace, you gave your word."

He turned to stone before her eyes. The silence lengthened to a full minute. "Aye, I did." Rising to his feet, he left the room without looking back. If he bothered to turn, he would have seen his houseguest grinning an impish smile as she finished her dinner with relish.

Chapter Four

No kissing tutor appeared.

Although not surprised, she did frown over the duke's continued distant manner toward her. She got to him the night he returned from his country estate and could recall with clarity the flash of desire in his eyes when she mentioned kissing.

He took great care to avoid her, and the subject did not come up again. When next they spoke, he outlined his plan for her debut into society and the acquisition of a husband.

First, she must be presented to the king, and then there were certain balls and suppers to attend. The duke gave her a list of hostesses he deemed worthy of their attention. Any others, she would make an excuse for their absence. He followed this list with one of suitable suitors with special instructions should she attract one of their interests. Lastly, he presented her with a list of lords to avoid and the possible consequences of ignoring his instructions.

"Am I to carry the names with me and check each list when I am introduced? How am I to know if I am dancing with an acceptable or non-acceptable partner?"

He stared at her as if she had grown an extra head. "Do not most women have an instinct for this sort of thing?"

"Perhaps, but my instinct may be tarnished by lack

of experience."

Leaning back in his leather chair, he studied her face across the broad expanse of his desk and sighed. "If you have a question, ask me. I shall not leave you to the wolves."

True to his word, he accompanied her on every outing with Mary sitting ramrod stiff beside her as chaperone.

Tonight, she made her official curtsy to the king, after which they would join his royal guests for dinner and entertainment.

Dressed in a pink silk gown with a tiara riding high on her dark curls, the duke escorted Amora into the palace and down all the long corridors to the throne room without saying a word, his manner impeccable and his face devoid of expression. Tripping with nervousness as they neared the throne room, the duke paused and steadied her. "Amora, you have dealt with the roughest of men in your brother's parlor. The king is both kind and understanding, and the men at court equally so while in his presence. Take a deep breath and hold your head high. I shall be right here beside you."

They stood side by side facing front.

The duke's words calmed the frenzied beat of her heart and the knocking of her knees as they waited to proceed.

"His Grace the Duke of Ravencroft and Lady Amora Elizabeth Hargrove." The palace herald announced their presence, and the king motioned them forward. Down the steps and across the massive, tiled floor, they walked through the groups of courtiers and past the royal guard until they faced the throne. Gilded portraits, gilt-edged mirrors, and pale blue silk walls danced before her eyes.

Golden chandeliers dripped from the elaborate scene of God and the angels painted on the ceiling. Her gaze dropped to the king, resplendent in his royal purple robes on a jeweled throne.

"Sire." Amora dipped to the floor and waited for permission to rise.

He motioned, and she rose.

The king studied her face. "A true beauty like your mother. I am delighted to make your acquaintance Lady Amora. I have no doubt you will make one of my lords very happy. "

He grinned when the duke bowed. "I would hold on to this one, Ravencroft."

The duke inclined his head in acknowledgment and led her away.

As she turned, her gaze met the heated stare of a distinguished man with graying hair standing at the back of the throne room beside another gentleman sporting an inch-wide white strip through his gleaming black hair. Both gentlemen studied her with intense scrutiny.

Terror weighed her down like a stone as the icy fingers of dread gripped her throat.Sucking in a breath, she concentrated on putting one foot in front of the other.

The larger man's gaze narrowed on her face and swept her body with a lascivious expression, coming to rest on her bosom, lifted high against the low neckline of her gown by her tight corset. She remembered him coming to her brother's house the week before his arrest. Both men and one other came to dinner.

****

When she walked into the room later the same night, the atmosphere crackled with tension. These men differed from Nathan's usual crowd as night from day.

Older, dignified, and quiet, they studied her every movement, making Amora nervous. No raucous laughter or drunken jokes echoed in the dining hall, just the silent regard of the dinner guests and several whispered conversations with her brother out of earshot, followed by hostile glares. After dinner, her brother demanded she sing for them, which brought about more secretive conversations and glares. The third man left, following a heated conversation wherein he threatened to expose the others if Nathan did not agree to his terms, and after the door slammed shut behind him, silence filled the room.

Amora had no idea what the men argued over but had no time to ponder before her brother ordered her to change for Pudding Lane. Unsure what more the night would bring, she changed into her costume and joined Nathan and his two guests in the carriage for the ride to her brother's favorite tavern.

When she played cards at the tavern, she masqueraded as Madame *Pari*, the French word for gamble, wearing a red velvet dress and a black domino mask to hide her identity. She played game after game as the night wore on, and her brother gave no indication he planned to stop her anytime soon. With a sigh of resignation, she dealt another hand, noting the distant dong of a clock announcing the midnight hour.

"We are done after this hand." Her brother stood beside her counting her winnings and smiling.

Relieved, she changed the game and dealt the cards.

Afterward, when she rose to leave, this man grabbed her backside, tugging her onto his lap, where he groped her breasts. Grabbing the nearest thing, she hit him over the head with a beer tankard and ran out into the street, where she hailed a hackney carriage to take her home.

Her punishment did not fit the crime. Nathan whipped her the next morning, saying he changed his mind about leaving and bet on two more games that he had to forfeit because of her absence.

Amora would rather take the beating than be at the mercy of the men he invited home. Shivering at the memory and the terror she endured, her knees grew weak.

****

The two men staring at her from the back of the throne room would be titled and of noble birth to be allowed so near the king. They knew her secret identity, and fear shivered over her. Would they make it known? Nausea rose in her throat. Her brother's trial began in one week, and if the duke discovered her talent at the tables, he would ask her to leave. He despised gambling and playing cards, using them for the sole purpose of revenge on his nephew's antagonist, after which he had no further use for them and made his opinion known.

Sucking in a breath, she kept her gaze on the floor. On the other hand, if the magistrate let her brother go, she would be forced to live the horror again, and men like this would be her future.

Halfway across the throne room, her quaking knees gave out. She stumbled and would have fallen, but the duke caught her against him and held her until the shaking stopped.

She gulped in air, anxious to keep her composure. The memories flooded back threatening to drown her, each laced with emotions and the reminder of her previous life.

"What is wrong?" The duke whispered the words in her ear.

Gazing into his dark blue eyes, secure in the circle of his arms, she shook her head. "I recognize two men who came to the house the week before Nathan's arrest. For a moment, I forgot how my life used to be, but the memories returned with one look at their faces."

The duke took her by the elbow and helped her to a chair. A frown furrowed his brow. Leaning over, he handed her his kerchief. "What do they look like."

Amora described them as best she could while dabbing the fine mist of terror from her forehead.

The duke nodded. "I am beside you, and there are guards at every door. I do not see the men you describe but if we become separated, make your way to one of the palace guards. They will see to your protection. No one will disturb you."

Those were the last moments they had alone all evening. Lord after lord asked introduction before sweeping her away to introduce her to more people. Twice she caught glimpses of the two men staring at her through the crowd, only to turn away when she faced them.

Her dance card soon filled with names as faces blurred, and she gazed around for the duke.

She lost track of him in the onslaught and sought to point out the objects of her concern but could not find him. Anxiety tightened around her chest like a too-tight corset.

The clang of a staff tapping against the tile floor stilled the room as the Major Domo announced dinner.

Stiff with worry, she hovered for a moment beside a marble column as the throng of guests made their way past her. She recognized none of them and decided the best plan would be to follow along for the duke would no doubt make his way to dinner.Turning toward the dining room, Amora leaned side to side around the crush, hoping to see the duke. She stopped short when a young man in a gray and mauve topcoat stepped into her path, bowing and offering his escort.

Her blood froze. *Good lord, one of Nathan's friends and the third man in attendance at the fateful dinner stood before her.*

"I have the most intriguing feeling we know each other, but I cannot put my finger on an exact time or place."

The band around her chest tightened for a moment or two, then his words penetrated the haze in her mind. Thinking quickly, she responded. "How so when I do not know you?" If he could pretend they never met, so could she. Unless he truly did not remember. Amora examined the thought. He came but the once and left before they traveled to Pudding Lane with her in costume. So, he may not know about Madame Pari. Curious about the man's intentions, she waited.

"I am the Earl of Pembsy, my lady, at your service. May I say your loveliness takes my breath away? And you are Lady Amora Hargrove, the most beautiful woman in England. I have it on good authority you sit next to me at dinner, and I came to fetch you."

Amora's breath hitched, and her smile faltered. He remembered her name. Any fanciful notion she entertained about his memory vanished like the missing card to a winning hand in the heat of the game. *Oh God*! What else did he know?

Leading her to the dining room, the earl appeared to be engrossed in the table décor until he stopped beside two settings with place cards indicating his information correct. Flowery compliments flowed from his lips like wine from a bottle the entire time, but he made no mention of Nathan or her in connection to him. "No other woman in the palace can compare to your beauty. I am quite infatuated with you to the point I cannot breathe. Allow me to pay tribute to your beauty."

She gaped in stupefaction. Dare she hope he knew nothing but her name?

The earl lifted her hand to his mouth and kissed her fingers one at a time while she searched frantically for something to say.

Heat rushed to her face as she considered removing her hand to spare it more moisture when she glanced up and met the hot stare of the Duke of Ravencroft from his seat at the other end of the long table.

So, this is where he got to. Her gaze rested on the dark-haired beauty beside him for a second. The woman spoke close to his ear, wrapping both hands around his masculine arm, and the duke laughed, his deep, rich voice creating flutters in Amora's stomach.

The earl slid her chair out, and she sat, dropping her gaze to hide the tinge of jealousy.

As a wealthy, handsome unattached man, the duke could dine with whomever he chose, whenever he wanted, and the act had little to do with her. Unless she had need of him, she amended and then he better be available and not off dallying. Had he not given his word to keep her safe?

Lost to her thoughts, she jumped in surprise when the earl's hands rested on her shoulders, and he leaned down to whisper, "I arranged to sit beside you tonight so we could become better acquainted."

Fear created a lump in her throat as she struggled to

produce an appropriate answer for the situation. In Nathan's parlor, she would have swung the poker at the earl's head.

Peeking at the duke, she flushed when anger shot from his eyes, and he shook his head at her.

She agreed with his rejection of the Earl of Pembsy wholeheartedly on the one hand, but on the other, the fact his nearness made the duke angry lightened her mood. If his grace did not like the attention she received, he should not be in such a hurry to place her on the front row of the marriage market. As for her, she would rather be anywhere than here. Slipping her hands into her lap, she used the fine linen napkin to dab at her moist gloves. Thank God for the layer of cloth between her delicate skin and the earl's drooling mouth and for his apparent memory loss.

Her dinner companion continued fawning the entire meal. Just when Amora decided she could take no more and grew quite nauseated by the exaggerated praise, the Major Domo tapped his staff and announced dancing in the ballroom.

Relieved, Amora sat her napkin on the table and rose to her feet.

"Allow me, my lady." The earl caught her elbow and turned her toward the door. "I shall have every dance and protect you from the bevy of lords shoving their way toward us. None shall touch you but me."

She glanced around. Several lords did appear to be headed in her direction. Time to make a hasty withdrawal before this situation exploded in a bevy of truths the duke need not know, along with the true thoughts of her mind. One could bite their tongue for so long, before an eruption occured. "I cannot dance with you, sir, nor can

I remain by your side, for all my dances are spoken for. Thank you for entertaining me at dinner, but I must find my guardian."

Tugging her elbow from his grasp, she turned to discover the duke standing behind her.

"You cannot escape so easily, my lady. I shall—"

"Thank you, Pembsy, but the lady is my responsibility." The duke's gaze narrowed on the earl before he turned to her. "Your hand, Lady Amora." His tone brooked no argument as he escorted her from the dining hall.

She sagged with relief as they walked away from the earl.

"Did you enjoy dinner? Pembsy seems quite taken with you. Although he is not to be encouraged in his pursuit of you. We can do far better than him."

We. What a wonderful word. Especially when used in any other sentence. Waiting for the stone in her belly to dissipate, flippancy seemed a good way to steer the conversation away from her dinner companion. "I could wring my napkin from the drool he dribbled on me throughout dinner. Are all lords so free with their compliments? I cannot fathom how my eyes could rival the stars in the heavens or how my skin is as pale as moonlight shimmering across the water."

"He is young and has not learned sincerity is the best form of flattery. When I tell a lady of her beauty, I do so in honesty."

Amora turned. "So, would you say my lips resemble rose petals, and my skin is as soft as down?"

His gaze rested on her mouth for several heart-pounding moments. "I would not suggest such a thing unless I knew them to be so."

Fluttering filled her belly, and languid heat stole through her body. She stared up at him and wondered if his mouth would feel as firm as it looked. If she stood on tiptoe and put her mouth on his, would his lips slide against hers? Would he hold her as he had in the throne room, where heart beat next to heart, with his heat surrounding her and his scent filling her senses? Her lips parted when he leaned close, and her breathing quickened. Closing her eyes in anticipation, she lifted her face—.

"My lady, I believe the first dance is mine."

She jumped and turned to find Lord Antony Dalton behind her grinning like a cat in the hen house, bowing low from the waist. In his twenties, with dark hair, of thin stature, and as tall as the duke, he cut a fine figure in his wine-colored jacket with white embroidery, white breeches, and shiny black heeled shoes with a jeweled buckle. The young lord signed her card first, and this dance belonged to him.

With a sigh of regret, she nodded at the duke and allowed the lord to lead her away.

Lord Antony proved to be a delightful dance partner and whispered droll comments about the other guests in her ear until her next partner claimed her.

She did not see the duke again until well after midnight. One dance remained, and her partner did not appear to claim her, so she made her way to the garden for some fresh air. The palace guard stood at attention in the halls and out on the terrace as she made her way down the lighted steps.

The beauty of the moonlight slanting across the grass and the scent of magnolias were bliss to her soul. A breeze touched her cheeks and cooled the beads of exertion the dancing created on her forehead.

The sound of tinkling water drew her to a three-tiered fountain, where the moon sparkled and glimmered on the surface of the water. Standing still, she let the solace of the silent, perfumed night fill her mind with serenity. If she could stay right here, in this moment, life would be perfect.

"Lady Amora. What a delightful surprise." The tone of his voice suggested otherwise.

Amora jumped at the sound of the Earl of Pembsy's voice and turned, frowning. Apprehension tightened her chest as she met the knowing gaze of the strutting young lord. Shivering with revulsion, she lifted her chin in challenge. She thought she got rid of the earl after dinner.

Glancing around, the earl surveyed their surroundings before narrowing on her. "Here you are all alone in the garden with no one to call for aid." His lips turned up in an evil smile. "This works out well for what I have to say."

Swallowing, she tilted her chin higher, refusing to fear him or anything he said. "What could you possibly say to make me call for help?"

A hollow chuckle escaped him. "A great deal, my dear. You see, your brother robbed me of my inheritance the week before the duke had him arrested. My family would not understand my involvement with someone of Hargrove's caliber, so I cannot appeal to the magistrate to recover what is rightfully mine."

Queasiness filled her belly and chest. She remembered the game and Nathan's delight when she won. The earl met them in Pudding Lane and gave no indication her knew her other identity. "What does your foolishness have to do with me?" She must determine if the earl recognized her as Madame Pari. Very few could because of her mask, and she spoke little or not at all when in costume.

He smiled. "With what Ravencroft offers for a dowry, my coffers would be replenished to overflowing. You owe me, and I intend to collect."

"Me?" Amora gaped. "You cannot be serious. Whatever my brother did or did not do, you are a competent *man* and made your own choice. I did not force you to gamble away your inheritance on a game of chance, nor did I cause your loss." She crossed her fingers and hoped the gods forgave her for her little lie. The earl played cards like a petulant child, easy to fool and screaming in anger when he lost a hand. She half expected him to lay face down on the floor, pounding his fists and kicking his feet, or hold his breath until he passed out.

The earl's smile dropped, and he took a menacing step toward her. "You are his sister, so I hold you responsible for repayment."

Stiffening her spine and locking her knees, she returned glare for glare. "As a *female*, society deems me inferior and therefore not liable for the mess Nathan made."

Moving with surprising speed, the earl caught her in his arms, pinning her to him. "You shall repay what is rightfully mine one way or another. Even if I must force a marriage by compromising you to collect the money owed me."

Horror numbed her mind at his intention, and she struggled against him for a second before going still. No way in hell would she be his pawn. "I will offer one warning. Let me go, or I will bloody your nose. No man forces me to do aught against my will as you shall soon learn."

"Your brother did."

Before she could think of a proper response, he tightened his grip and leaned toward her.

She struck out as if it were second nature, planting a blow on his nose with her fist.

The earl screamed with pain and let her go. Stepping back, he grabbed his kerchief from his jacket pocket. Holding the item to his nose to stem the flow of blood, he glared. "You will pay for this."

Amora straightened her gown. "I think not. Next time a lady tells you no or demands to be released, listen to her."

She hurried away while the evil little lord dealt with his injury, whining about the stain his blood made on his new jacket.

Chapter Five

Halfway back to the palace along the garden path, Amora twisted her foot and lost a slipper.

"Balls!" Holding her right foot up, she searched for the errant article, hopping on the other foot as she inspected the grass beside the path. A glimmer reflecting the light of the silver moon caught her attention. Retrieving her shoe from the bushes beside the path, she searched the area for somewhere to sit so she could lift her skirts and inspect her injury out of sight. Earlier, on her way through the garden, voices came from within a secluded arbor suggesting a hidden area for conversation.

Upon investigation, she discovered a carved bench, and she sat, lifting her skirts. Her ankle did not hurt when she walked, and no visible injury appeared. Sighing with relief, she bent to replace her slipper and stopped.

"Damn it!" In her hurry to retrieve her slipper from the path, she failed to notice the missing heel. "Bugger. Now what shall I do?"

"Where have you been?" The duke strolled into view at the same moment scaring her into dropping her slipper with her skirts still hiked to her knees.

Staring down at her silk stocking-covered legs and missing slipper he growled, searching the area behind her. "What has happened? Where is the scoundrel who accosted you?"

She realized the picture she must present with her ruined heel, and her skirts hiked halfway up her leg. For a second, she considered telling him about the earl but changed her mind. Any conversation with the erstwhile earl might lead to Madame Pari, something she would avoid at all costs. The duke must never know of her skill or her involvement in Nathan's obsession.

"I am alone."

"Then how do you account for your broken slipper and mussed skirts. No lady sits alone in the palace garden looking as you do. Point out the direction the villain took."

The earl no doubt cried on the walkway by the fountain even yet. "There is no one here but me, and no one touched me." Amora crossed her eyes as she lied because her hands were busy with her skirts.

Disbelief hardened the duke's face. "Tell me the truth."

"Fine. There are twenty dukes, a prince, and three earls beneath the bench. The viscount left a moment ago, after dallying with me. The prince asked for my hand in marriage but withdrew his proposal after the viscount's confession. His majesty swore a holy oath to avenge my honor before allowing me to tuck him away beneath me, thus righting a grievous wrong. Whereas, all three earls merely wanted to take me for their mistress, and I have not had time to discover the nature of the twenty dukes." Dropping her skirts, she lifted her chin in defiance, not wanting to speak of her own clumsiness or the situation with the Earl of Pembsy. "What difference does it make?"

Voices approached, and the duke slid onto the bench beside her, his voice dropping to a whisper. "It makes a great deal of difference. You cannot be found in a compromising situation. Think of your reputation. You have one strike against you already with the scandal and reputation your brother created. Many do not know you are blood relatives, and this is a good thing."

Amora tossed her head in defiance."I had nothing to do with his cheating." She taught him to count cards, when to hold, and when to draw. He lacked her intuition for the game, and his fraudulent activities were his own.If she said the words enough, she might believe them true.

"Because he is your male relative, you are elevated or sunk along with him."

Folding her arms over her chest, she frowned. His words were the understatement of the century. "Is this why you are in such a hurry to marry me off? You are hoping to sign a marriage contract before anyone realizes who I am?"

Silence followed her question. "I wish to sign a marriage contract before your brother has a chance to be free. I cannot bear to think of you at his mercy."

"Were anyone interested in *my* wishes, I would ask for a man who wants me for me, who meets me on every level of my mind, and understands the yearning of my heart. The rest of the dandies or whatever they are called can go whisper their insincere words of nonsense to someone else."

Deciding she cared not whether the duke gazed upon her knees or not, she lifted her skirt, and slipped her foot into her satin slipper. When she turned and gazed up at his face, the breath caught in her throat.

His eyes darkened as he leaned close and brought a gentle finger to her cheek, stroking her skin. "How can you be so beautiful? The magic of the moonlight cannot compare to the mystery I find in the depths of your beguiling eyes or the allure of your soft, delicate lips. I want to drink the nectar of your mouth and lose my soul in the entrancing spell you weave around me. I cannot get your scent out of my mind and wonder how your softness will feel when I hold you close. Did your twenty dukes, a prince, and three earls speak frivolous words of love before you stuffed them beneath your bench?"

The arbor created an intimate atmosphere, and the smell of his skin coupled with the heat of his body so close to hers turned her legs to jelly. His words made her breath come fast, and her lips parted as she gazed up at him.

"And if they did?"

He smiled. "Forget them. They would not be stuffed beneath us if they spoke truth. I do not make the same mistake." Desire glittered in his eyes. "I gave my word."

She nodded, unsure of what word he spoke. Her blood caught fire when she gazed into his eyes. Butterflies filled her belly, and her heart sped up when he lifted her face to his.

He stared at her mouth as he ran a thumb over her bottom lip. "I have wondered for days what you taste like. You asked if I thought your mouth resembled a rose petal, and I have decided I must know the answer."

Her lips parted in anticipation, and she dare not breathe for fear the spell would break.

He leaned close, blocking the moonlight above her as his warm lips covered hers. Afterward, she would always equate the scent of magnolias with her first kiss, for they surrounded her along with the duke's heat beneath the magical night sky.

He slid his firm mouth over hers, searching and applying gentle pressure while his hands caressed her face. She could not believe this was happening and leaned against him, wrapping her arms high around his neck. His embrace comforted her as no one else had, and for the first time since Nathan dragged her to London, she felt safe.

With a groan, he tipped her head to the side. "Open for me."

She opened her mouth to ask what he meant, but never got the chance, for his tongue slid between her lips and stroked along hers, sending shivers of delight through her body.

She trembled against him, wanting each moment to last for an eternity. The taste of him in her mouth intoxicated her, and she could not get enough. Her blood sang, and heat filled her belly.

Then his arms hugged her tight against him, and she sighed with pleasure. He drank from her mouth as if starved for the taste of her, and she opened her mouth further, anxious to see what other pleasures he would share.

But he lifted his head before she could discover more and held her against him while he dragged in a ragged breath. "God's teeth, you tempt me, and it takes all my self-control to not take what is mine."

Amora lifted her head from his shoulder, confused. "Do you speak of me?"

He brushed a hand across her flushed cheek, and his lids dropped over his eyes, ignoring her question. "Lesson one, delivered as promised."

She shook her head. "I do not understand."

"I gave my word to find a man to tutor you in the art

of kissing. Who better than I?" He stroked her cheek once more. "I hope your many suitors cramped for space beneath us realize the futility of their suit."

He exited the arbor and tugged her along with him toward the terrace at the top of the stairs.

Bemused, she hurried to catch up. "So, you are to be my kissing tutor?" Excitement spiraled inside her, and she could not wait until lesson two.

He ignored her question. "Did any of the lords vying for your favor this evening, other than the unfortunate ones in the arbor, catch your attention?"

Her anticipation of future kissing lessons dropped like a rock off a tall cliff. "No. None of them were sincere, although Lord Antony is quite entertaining."

He nodded and led her through the palace in silence to the entrance where his carriage awaited on the cobblestone drive. "He comes of good blood and is an acceptable match."

How could he hold her so close, kiss her so thoroughly, and then approve another man as her suitor? Disgruntled, she hobbled along beside him, one foot taller than the other, wondering what she had to do to catch his fancy when they came upon the Earl of Pembsy simpering to an older woman about his bloody nose.

Her mood lightened in an instant, amused at the sight. He would do well to remember she tolerated no abuse from any man. Smiling wide as they passed, she giggled when the earl flattened his body against the side of the corridor to make more space between them. The night proved a grand source of information, showing her who to trust and who to avoid.

****

Forgetting all about the man who frightened her in

the throne room, she accepted invitations to several outings with Lord Antony, unaware of any danger until a week later, when she accepted his invitation to the theater.

The Earl of Pembsy avoided her whenever they attended the same event, and she breathed a sigh of relief, putting him out of her mind. Her blow must have convinced him of her sincerity in being left alone. His lack of interest must mean he had no knowledge of her alter ego.

Amora sat beside Lord Antony in his box while the duke sat across the way in his. All through the first half of the play, the heat of his grace's dark gaze rested upon her, and she resisted the urge to turn her head. During intermission, she made her excuses to go in search of the women's loo and slipped through the entrance hall and corridors filled with London's elite, standing in small groups gossiping.

With her mind on the amusing comments of Lord Antony, she must have taken longer than she supposed, for on her way back. She noted the emptiness of the corridors. *The play must be starting again.*

Hurrying toward the theater door, she ran right into the monster man from court. With an exclamation of dismay and a quick step back, Amora turned to run but did not escape his quick hands.

With a twist of her arm, he propelled her into an empty closet and shut the door behind them, pressing his large body into the back of hers from lack of space. His heavy breath smelled of stale port and cigar, moistening the back of her neck and making her shiver with revulsion.

The confined area had no outdoor vent, and the air

grew thick with their combined breathing in a matter of minutes.

Nausea rumbled in her stomach, and fear pounded in her chest.

"Now then. I want what I paid for. I won the bid and paid the money your brother asked for you. I never got the chance to collect you before the constables took him to Newgate, but I am here to collect you now. I lost ten thousand pounds because you were not in the games I counted on."

"You bought me from my brother to play cards for you?" She shook her head in amazement. Nathan deserved everything the duke did to him and more.

"Aye, and now you will win the money back for me."

Not if she had any say. Taking a deep breath, she screamed as loud as she could, earning a blow on the back of her head. Staggering, everything dimmed, and black dots swam before her eyes. The room twirled around her head, and her heart thudded in her ears. Amora dropped her head and thought hard, gasping in pain.

The man laughed. "Now then. You will do as I say. Do not give me any more problems, or you will earn more blows. The earl said you did not know your place, but you will." Searching the area behind him, he opened the door a sliver.

She sucked in as much fresh air as she could while she searched the area for a weapon.

The closet contained a broom, nothing more, and smelled of vinegar. She closed her free hand around the handle and waited.

The man clapped a hand over her mouth. "We are

going to walk out the front doors together. No noise and no fighting, or I will cuff you hard enough to make you sleep until this time next week, understand?"

She nodded, understanding once he propelled her past the ticket booth, her fate became sealed. Even though, Lord Antony, the duke, and help lay a hundred feet in front of her behind the closed doors, they would be too late.

Relaxing in his hold, she let him steer her out of the closet, appearing as docile as she could.

The man turned his head to see behind them and missed the fact she brought the broom with her. When they entered the corridor, she swung around to face him, untwisting her arm. With a quick hard jab to his mid-section with the handle of the broom, she lifted her knee into his groin, before whacking him over the head with the handle.

He dropped to his knees in pain, and she tossed the broom, using the opportunity to slap him across both ears at once, open-handed.

The man fell to the floor, gasping with pain. "You broke my ear drums! I will make you pay for this!"

Amora did not wait around to hear more but hurried to the theater door, walking into the solid wall of the duke on his way out.

"Where have you been?" His gaze roamed her too hot face and frightened expression. "Are you all right?" Leaning to gaze behind her, he stepped around her to stare at the heap of man on the floor.

"I am fine. I cannot answer the same for the person behind me. He attempted to abduct me, but such an outing did not appear on my schedule for today. So, I declined his offer."

The duke frowned and took her elbow, guiding her to Lord Antony's box. "Stay here. I will take care of whoever he is."

He returned fifteen minutes later and took his seat across the way, giving her a brief smile.

Relaxing in her seat, Amora determined the threat taken care of, or the duke would not have returned. She made the decision not to let the incident ruin her night and turned to Lord Antony with a smile. Her past would remain in the past if she had any say.

He responded by leaning close. "This is my favorite part."

She frowned. "I thought the play opened tonight. How can you have a favorite part if you have not seen it before?"

"I can have a favorite when I sit next to you."

The silly statement made her smile. Some of her suitors were extravagant, some were overly complimentary to the point she wanted to gag, and others made no secret of the fact they courted her dowry instead of her, considering their ancient lineage a huge favor they bestowed on her in return.

Lord Antony made her laugh with his silly antics and comments. Of all the men who sought her out, she liked him the most.

The lord whispered silly anecdotes about the play and actors in her ear until the curtain dropped. Laughing, they rose to find the duke standing beside their box in silence. He informed Lord Antony in quiet tones of her would-be-attacker. "I shall see Lady Amora home."

With a slight nod, they walked out together, and Lord Antony kissed her hand farewell.

"Until next time, my lady."

She sighed wistfully, staring after his retreating form and wishing they had more time to talk. His jests and smiling countenance made her forget her own problems and the worry for the future. Turning, she caught the duke's dark gaze resting on her face. With a shrug of regret, she allowed him to help her into his carriage.

"I apologize for disturbing your romantic evening with Lord Antony. After your near abduction, I made the decision to escort you home, so I know you are safe."

Amora turned from gazing out the window. "Lord Antony and I have some things to discuss, and I did hope for a quiet moment with him, but it cannot be helped. Did you find the man who attacked me in the theater?"

The duke shook his head. "He disappeared by the time I returned, but one of the theater guards knows him. He is the Earl of Chauncey and has long been suspected of being involved in a human slavery ring here in London with connections to Singapore and Asia."

Amora stared at him as horror gripped her throat. When she won the money he desired, did he plan to sell her into slavery? Other memories surfaced, and she swallowed. "He came to the house with two other lords. Nathen made me stand in the center of the room while the men walked around me. One sniffed my neck, two of them touched my hair…" She shivered to her toes. "Now I know two of their names, the Earl of Pembsy and the Earl of Chauncey. The earl said he came to get what he purchased…" How many times did Nathan sell or barter her away? Nausea rose in her throat. "Please ask the driver to stop. I am going to be sick."

The duke rapped on the roof with his cane, and the carriage came to a stop on the side of the cobblestone road.

Amora slipped from her seat and stumbled out into the night, retching behind the carriage wheel until her stomach held no more.

"Your rejection of Pembsy at the palace now makes sense. Why did you not tell me about his involvement with Hargrove?"

Because of Madame Pari. She retched again.

A soft linen kerchief appeared beside her with an elegant "R" embroidered in the corner. She wiped her mouth as his strong arms turned her, holding her against his broad chest.

"I did not think he recognized me at first." She could not explain the rest and dropped her head as the emotions of the evening rolled down her face.

He let her weep all over his perfectly tailored evening clothes, sopping his cravat and vest.

When she stilled, he rubbed lazy circles on her back, calming her.

"Do not entertain any connection with either earl should they approach you again."

She shivered against him. "I do not think I could. Especially after what happened. How could my own brother…" Terror clutched her chest, and she could not finish the sentence. "If you had not come for him when you did, God alone knows where I would be by now."

Chapter Six

Amora closed her eyes and willed the evil away. "Do you know how much he paid for me?"

They stood in the red salon the following evening discussing the report William handed the duke moments earlier concerning the Earl of Chauncey. Her attacker produced a receipt signed by the Earl of Hargrove acknowledging the sale of his sister. He claimed to be within his rights to collect the property purchased. The magistrate disagreed and after a stern discussion about human slavery, and because he came from a family of the bluest of blood, let him go.

Pacing, Amora stopped beside a small table and picked up the deck of cards lying there. Agitated, she shuffled them without thinking.

The duke shook his head. An odd expression crossed his face as he gazed at her. "The amount does not matter. How do you place a monetary value on a human life, especially a sister?" He remained silent for several minutes as he studied her. "I will have extra guards posted, and I want your word you will not venture out without my permission."

Amora stared. "You think there is still danger?" Setting the cards down, she walked to the nearest settee and hovered, staring out the nearby window with unseeing eyes.

The duke's compassionate gaze followed her.

"Nathan sold you to Chauncey and used you to ante up in a game of chance with me. My concern is who else he may have bartered you to."

A new worry tightened her chest. "Since he sold me to the Earl of Chauncey first, are you no longer responsible for me?"

She swallowed and fought back the panic racing through her veins, pacing to the hearth.

"Nay. The magistrate named me your guardian until you marry, or he changes his decision. Should he be so inclined, I would be the first to know, and I have received nothing to indicate a change."

Thinking of his previous comment, icy fear tingled down her spine. "What if there *are* more men who bought me?"

Trembling with terror, she held her hands to the flames to warm them. A shiver worked its way through her body as though a dark cloud encompassed her world, smothering her in evil.

She did not know the duke approached until he lifted her chin with a gentle finger.

"You are my ward, and no harm shall befall you. I will not allow it."

She wanted to believe him with all her heart and soul but failed. How could he know the depths she sank to while in her brother's home? Or who might come for revenge?

"Get some rest, Amora. We will work out the difficulties tomorrow."

Numb with disbelief at the sudden turn of events, she walked on wooden legs to her chamber and allowed Mary to help her undress and don her night rail.

"Have a good night. m'lady. Sweet dreams." The

maid's cheery voice drew her from her reverie with a start.

"Thank you."

Mary blew out the candles and closed the door behind her.

Amora lay in the flickering light of the fire, staring at the stars through her chamber window. "Help me, Mama. I know you are there, and I need your help. How can I fight the evil if I know not from which direction it comes? I know you see more from your position in the sky and ask you to send me what I need when I need it most."

She found comfort in imagining her mother looking down from the heavens and guiding her path through the pitfalls of evil surrounding her. Amora fell asleep a few minutes later and dreamed of angels with fairy wings, her mother playing the pianoforte, and the duke.

Scratching at her window woke her, and she sat up as icy terror raced down her spine. "Who is there?"

No sound came except the whisper of the wind through the panes of glass and the snap of the fire. Clutching her coverlet to her chin, she stared at the window and waited.

The scratching came again, followed by a thump.

Amora jumped from her bed and tip-toed to the window to peek out the heavy velvet drapes, still drawn back as she asked Mary to do the night before.

A ladder leaned against the side of the house, and a rough-looking man clung to the sides as he made his way up the rungs.

Not waiting around to see if he made it or not, she sped to the door and flung it open.

No guards stood in the corridor to aid her, and panic

gripped her. With a silent cry, she fled on winged feet down the long, cold corridor to the duke's chamber.

Knocking, she waited two seconds before lifting the latch and slipping through the door. Shivering with fear, she hurried to the side of the massive bed.

The duke lay in the center, his dark hair prominent against the white of his pillow. One naked tanned arm rested on the heavy navy velvet coverlet covering the lower half of his chest and body.

She touched his arm. "Your grace." Her cold feet brushed against each other beneath her night rail, and her ears searched the darkness for intruders. "Have you a sword or a pistol nearby? I need a weapon."

The duke lay still as stone.

"Your grace, someone is at my window with a ladder and shall discover my absence. I must have a weapon or find a place to hide." Her knees knocked together, and her throat tightened. She could not hear past the pounding of her heart in her head. What if the men came in the window and followed her down the corridor? She had not stopped to close her door, and the intruder would know she left. Without a weapon, she would be easy game.

A door closed, and Amora jumped. Her decision made, she hurried around to the other side of the bed, slipped beneath the covers, and lay behind the duke's back. If the intruders entered his chamber, they would not see her behind him.

Men's voices drifted toward her, and the sound of their footsteps thudded against the wooden floor of the corridor.

Amora snuggled closer to the duke, trembling, and received her second surprise for the night. Naked to the waist, his warm skin glowed golden in the flickering light of the fire. Hesitating, she stared at his back until another closing door in the corridor sent her shivering up against him, ducking beneath the fine linen covers. Did the intruders search for her chamber by chamber? And where were the guards? She would be safe here for the duke would not let them hurt or abduct her. Not daring to breathe, she waited, but nothing happened.

The footsteps stopped, and all grew silent. Minute after breathless minute passed, but nothing moved or stirred.

A log settled in the hearth, and she jumped with terror. Lifting her head from beneath the covers, she stared at the fire, listening intently to the darkness, clutching the broad back beside her. The heat of his hard body drew her like a warm fire on a snowy night, reassuring her while his masculine scent surrounded her. Amora swallowed. God, he smelled good. Putting her nose close to his back, she took a deep breath and sighed. The silence of darkness settled over her in an intimate blanket, making her keenly aware she lay beside the duke's naked back, in his bed, in nothing but her night rail.

Propriety demanded she lay on the chair before the hearth or go check the corridor. Not wanting to do either in case the villains returned, she hesitated.

The duke turned, murmuring in his sleep. He hesitated when he encountered her still form beside him, and then warm arms closed around her, drawing her to his broad chest.

Amora gasped at the contact, and languid heat seeped through her body, setting her on fire.

Her breath caught in her throat as one hand caught

her chin and the other ran the length of her back. Not daring to breath in case she broke the spell, she trembled, willing him to kiss her, and make her feel wanted, alive, and safe.

Looming up one elbow, his lips descended on hers while his hands searched her figure, running over her unbound breasts and down to her hips before closing around her buttocks.

Gasping, Amora arced against him, biting back the moan on her lips. Her heart sped up like a racehorse as he caressed her body. Running her hands over the rippled muscles of his chest, she sighed with pleasure.

A moan escaped him. Holding her against the hard length of his arousal with a murmur of satisfaction, the duke drank from her lips in long, open-mouthed kisses setting her soul on fire.

Needing no further invitation, she wound her arms around his neck and kissed him back with all the frenzied anxiety she suffered in the last few minutes, wanting to soak in the reassuring heat of his hard body and the security of his chiseled arms.

"Amora." He sounded bemused and frustrated.

Butterflies filled her belly, and wanton curiosity gripped her. What did a man do to a woman in bed? She clung to him, trembling with anticipation, and protested when he lifted his head to gaze down at her. "Do not stop. Do not let me go."

"Why are you in my bed?" His husky voice made her mouth go dry. With his hair ruffled from sleep and his droopy eyes gazing down into hers, he made all other men pale in comparison.

Then she remembered. "I did not want them to find me."

"Who?" Alert in an instant, sensuality vanished as he stiffened against her, lifting her chin to gaze deep into her eyes. "Who searches for you?"

Shivering, she told him about the ladder and intruder.

"This is why I awaken to find you in my bed?"

"I shook you, but you did not answer. When a door closed in the corridor, beside you seemed the only safe place to be."

"Stay here, and I will see who dares break into my home." Dropping a quick kiss on her upturned lips, he slid from the bed. Naked to the waist, he tugged on a pair of breeches and left the chamber on silent feet.

She lifted his coverlet to her chin and waited. Silence filled the night. The crackle of the fire and the whisper of wind against the window filled the empty space of the chamber.

A good half hour passed before the duke returned, closing the door behind him. "All is clear, except the fact you are here in my bed in your night rail. The police will be here any moment. So let us get you to the duchess' chamber to protect your reputation. I do not want it known you entered this room."

Amora sat up. "Did you find the villains?"

"We will speak in the next room. Up you get."

He had her under the coverlet in the duchess' bed before she could blink and reappeared a moment later, tucking a tunic into his breeches. "Now then. This is what you will tell the police and anyone else who asks. You heard a noise, got frightened, came to my door, and knocked, whereupon I sent you to the duchess' chamber while I slipped out to investigate."

She nodded. "What about the man outside my

window?"

"He got away. We found nothing of the attempted break-in except the ladder leaning against the side of the house. I sent for the constables, and they should arrive any moment."

Mary hurried into the room a few minutes later, exclaiming over her mistress. "Ye should have rung the bell, m'lady. I would have come to help ye."

"And would have walked into a bad situation. The villain is quite a large man, judging from the deep ruts his ladder made. Lady Amora made the right choice to come to me and let me handle the situation. I would not want you hurt either, Mary."

Her maid flushed and bobbed a curtsy before disappearing down the corridor to order a tray of tea for her mistress.

The officers arrived a few minutes later and asked questions until the first rays of the sun burst over the sea of housetops.

Amora grew so weary, staying upright took all her concentration. The officers found no evidence other than large, heavy footprints leaving through the outer fence and disappearing into the street.

Amora sipped her tea after the officers departed. "What am I to do? I cannot go to balls and accept dinner invitations if I do not know if one among the guests plans to harm me."

"Perhaps it would be best to limit our social engagements for a week or two until we catch the intruder and anyone involved in this." The duke studied her face with a closed expression. "If we do so, you would not be able to see Lord Antony unless he called here."

Amora sighed and shook her head knowing Antony would call if she asked him to. "It will mean you are responsible for me longer than you planned. I cannot be selected from the marriage market if I am unavailable."

The duke turned from his position in front of the hearth. "Your safety is of greater concern."

Relieved, she smiled and slid down in the bed, drawing the covers to her chin, happy he said as much.

Mary gathered up cups and saucers while they spoke.

"Did you suppose I would cast you out at the first sign of trouble or that my offer to help you obtain a husband has a time limit?" The duke's quiet voice held a note of disbelief.

Opening her eyes, Amora gazed up at him. "The first morning I came, you mentioned your need to marry me off as soon as possible."

"I recall no such thing. The magistrate made his ruling clear, and we shall both abide the terms. I will see to your welfare until you are wed." His intense blue gaze pinned her to the bed telling her he meant every word.

Amora nodded, and the duke left the chamber, murmuring he would see her after she rested.

Perhaps she misunderstood his intent when she first stepped beneath his roof. He seemed in such a hurry to get rid of her. Unsure whether she liked his comment about abiding by the magistrate's terms, she drifted off to sleep until Mary woke her to dress for tea.

****

The usual array of flowers sent by would-be suitors arrived with the usual invitations to various events. The Duke of Ravencroft never socialized, and when the dowager hostesses of London realized his grace accompanied the lovely Lady Amora Hargrove to every engagement, the number of requests for their presence grew a hundred-fold.

His grace took time out of his busy schedule to go over every invitation and hand-picked the few he would accept. A great number of his friends had an adequate number of household guards to satisfy him, and those he accepted.

A large bouquet of roses, hyacinths, magnolias, and forget-me-nots arrived at teatime with a handwritten note from Lord Antony asking her to the opera, and her spirits sagged, knowing she must decline. He sent flowers when he had some new information to share or some crazy scheme for his quest to win the hand of a specific lady he fancied, and now, she would miss out.

"Is not seeing Lord Antony for a few days so hard to bear?"

Amora had not realized the duke stood in the entry hall until he spoke. Turning, she set the flowers on the table and handed him the accompanying note. "I would trade the lot of them for one evening out with Lord Antony and a bit of merriment." She waved an arm at the mountain of bouquets and sank onto a velvet chair. Shuffling the note cards, she sighed.

Silence filled the entry as the duke studied her. "I am surprised you consider leaving the house after the events of the past night and our discussion earlier."

"Ordinarily, I would not, but this is Lord Antony, and he needs me." When she glanced up at the duke, his impassive expression gave her pause. Thinking he must be displeased with her comment when he meant to keep her safe, she hastened to add. "I do understand why I cannot accept, but no one said I had to like it. Lord

Antony has something new to share with me."

Another long silence filled the room, now heavy with the perfume of dozens of flowers.

"Does he often share 'something new?' "

"Of course. Some of them are quite shocking but so much fun. The man has quite the imagination, and he is so romantic."

The duke's stillness deafened her, and she gazed up with concern.

"Do you care for him?" The soft-spoken question took her by surprise.

She had not thought on it until now. "Yes, I suppose I do."

Lord Antony pined away for Lady Sarah Winchester, daughter of the High Chancellor, betrothed to some duke since her youth. Unhappy with her parent's choice of marriage partner, Lady Sarah let it be known she wanted to make her own choice, and after partnering her to several balls and dinners, Lord Antony became quite hopeful the lady felt the same of him as he did her.

He spilled his heart to Amora one evening, following an outing to the theater, sounding so forlorn in his quest, she agreed to help him. For she knew the pain of being unwanted and unworthy, and her heart twisted in anguish for him.

The duke studied her face. "Then accept the invitation. I shall not keep the two of you apart. But make the fact known to Lord Antony, I will accompany you. Any further outings must be kept to a minimum until we discover if Chauncey acted alone or if others have claims."

Her eyebrows rose. "You plan to join us?" The duke never attended the opera describing it as a bunch of stuffy overweight individuals who sang foreign songs for money and were extremely boring.

"Do not worry. I shall not interfere with your outing. I come to see to your safety, nothing more."

Turning on his heel, the duke left the room.

Bemused, Amora analyzed their entire conversation and shrugged. His grace could be so unpredictable at times, wanting her to stay indoors and then offering to escort her out.The man had a devil of a time making his mind up. Hurrying to the conservatory for ink and a pen, she accepted the invitation, and added the duke's conditions.

Handing the note to a footman with instructions to put it into Lord Antony's own hand, she wandered into the red salon to pour tea for the duke.

Chapter Seven

Lord Antony's carriage arrived at six forty-five and drew to a stop in front of the townhouse.

A footman answered the door as Amora descended the main staircase in her red opera gown with the low square neck. With her dark, curly hair piled high on her head and threaded with pearls, she wore a matching pearl necklace, drop pearl earrings borrowed from the Ravencroft jewels, and long white gloves. Her satin slippers matched the blood red of her gown and the lining of her black cloak.

Pausing at the foot of the stairs, she held her hand out to Lord Antony and smiled when he kissed her knuckles. "You are a goddess, Lady Amora, fallen from the heavens. An enchantress sent to craze men with your grace and beauty, and you fair take my breath away."

She nodded. "Thank you for the compliment, kind sir. You are as handsome as you are poetic."

The duke stood on the other side of the stairs with a strange expression on his face, his eyes glittering in the candlelight.

Amora glanced at him and caught her breath.

Dressed in full evening clothes, he made her mouth go dry. He wore his black hair slicked back from his broad forehead, drawing attention to his straight nose and square jaw. A snowy white cravat tied in an impossible knot at his throat contrasted sharply with the perfection of his expertly tailored black evening jacket and trousers. He wore a royal blue vest beneath the jacket, echoing the blue of his eyes. Handsome as sin, masculine as the gods, and dangerous as a predator, he studied her through half-closed eyes.

Nervous, she said the first thing to cross her mind. "Do you like my new gown, your grace? The dressmaker sent it over today, right after tea. I think the color a bit bold, but I like it. Mary says she likes it, and Lord Antony likes it. So, what do you think? Do you like it?" What she would give to make her mouth stop talking when she got uncomfortable. An awkward silence followed her outburst.

Then, he cleared his throat. "I think it adequate."

Disappointment tightened her chest, and she resisted the desire to pout. Only the discipline of maintaining a neutral expression as she played cards rescued her.

She would give all her possessions to have him speak to her like Lord Antony did. Staring at him as he walked past her, she thought of the moment earlier this morning when he held her in his arms and kissed her. Such moments were fleeting and too far between. Stuffing the memory to the back of her mind, she hovered at the bottom of the stairs hoping to maintain a disinterested air to hide the direction of her thoughts.

The duke shook Lord Antony's hand. "Good evening, sir. We will take my carriage if you do not mind. It is larger and more secure. My outriders shall also accompany us."

Her eyebrows rose. Outriders? To the opera? Who ever heard of such a thing?

"Amora?"

The duke held the door, and she followed Lord

Antony out into the night, allowing the footman to help her into the duke's magnificent carriage.

She sat opposite the two men as they trotted off and struggled to find a natural position for her hands, putting them first in her lap, then on either side of her.

The men discussed pleasantries, horses, the weather, and then politics, and all the while, she turned to the left and then to the right trying to appear as relaxed as possible.

Every time she glanced up, the duke's gaze rested on her with an unreadable expression. Until, in desperation, she turned to ask Mary about her married older sister and her grievous confinement.

Their arrival at the opera caused quite a stir, and Amora took her seat beside Lord Antony with a sigh of relief.

The duke took a seat behind, and to the side, so anyone entering or exiting the box had to pass him. While Mary sat directly behind Amora, exclaiming over the grandness of the theater.

The dowager hostesses of London appeared at their box a few at a time, complimenting the duke on his appearance and twittering with delight.

Amora rolled her eyes and listened without shame to the talk behind her until Lord Antony whispered in her ear.

"There she is." His forlorn expression made her frown.

Glancing around, she spied Lady Sarah on the arm of the Earl of Pembsy and grew quiet. The only other dowry nearing hers in size belonged to Lady Sarah, making her the earl's new target. "I do not think you have cause to worry. The Earl of Pembsy seeks to refill his coffers. He wants Lady Sarah's dowry, not her."

A long silence followed her statement.

"I have plenty of cause to endure sleepless nights. Lady Sarah is betrothed of sorts to the Duke of Huntington, a loathsome bore who has called on her only once all season. The man is twenty years her senior and a widower with no heir. The word among the Ton is he is in love with an actress and seeks a young wife to continue the family lineage. Unable to father one with his last wife, he hopes a nubile young debutante will produce the desired offspring. After which, the duchess shall be sent to his country estate to raise the child. She shall be put out to pasture, if you will, leaving him free to be with his actress. Sarah refuses to be a brood mare, and though she made her thoughts quite clear to her parents, they persist in pursuing the matter. So in response, she attends events with different lords hoping to receive a counter proposal her father will agree to."

Amora thought hard. "How is one betrothed 'of sorts?' "

Antony rolled his eyes. "There is no marriage contract. Her parents and the duke made a verbal agreement at his wife's funeral six years ago. Lady Sarah believes the whole thing archaic and revolting. The Duke of Huntington should have remarried a woman more his age well before he bent over Sarah's twelve-year-old hand and asked her father for his consent. For a man of fifty to make arrangements to wed a young girl on the day they bury his wife is nauseating, evil, and fills me with disgust."

Silence filled the space between them. Amora could not agree more, although women were bought, sold, and traded on a regular basis in society, as her own situation bore testimony to.

"So, the Duke of Huntington never produced an heir, and now he nears his fiftieth year, he seeks a young wife to fulfill the purpose? Why not wed as soon as his period of mourning ended? He would have a better chance as a younger man."

Her companion shrugged. "Some men do not consider marriage an admirable state and avoid the altar at all costs. I do not. Marriage to me is a blissful event, something to be cherished and honored. I think of little else and yearn with all my heart to make Sarah mine. She whispered to me one evening of her desire to find love, true love, and if found, she would consider elopement. I believe she meant with me, but what if I am wrong? This is the third time this week she has allowed Pembsy to escort her. What if she fancies him and not me?"

Amora studied the pair on the lower level with new eyes and shook her head at Antony. "Trust your instinct. As for the earl, he does not possess the rank nor the money to woo Lady Sarah to her father's satisfaction, and I do not believe she likes him. Pembsy gives the most exaggerated compliments and whines over every spill. How could a woman of Lady Sarah's intelligence admire such a man?"

"Look how she gazes up at him and touches his arm when she laughs. I cannot bear to watch, yet I am compelled at the same time. My chest aches when they are together."

Tilting her head in observation, Amora thought of her own stirrings of desire. "'Tis an act. If she cared, her gaze would linger, as would her touch. You must tell her how you feel before her duke convinces her parents to force the union. Let her feel the extent of your ardor. If she loves you, she will not care you are a lord."

Lord Antony squirmed. "I am not what her father wishes for her either, or what if she rebuffs me? I do not know if my heart could withstand such a moment."

"What if she accepts? Some ladies strive to make the man they fancy jealous. Lady Sarah laughs too much, and the sound is quite fake. I have spent time with the earl, and I can assure you, he is not so entertaining." Leaning close, she whispered. "See how she glances in our direction when she laughs? The lady plays with your affections."

Lord Antony touched his head to hers. "God, I hope you are right."

They stayed close together for a few minutes, studying Lady Sarah through the crowd, until the first opening strains of the orchestra filled the theater.

Suddenly aware of the stillness behind them, Amora turned to see if the duke remained in the box.

His dark gaze stared back at her, and a wry smile twisted his lips.

She nodded, smiled, and turned back to enjoy the show, conscious of his regard throughout the entire evening.

Dante, one of the duke's outriders, joined them in the box, dressed in evening clothes. He followed Lord Antony and her when they mingled in the corridor during a performance break. No one approached her, and no one stared at her.

Relieved, Amora joined the conversation closest to them until one of the ladies smiled and said, "I hear the Earl of Hargrove goes on trial this week. Such a to-do over him I have not seen in some time. Did you know he killed five lords in the last two years? He outright murdered the lot, right in his own townhouse outside Mayfair."

The five-minute warning sounded.

Amora's blood boiled. Her brother may be a scoundrel, but he never killed anyone. She opened her mouth to argue with the lady, but Lord Antony caught her hand and excused them. "We are going back to our seats. Thank you for the conversation."

Leading her out of hearing distance, he stopped beside a decorative side table holding a vase of fresh-cut blooms. "Do not say a word. Women of her character create drama, and commenting gives them more to use against you. The gossips say what they like with no regard to other's feelings, and if you give them attention, their boasts get worse."

"My brother is not a murderer. He is guilty of cheating, drinking, gambling, and whoring but not taking another man's life in cold blood." She spun away from curious patrons as they wandered toward the theater and their seats. She gasped when the sound of ripped fabric rent the air and gazed down. Her beautiful red gown hung askew, ripped from the waist in a four-inch section where the bottom of the skirt hooked on a circular pattern on the bottom of the table leg. She clapped a hand to her waist to hide the disaster and smiled at several women as they traipsed past.

Lord Antony escorted her down the opposite corridor away from the crush.

Alone, he touched her cheek. "Because someone says a thing does not make it true. Even if all of London yelled it from their chimneys, nothing would change the truth. We may have to avoid going out for a fortnight until the trial is over. People will have their say, and I do not like to see you hurt."

Amora bowed her head and drew in several deep breaths. "I am fine now. Thank you."

He leaned toward her and studied her face. "Right then, we shall find our seats before our absence is noticed."

Smiling, she took his arm, and they returned with Dante, who waited several feet away.

The duke raised an eyebrow at their tardy entrance but said nothing, and the rest of the opera proceeded without incident.

Amora knew prominent families were involved in her brother's case but somehow did not realize she would be the subject of scorn. Considering how best to act during future encounters, she stared out the carriage window at the passing city. Candlelight from the street lanterns flitted across the cobblestones as the horses clopped down the empty streets toward the duke's townhouse.

The breeze smelled of coal, oil, and wood smoke, and Amora closed her eyes to think.

"How did your dress become torn?"

Her eyes flew open, and Mary clucked her tongue in disapproval.

His grace studied her face and then Lord Antony's. "Do I thank the lord for rescuing you or challenge him to a duel for putting you in a compromising situation?"

Her gaze jumped to Lord Antony's and then to the duke. "I, uh, caught it on a table in the corridor. Lord Antony has been a perfect gentleman, nothing more."

"I am glad to hear he watches out for you. For a moment, I wondered if a duel were in my near future."

Amora gazed at him to determine if he jested with

her. Would he truly fight a duel on her behalf? The sincerity of his tone and the gleam in his eye said he would, and she filed the information away in a corner of her heart where no man tread before.

"I would never do anything to cause Lady Amora harm or discomfort." Lord Antony's quiet tone broke into her thoughts.

"I am relieved to hear it. With the earl's trial starting in two days' time, the lady requires added protection from the gossips and tale mongers."

They told him of the situation during intermission, and the duke nodded his head. "I shall be busy with the trial and unable to see to Lady Amora's protection. I trust you will look out for her with Dante's help?"

Lord Antony assured him he would.

Once they arrived home, Lord Antony took his leave, and Amora followed the duke into his study. "Should I refuse all further invitations until after the trial?"

The duke strolled to his drink trolley and splashed whiskey into a glass. "I do not think such a thing necessary. You may find the number of invitations dwindle until the magistrate passes a verdict."

Walking toward the fire, he leaned an arm on the hearth. "Or they could increase in number depending on the general opinion of society. Although I would be careful to avoid any invitation unless you have been introduced before this and know the person. A great many gossips masquerade as ladies, and their talk can be brutal." A deep sigh escaped him. "This is why I wanted to get you engaged, and a marriage contract signed. The tales will be wild and grossly exaggerated, each one adding a new twist or detail others know nothing about."

The duke stared into the flames for several long moments. "I cannot be there to protect you from scandal, so you must do so on your own conscience. Your behavior in any public event will be picked apart and inspected for flaws. There can be no more canoodling with Lord Antony, or anyone else, unless an engagement is announced. Your reputation and future life depend on you."

Amora nodded. She knew the same. "I will be the model of propriety." Unless word of Madame Pari reached the ears of the Ton, then all bets were closed.

The duke's lips twisted wryly as if he did not believe she could. "I asked earlier today if you had feelings for Lord Antony, and you confessed you did. Please explain the nature of your relationship with him. The two of you sat so close all through the performance, it is doubtful one could slip a parchment between you. I am concerned about the gossip. Have you discussed a future together? Has he spoken of love or kissed you? Does he plan to ask for your hand?"

Silence filled the chamber.

"Nay. We are friends, nothing more."

A frown furrowed his forehead. "Has he touched you or been too forward?"

"I spoke the truth. He is but a friend." She would confess Lord Antony's infatuation with Lady Sarah, except he swore her to secrecy.

The duke swirled the amber liquid in his glass and took a sip. "I do not know how bad the gossip will be, and I must be sure Lord Antony will look after you."

"He protected me tonight and will do so again. Dante never leaves my side when I step outside this door, so I am quite safe. Thank you for your concern, but I shall say good night." Turning away, she took two steps toward the door.

"Amora."

Turning toward him, she stopped.

His dark eyes glittered as he gave her a long-heated look. "Come here."

Trembling, she approached, curious about why he called her back.

Setting his glass back on the drink trolley, he strolled toward her and stopped. His gaze wandered over her hair, her lips, and her breasts before gazing deep into her eyes.

Amora licked her lips and shifted her feet. "Yes?"

"I do not know when I will have time after tonight to tutor you. Are you ready for your next lesson?"

Trembling with anxiety and anticipation, she nodded and lifted her head as he bent toward her. Heated lips covered her own as he caught her and held her tight against him. Butterflies filled her belly and rose in her throat as his heat surrounded her. He tasted of whiskey, temptation, and danger, and she shivered in delight. Lifting a hand to stroke his jaw, she wrapped the other around his neck and poured her heart into the kiss.

His response took her by surprise. With a growl, he tightened his hold and ravished her mouth. She opened her lips and let his tongue stroke along hers, whimpering with need. The fluttering in her belly increased, and her heart pounded in her ears.

"Your beauty draws me until I can think of nothing else. All night, I yearned to hold you in my arms and tell you how you make me feel." The raw desire in his kiss, coupled with the urgency of his hands as they roamed her body, caught her blood on fire. She gasped into his mouth when he squeezed her breasts above the binding of her corset, and her breath quickened.

She needed to touch him, to get closer to his heat.

Trembling, she undid his vest and untucked his tunic, sliding her hands over his hard, rippling chest.

The duke moaned, catching both her hands in his. Lifting his head to gaze deep into her eyes as he rubbed her back with slow lazy circles, making her squirm against him. His breath blew across her face. "Your lips entice me as few have, but we must stop, or I shall not be able to. I could not take my eyes from you all evening. Your beauty outshone every other woman in the theater. But you must not take any chances. If you see anything or anyone out of the ordinary who makes you uncomfortable, tell Dante, and he will get word to me. With any luck, the trial will be fast, and justice will be served. During the process, we will be able to ferret out any other questionable connections your brother had. I am anxious to discover if he sold or bartered you to any other person so we can apprehend them. Your life must be your own before we can move forward."

Amora stared up at his handsome face, still quivering. "Do you think there are more?"

She liked having him a few feet away. Something about his presence made her feel safe, and thoughts of going anywhere without him concerned her.

He shrugged. "None have shown their hand, but it does not mean they do not exist."

"I could stay home and invite Lord Antony to tea."

"For an unspecified amount of time? There is no need to make you a prisoner."

"What are your thoughts on the high chancellor?"

The duke stepped back to study her face.

"Winchester? He is a bit stuffy but a good man and loyal to the king. Why do you ask?'

"I have an invitation to tea tomorrow afternoon."

"If Lord Antony goes, I see no problem."

She grinned. "He is invited, but I wish you could come, too,"

"I must attend your brother's trial and make sure the bastard gets the sentence he deserves. Tomorrow is the day the magistrate goes over the charges."

She shivered. "I do not know what I will do if they let him go. I have no wish to return to him."

He stroked her cheek. "I will not let him have you. One way or another, I will keep you safe.

Chapter Eight

The trial had everyone's attention.

At first, Amora received pats of condolence and words of encouragement from the hostesses and ladies she met. As more information came out about her brother's illegal activities and the prominent families involved, people chatted about her, not to her.

As one unpleasant evening ended, a dinner hostess requested she empty her reticule before leaving the home to ensure she did not slip any valuables or silver cutlery into her bag.

"One can never be certain of someone's character when bad blood is involved. After what we have learned of the earl, how can we be sure of his sister?"

"Lady Amora had nothing to do with the earl's activities." Lord Antony drew up to his full height and demanded an apology, promising he and everyone he knew would never darken her door again if she refused. Though but a lord, his family had the bluest of blood, and such an insult would ruin the lady's chance in society. She capitulated and offered a profuse though insincere apology.

Once they took their leave, Amora sank into the cushion of Lord Antony's carriage, shaking from the confrontation. "My brother is a liar and a cheat, so it is to be expected, I suppose. But why do they condemn me when I had nothing to do with it?" Other than masquerading as Madame Pari and relieving foolish young men of their wealth or being beaten senseless by her brother. Amora glanced out the window and sighed, wishing for the carefree days of her youth when resting in the afternoon was the one thing marring her day. Things were different as an adult and much more complicated. She did what she must to survive while living with Nathan, and her games were skill, not subterfuge. Although the chances of anyone else seeing the situation from her point of view were slim if any.

"Wait until his grace hears of this." Dante's lips twisted. "I should not want to be in Lady Charlotte's shoes when he does."

Amora's chin lifted. "His grace is too busy with the trial to take much notice of my little problems. I shall be fine, and if I am to endure the war, I must not falter during battle."

Dante shook his head. "His grace is busy, yes, but he does not retire until I make a complete report about you each day, my lady."

She did not know what to think of his statement. Following her last encounter with the duke in his study the night of the opera, she had not laid eyes on him. He rose in the wee hours of the morning while she slept and retired long after she retired to her chamber at night. A fortnight passed without any communication between them.

Lord Antony proved a true friend during her trying times and teased her out of her melancholy. His courtship of Lady Sarah took a turn for the better following tea at her father's London home the day Nathan's trial began.

The Duchess of Winchester gazed down her nose at Amora and sipped her tea, her sharp eyes missing nothing.

Frantic to create a distraction so Lord Antony could slip a note into Lady Sarah's hand unobserved, she rose and wandered over to a pianoforte in front of the window overlooking a fabulous flower garden.

"Do you play, your grace?" Stroking the gleaming finish of the instrument, she glanced back toward the others.

The duchess sighed. "Not anymore. My arthritis keeps my fingers stiff and makes playing impossible."

"May I?"

When the duchess nodded her consent, Amora sat on the tufted velvet bench and ran her hands over the ivory keys. "My mother used to play and taught me a few songs."

With a slight nod in Lord Antony's direction signaling his opportunity, she plucked out the opening strains to a popular ballad, adding her voice to the song.

Lord Antony passed his note under the duchess's unsuspecting nose and followed the ladies to a settee nearer to the pianoforte.

A small smile of satisfaction tugged at her lips when he wiggled his eyebrows, signaling success. Relieved, she threw her heart and soul into the old ballad and found the exercise calmed her own troubled heart.

When the last notes died away, Amora rose to find all three of her companions staring at her.

The duchess sighed and gave her a warm smile. "Oh, my dear, you have an angelic voice. I have not enjoyed company for tea so much in years. My old heart skipped a beat when you played the ballad, and I shall never forget the way the hair on my neck stood up when you sang the chorus. You fair gave me goosebumps."

Goosebumps were a good thing, forever after the Duchess of Winchester championed her cause.

Thrilled with their success, the duo hurried back to Ravencroft Townhouse to make plans for the ball later the same night. Lord Antony's note asked Lady Sarah to meet him on the balcony at midnight.

Nervous as a chicken in a famine, Lord Antony paced back and forth in the library until Amora demanded he sit. "You are making me nauseous. If she cares, she will come. Either way, one thing will happen for sure. After tonight you will know."

Grinning, he plopped down beside her. "How shall I let you know if she agrees to walk in the garden with me?"

"I plan to be in the garden beforehand, watching from a distance, and if she comes, I will keep guard for you. Think how suspicious I would look if I followed her out. "Amora shook her head. "I do not want to frighten her off or alert her mother."

"You know I will do the same for you as soon as you find a suitor."

Amora laughed. "I doubt I shall have one anytime soon. Most of my suitors want to take my gold to the garden and kiss the coins in the moonlight, not me."

Lord Antony squeezed her fingers. "There is someone for you out there somewhere. Our goal is to find him. In the meantime, do I wear my burgundy jacket with the white embroidery or the navy one? And do I wear white breeches or black? My valet learned a new knot for my cravat, and I have two new vests, one gold and one black."

"Wear the navy topcoat with the gold and burgundy embroidery, the gold vest, and the burgundy breeches.

You will make her swoon with the masculine picture you present."

"But I do not want lady Sarah to swoon. I want to kiss her." A lustful gleam entered his eye, and he sighed. "I cannot get her lips off my mind."

"Have you kissed before?"

He glared. "Of course I have. The act is just a matter of putting lips against lips."

She gazed at him, hiding the smile tugging at her mouth. "If you view kissing thus, how do you plan to convince her to marry you?"

Her friend shrugged, adopting a haughty stance. "With my handsome face and perfect lineage." He seemed serious, and Amora shook her head again.

"Your lineage will not be the one kissing her. You must put feeling into the action."

His mouth twisted as he sank onto a settee. "I have the emotion but not the expertise. Most of my friends used the housemaids for practice. My mother never took her eye off me long enough for me to get good at it. What if I lose her for lack of technique?"

When he jumped up to pace again, she rose. "You may practice on me."

Lord Antony stopped cold. "Are you sure? I mean, what if the servants come in, or the duke? He may not understand my lack of knowledge, and I do not want to have to duel with him."

"No one will know." Walking away, she closed the door and twisted the lock, adding the back of a chair beneath the latch so no one could force their way in.

"Ready." She walked to the hearth and faced him. "Here I am, Lady Sarah. Now kiss me."

Lord Antony stared at her. "I am not sure this is a

good idea." Shifting from one foot to the other, he glanced at the door.

"Of course, it is. Who else are you going to practice on? Come on, kiss me."

With a nervous glance toward the window and back at the closed door, he approached and took her gingerly in his arms.

Amora lifted her face and pursed her lips, waiting for him to comply.

When he refused, she groaned in annoyance and tugged his head down to hers.

Sliding her lips over his, she held him tight against her. "I am Sarah, and you love me. Come on, Antony, pretend."

He opened his mouth over hers and kissed her deeply.

She experienced none of the breathless anticipations she did when the duke kissed her. Her heart did not speed up, no nervous flutters filled her stomach, and no breathlessness overtook her. Tucking the methodical experience away, she dropped her arms.

Lord Antony lifted his head and stepped back. "So, how was it?"

"I think your kisses wonderful. Lady Sarah will be hungry for more." Lying did not come easy, even for the sister of a cheat. Amora prayed her brilliant smile convinced him.

"I hope you are right. I do not know what I will do if she does not come out on the terrace. I cannot live without her, and it has been torture these past weeks to see her with one lord after another. I do not know how much more I can take."

"And thus, the reason we gave her the note. Now, go

home and get ready. I shall have my bath, dress, and meet you in front of the townhouse in three hours' time, ready to make this plan work."

When they replaced the chair and unlocked the door, Amora swung it open to see the duke, standing before her.

His stare turned to a frown when Lord Antony stepped from behind her and offered his hand. "Good day, your grace."

A muscle ticked along the duke's jaw as he gazed from one to the other. "Why were you alone with Lady Amora behind a locked door?" His sharp gaze inspected her flushed face and windblown hair before dropping to her lips. Fury shot from his eyes. "Have you compromised her?" He took a menacing step toward her companion.

"No, he did not." Her words stopped him mid-stride. She met the anger in his with the calm of hers.

The duke inspected her face again. "Your lips are swollen, and your cheeks are flushed, telling me he kissed you."

Her chin rose. "He did not."

Lord Antony glanced at her and took a step forward. "We should tell him the truth."

The duke's expression darkened. "So, you did compromise her. Go to your chamber Amora. I will deal with this."

"No. You want the truth. Fine. Answer the question, my lord. Did you touch me inappropriately, as in, anywhere on my body but my face or hands?"

Lord Antony glanced at her shaking his head. "No, but—"

"Have you compromised me or violated my virtue

in any way?"

"Good God, no. But—"

"And the last question. Did you kiss her?" The duke took another step forward.

Amora stepped in front of him. "No, he did not."

"We did kiss, my lady." Antony shook his head at her and stepped around to face the duke. "I am ready to offer for her hand, your grace."

She knew what the effort cost him, and although his courage impressed her, she would not marry a man who loved another.

"Aye, we kissed but 'twas me who did the kissing, not him. He stood still as a statue and did not kiss me back. So, he cannot be held accountable for my actions."

The tick in the duke's jaw grew more noticeable as he stared holes through Antony. "I will hear it from you. Who initiated the kiss?"

Lord Antony ran a hand through his hair and sighed. "Lady Amora, your grace."

"See? Lord Antony did nothing wrong. I am the aggressor, not him. Now, if you will excuse us, we have a ball to go to."

"And if I refuse to allow it?" The tick along the duke's jaw grew more pronounced.

"I will go anyway. I gave my word to help with a particular situation, and I shall."

Their gazes locked, and neither backed down for several long minutes.

Lord Antony stood still, his expression saying he wished to be anywhere but here.

A tense silence filled the corridor. Then, for whatever reason, the duke capitulated. "Do not leave Dante's side. We found more evidence today tying your brother to Singapore. I cannot elaborate without giving away key information." He searched both their faces before pinning Antony to the floor with his narrow gaze. "Do not let her out of your sight, or you will answer to me."

"You have my word, your grace."

"And no more kissing or touching unless you intend to offer for her hand."

"Aye. My hands shall remain by my side all evening, and my lips as well. If Lady Amora attempts to kiss me again, I shall dissuade her."

"I have your word and shall hold you to it. I am an excellent shot and have not lost a duel yet." The duke strode toward his study without a backward glance.

Once alone, Lord Antony gave an audible sigh of relief, wiping terror from his noble brow. "Do not ask me to kiss you again, Amora. I do not fancy meeting the duke at dawn across an open field. Although I like you a great deal, I wish to enjoy a long life and marry Lady Sarah."

"And you shall. But first, you must get dressed for the ball, and so must I. See you at seven."

He nodded and all but ran from the townhouse.

All the way up the stairs to her chamber, Amora thought on her kiss with Antony. Pleasant, mechanical, warm, and wet, but nothing of note to think about. She experienced none of the pleasure nor the need to get closer. Thank the gods Antony did not try to stroke her tongue with his. Nausea rose in her throat at the mere notion.

Heart-pounding, breathless, anticipation, fluttering belly, heated desire, and the need for more ran through her body like liquid fire when she exchanged kisses with the duke. Just thinking of him in this way made her squirm. Who would have guessed kissing different men could have such extreme reactions. Bemused, she walked away to bathe and dress for the ball.

The duke did not come out of his study when William announced Lord Antony's arrival for the ball.

So, Amora tapped on his door and called, "good night."

The door flung open before she took two steps. Catching her by the elbow, he steered her into his study and closed the door behind him.

Before she could think, his hot mouth descended on hers, ravishing her lips with hungry, carnal kisses, while his hands caught her waist and held her against him.

The heat of his body, coupled with the taste of his kisses, intoxicated her. His musky scent surrounded her, sending her senses dancing with longing and desire. Flutters filled her belly, and her breath came fast. "Your grace." Anticipation and wild excitement raced through her bloodstream.

He kissed her again, his hands dropping to her hips while his tongue stroked hers. "Does Lord Antony make you breathless with desire? Do you dream of his kisses at night and yearn to feel his hands on your body? Do you go crazed for one glimpse of his face and count the hours until you see him next? Does your heart speed up whenever he is near? Does your soul know you cannot live without him?"

Quivering with desire, she shook her head. "Nay. None of the things you mentioned. We are but friends."

Dante knocked on the door, making her jump in alarm.

"Your grace, my lady, Lord Antony waits in the red

salon."

The duke stared down at her for long seconds. Then he stroked her cheek as he called to Dante. "We will be but a moment."

"Very good, your grace." His footsteps retreated, leaving them in silence.

"Do you plan to marry him?" The duke's gaze darkened as he stared at her lips.

"Nay." Her mouth dried, making the word difficult to say. Amora swallowed, unable to tear her gaze away from the hunger in his.

Satisfied with what he read in her eyes, he stepped back, dropping his hands to his side." I planned to go to the country to see my mother this weekend. I would like you to join me."

Surprised at his sudden invitation, she nodded. "I would love to."

A curious look passed over his face. "Do not take any chances tonight at whatever function you attend. I will have your word you will behave in the proper fashion."

"Aye." She had no need to kiss anyone but him.

"I will see you early tomorrow morning, then. Good night, Amora."

"Good night, your grace."

In the carriage, Lord Antony took her hand in his. "We took an awful chance today and nearly lost both our dreams. I appreciate your help getting out of the mess, but I could have defended my actions with the duke."

"Not without losing Lady Sarah and marrying me. I, for one, have a different future planned, and I refuse to give it up for something so silly. Although I love you dearly, my love is as a friend, not a lover or husband."

"The same for me. My heart belongs to Lady Sarah."

"Which is why I would rather sacrifice your pride in front of the duke than see you lose your chance at happiness."

"It *was* my pride. I doubt his grace considers me much of a man when I hid behind your skirts."

"You did not hide. I stepped in front. Now, about our plans for tonight…"

Chapter Nine

At eleven in the evening, Amora slipped away from Dante and out of the ball, hiding beneath a tree flanked with flowering bushes. She could see the terrace and the steps down into the garden without revealing her presence.

Lord Antony appeared on the terrace fifteen minutes later and paced. Clasping his hands behind his back, he stopped every couple of minutes to glare at the door before resuming his activity.

Sighing, she leaned her shoulder against the trunk of the tree. Nothing more could be done but to wait.

Amora understood his frustration.

Earlier in the evening, when they arrived, Lord Antony danced the first dance with Lady Sarah and then stood in different groups around the ballroom as the object of his affection danced until dinner. Whereupon, he sat directly across the table from her and the Earl of Pembsy, keeping his gaze on his plate rather than on the love of his life.

The Duke of Winchester hoped to find a suitable match for his daughter among the titled gentlemen at court. Being the second son of a mere lord did nothing to encourage his suit, and the duke warned him away from his daughter at the first of the season.

Undaunted, Lord Antony took dances when he could and offered tea and punch when the occasion arose.

Now, he grew tired of being in the background and yearned to know if Lady Sarah reciprocated his feelings.

Her heart ached for him as they waited.

At last, the clock struck midnight, and Lord Antony stepped into the shadow of the terrace.

Amora's gaze sharpened when the door opened, and a couple emerged, speaking in quiet tones as they made their way down the steps toward the garden and disappeared.

The door opened again, and Lady Sarah stepped into view. Her blonde hair gleamed in the light of the lanterns as she slipped onto the terrace and stopped. Gazing around, she took a tentative step and then another, gazing into the corners.

Lord Antony emerged from the shadows, and they spoke for several seconds before he took her arm and walked her down the steps.

Amora breathed a sigh of relief. For a while, she wondered if Lady Sarah would come and if not, what she would do to console Lord Antony. He swore he would never love another as he loved her, and she believed him. If the truth were told, she yearned to find the same all-consuming euphoria he did when he spoke of Lady Sarah.

Slipping out of sight as the two strolled to the arbor, Amora waited until they disappeared before coming from her hiding place to stand guard so the two could talk without being discovered.

For several minutes she hovered around the entrance to the secluded alcove before bending to sniff a foxglove.

A voice behind her startled her. "Lady Amora, all alone in the garden. This is the second time I find you thus."

It could not be! Swiveling, she faced the Earl of Pembsy with a sneer on his face. "What do you want?"

Graciousness and manners would be lost on the arrogant man, so she did not bother.

The earl shrugged. "Where is your lady's maid or escort? No lady walks alone in the garden unattended unless she intends to meet a man. Such a thing is simply not done. Think of your reputation. Have you a secret lover waiting in the arbor, I wonder? What fun the Ton will have if I were to let it be known I met you alone in the garden twice. Once at the palace and once here. One word to the right ears, you would be ruined, and the Duke of Ravencroft pitied for helping the sister of a murderer and a cheat."

She froze. If he said aught about their meeting either time, she would be ruined, and the duke pitied, as he said. Her chin lifted. "His Grace is not one to anger. He is my guardian and will call you out if you bandy my name about."

"Unless he thinks I compromised you and forces me to offer for you. In which case, all the lovely gold he donated for your dowry will be mine and worth every lie. I paid you a great compliment when we first met by inviting you to share your wealth with me, and you bloodied my nose. Is it not interesting how times change? Now, I hear your brother is going to hang for cheating at the tables and racetracks. No man of noble birth will want you following the trial and sentencing. I think it best to confess to Ravencroft how I have dallied with you."

Not while she lived and breathed. Amora narrowed her eyes. "Did you not learn your lesson the last time you threatened me?"

Feigning a fist punch, she kicked him in the groin when he leaned away to avoid her blow and followed with a punch to the nose when he fell forward after her kick.

"Damn you! Who taught you such a trick?" The earl dropped to his knees, gasping, and searching his pockets before withdrawing a kerchief. "I cannot believe you bloodied my nose again." Curling in a ball, he dabbed at his nose. "You will pay for this. Mark my words."

Anxiety tightened her throat. "As will you. I will not be kind next time. So stay away from me."

Turning, she came face to face with Dante.

The six-foot brown-haired outrider glanced from her to the earl crying at their feet. Picking the shriveling coward up by his embroidered jacket and fine linen shirt, he glowered into his face. "I would leave London if I were you. For when the duke hears of this, he will demand satisfaction, and you know his reputation with a pistol."

The earl paled and hurried away without looking back.

Dante turned to Amora. "You hit the earl before? I am forced to admit, your feigned punch impressed me."

"Thank you. And yes, I have hit him before, in the garden at the palace. I did not care for his conversation and let him know my thoughts."

"His grace will not be pleased." He shook his head. "If you let me know you required fresh air from the garden, I would have come, and Pembsy would not have dared approach you. This whole situation could have been averted.

"I know, and I am sorry, Dante, but I had to come

alone for a reason I cannot reveal. I gave my word."

A frown darkened his expression. "Do you have a clandestine meeting arranged?" Glancing around, he strode into the arbor.

"No! Do not go in there!" Amora rushed to catch his arm, but she came too late.

Dante peered through the vines surrounding the secluded area and then turned to her."

She fancied she could see him thinking and waited to see his decision.

"If we are going to stand guard for Lord Antony, we should find a more obscure place to do so."

Amora glanced at him. "So, you understand why I came out here?"

"Aye. Over here, we are in shadow." He led her to a bench beneath a large ash tree, where the shadows hid their presence.

"I must have your word you will not speak of this situation or the couple in the arbor to anyone, especially the duke." She wrung her hands as she made her request. "Please? It is important."

A full minute of silence followed her request. "You have my word unless his grace asks me specific questions regarding this moment, or your safety is in jeopardy."

After a moment, she agreed. Dante did owe his loyalty to the duke, after all.

Sitting, Amora breathed a sigh of relief and settled back to wait. Her peace lasted a full minute before the Duchess of Winchester sailed out onto the terrace. "Where is my daughter?"

Amora froze. The seconds ticked like the dong of a clock as her mind ran rampant with possible scenarios.

Not wanting to leave Antony and Lady Sarah unguarded, yet knowing the Duchess of Winchester's regard for propriety, she had no desire to be discovered in the garden without an escort, either.

Thinking her own plight, the lesser of two evils, she turned to Dante. "I will distract her grace while you help these two back inside unobserved."

"I have a better idea. Antony will remain in the arbor, and your man will escort us both to my mother. Problem solved."

Lady Sarah and Lord Antony appeared behind them, flushed and looking as though they caught a star from the heavens whose brilliance shone from their eyes.

So, the tete-a-tete proved successful. Amora slipped her arm through Lady Sarah's. "Try to look a little less in love and more like we wandered through masses of foxglove, or your mother will be suspicious."

"Right you are." The lady bowed her head and took several breaths as they approached the terrace. When she glanced up, her face appeared normal, but her eyes retained their gleam.

Dante kept his distance behind them, and when Amora glanced back, no sign of Antony could be seen.

"There you are, darling. Somehow, I missed your departure to the garden with Lady Amora. I have been searching everywhere. I am relieved to find you here and so well protected."

Her daughter smiled. "There are wonderous gardens here, Mother. Amora and I both needed a breath of fresh air. Since the duke's outrider follows her everywhere, I did not think you would mind my going without you. Her brother's trial has been quite hard on the poor dear."

"I have heard the gossip, dear, and I am glad you

offered her your sympathy. I have given the matter some thought and reached a decision. I shall host an extravagant soirée where Lady Amora shall sing for us. Society will change their opinion of her when they hear her angelic voice."

Amora frowned. "Singing seems a strange way to convince people of my innocence."

"Agreed, but I have dealt with the fickle hostesses of the Ton enough to know how to sway them. Not a one dares to cross me. Now then, I shall send the invitations tomorrow, and we will meet on Thursday evening next at seven. Come along, dear. It is time to leave." She nodded at Amora. "Good night, dear."

"Good night." As Lady Sarah and the duchess swept back into the ballroom, she stepped back into the shadows to decide her next play.

Antony bound up the steps to the terrace a few minutes later. "Oh, Amora, you cannot believe how ecstatic I am. Sarah loves me and has agreed to elope! She does not care for the Earl of Pembsy and allowed him to escort her to appease her mother. She wants me! And I am so in love I believe I could fly if I put my mind to the task."

"You both looked quite radiant when you stepped from the arbor. I am sorry you did not have more time alone with her."

"Me too, but the fact her mother came outside to the garden to search for her did not surprise either one of us. Now, all I need is to find the right opportunity for us to escape. I am so happy I could walk on a cloud."

"Do not fly off just yet. The clouds will have to wait until we make plans. The Duchess of Winchester invited me to come sing this coming Thursday at seven. You could escort me and get another moment alone with Lady Sarah."

"Thursday?" Antony frowned and grew quiet. "I shall think of a plan. We cannot let anyone know what we are about, or I shall lose her."

Amora shivered as the cool of the evening brushed over her bare shoulders.

"In the meantime, we should get you home. It is late. The last thing I need tonight is the duke hunting us down and demanding an explanation. One stern talk from him is enough."

Dante nodded toward the ballroom. "Most of the guests are leaving. I think we should, too."

They drove home in silence. When the carriage stopped in front of Ravencroft Townhouse, Lord Antony glanced up at her. "I shall come later in the day tomorrow to make plans."

And then she remembered. "Come on Monday. The duke invited me to the country estate this weekend to meet his mother and sister. I will not be home."

He nodded absently, and she accepted Dante's hand out of the carriage.

"Until Monday," Antony called as the carriage drove away, rumbling over the cobblestone road.

The lanterns hanging from elaborate posts along the narrow street sent slivers of light over the round stones lining the road. Silver shafts of moonlight outlined the rooftops and chimneys as far as she could see. A breeze stirred dried leaves at her feet, and the chirp of crickets filled the silence. The scent of wood fire, coal, and magnolias teased her senses. Somewhere close, a horse snorted.

Amora turned and walked up the stairs to the front

door, which Dante opened for her. "Thank you for your help tonight. Lord Antony is quite smitten with Lady Sarah, as you know, and asked me to help him with his suit, swearing me to secrecy. Knowing you know my purpose without breaking my word is a worry off my mind. I want to thank you for aiding me this night."

He turned to face her. "My job is to keep you safe, not to pass judgment. I cannot do what his grace requires if I do not know where you are."

She nodded. "I apologize, Dante. I shall not slip away from you again."

With a nod, he disappeared into the duke's study, and Amora climbed the stairs to her chamber.

****

Mary woke her before the sun. "Hurry, my lady. His grace is anxious to leave."

An hour later, she accepted the duke's hand into his carriage, and they were off with Mary and the duke's valet traveling behind them in a separate carriage. The clop of the horses' hooves on the cobblestone road filled the silence and the early morning breeze carried the scent of smoke, waste, and the Thames.

Amora leaned forward and peeked out the window at the houses sailing past and the lengthening shadows as the first rays of the sun filtered through the narrow empty streets. "How long is the drive to your country estate?"

Street workers doused the gas lanterns lining the road as they passed.

"Four hours if we keep going at a good clip." His dark eyes gazed at her in the faint light coming through the window. "Dante tells me you struck the Earl of Pembsy."

Her chin rose. "Only after fair warning. I do not

113

enjoy being touched, and he refused to let me go."

"Why did you not tell me?"

She shrugged. "What could you do after the fact? I needed help in the moment, not later. Besides, I learned how to get away from those kinds of situations the first two weeks I lived with Nathan."

He stayed silent. "The purpose of a guardian is to provide for your wellbeing. I apologize you had to take care of him on your own. The earl will never bother you again, and next time a man makes you uncomfortable, I will handle him."

"If you handle every man who makes me nervous or tries to pin me down and kiss me, you will take out half the riff-raff in London."

She wanted to take back her comment when the duke's eyes shot fire, and his lips thinned.

"Provide me the names, and I will exact satisfaction."

Amora shook her head. "You cannot challenge half of London to a duel, and besides, these men do not matter. I took care of the situations as they occurred, and I am glad for the experience. Otherwise, the earl would have overpowered and compromised me." A shiver of disgust rushed over her. "I would no doubt be wed to the cockroach at this moment. The revolting thought makes me quite nauseous."

"When we return to London, I will instruct you on a couple of defensive techniques. My hope is you will never need them."

"Mine, too."

Silence followed, and Amora turned to gaze out the window at the passing scenery, busy thinking of ways to help Antony pursue Lady Sarah.

They arrived at Ravencroft Estate three and a half hours later, hot and in need of a cool drink.

Large oak trees lined the long cobblestone drive, shading the road and creating a bowery of greenery. The drive curved in front of a sprawling stone two-story house with large paned windows facing the road. Servants lined the sides of the red-carpeted steps leading to the double oak door entrance.

The duke greeted each one and introduced Amora as they ascended the stairs. So many servants for such a grand house, and each one smiled with genuine happiness when the duke stopped to acknowledge them.

The butler, an older man with graying hair and piercing brown eyes, informed them the Dowager Duchess of Ravencroft awaited their arrival in the blue saloon.

His announcement surprised the duke a great deal. "My mother has not left her room since the death of my nephew." He slid a sideways glance at Amora. "Her curiosity about you got the better of her."

She did not know how to respond, so she said nothing. Curiosity could be both good and bad. Time would tell which one the dowager duchess entertained.

They handed their cloaks to the butler, and the duke escorted her to meet his family.

The dowager duchess, dressed in a dour black mourning gown with her gray curls piled on her head, sat on a white satin settee with a lace shawl over her knees and shoulders. Keen blue eyes studied Amora as she walked forward and dipped a curtsy.

"So, you are the Earl of Hargrove's sister." A smile lit the still beautiful face of the duke's mother as she took her hand with soft wrinkled ones. "Welcome, my dear."

A woman of her own height rose to her feet dressed in black, as well. Her brown silver-tipped hair curled around her beautiful face and rose high on her head. "Welcome to Ravencroft." Delicate hands took both of hers and squeezed. "I am Esme, Marchioness of Baxter and Alexander's older sister. Come, have some tea while the servants settle your things."

Amora sat next to the marchioness while the duke took a seat beside his mother.

They enjoyed tea and iced lemon cake while discussing banalities.

Ice blue silk covered the walls, and a thick rug of the same hue covered the wooden floor beneath their feet. White and gold etched furniture filled the room, complementing the gilded white plaster of the ceiling. Long gilt-edged mirrors hung on all four walls alongside golden curved lamps, and crystal-cut vases with fresh floral blooms filled the air with their sweet perfume. Heavy pale blue drapes trimmed with gold tassels and held back with a golden rope hung at the large windows overlooking the front of the house and the flower gardens.

"What is the latest word on the trial of the Earl of Hargrove?" The dowager's question brought Amora's attention back to the conversation.

"We have a couple more witnesses, and then the magistrate will give his verdict. I expect the whole fiasco over by the end of the week."

Amora's heart rose to her throat. The Duchess of Winchester's soirée could not be better timed, and she hoped the outcome would be all the duchess hoped. If her brother were set free, she would need friends.

After tea, the duke gave her a tour of the house and

estate before leaving her outside her chamber door. "I have some things I must attend to. Feel free to explore the house and gardens, and I will see you at dinner."

Chapter Ten

Amora took him at his word, and all afternoon, she allowed her heart to dictate where her feet would go next.

Ravencroft Country Estate delighted her senses and calmed her soul. The flower gardens stretched in endless rows, intoxicating her with their fragrance, while the winding paths beckoned her to come explore.

Her chamber boasted elegant shades of lavender with gold accents with a large paned window overlooking the park. Green grass rolled away across countless acres while silver birch, giant oak, and sweet chestnut trees dotted the landscape. She could stay here for an eternity and not feel she stayed long enough. If wishes came true, this is where she would be.

After a day and a half outdoors exploring and a horse ride around the park, Sunday evening came too soon.

With a sigh, Amora turned from the window and took a seat so Mary could arrange her hair for dinner. "I have forgotten how quiet the country is. My home is or was in Southampton, and I loved it there."

"Since the magistrate made ye his grace's ward, there is no reason why ye cannot come back here if ye've a mind to."

"Unless my brother is released, and I am forced to go live with him." Her worry stayed on her mind morning and night. Once she helped Antony win Lady

Sarah's hand, she would leave London. The duke graciously gave her a small amount each week for her needs. Since she had none except the need to be free, she saved it in a kerchief in her wardrobe at Ravencroft Townhouse. No one knew what became of her dowry, and Amora planned to travel to Hargrove Estate and track down her father's overseer. He would know what became of her gold. If her cause were lost, she would take her savings and play until she had enough to survive on her own.

After a succulent dinner of roast duck, pigeon, and goose, they retired to the blue salon for a quiet evening.

The duke stood before the fireplace swirling a glass of port while Esme worked needlepoint beside the dowager duchess on the settee facing the fire.

Amora sat alone on the other settee with her head buried in a book of poems she found earlier in her inspection of the library,

The butler stepped into the room. "Excuse me, your graces, there is a visitor here to see you."

"Show them in." The duke set his glass on the drink trolley and turned to the door.

"Do not be upset, Alexander. I invited Olga to the house this evening to introduce her to Lady Amora." The dowager's voice spoke from the settee.

The duke frowned. "Mother, you know how I feel about you inviting such persons into the house. If the authorities discover the gypsies' presence, they will be arrested."

"Which is the reason I let them stay on our property. We have vast forests and lands, and they hurt no one. I spoke with Olga about the girl, and she asked to do a reading on her."

Before he could reply, a frail, old woman with dark leather skin entered the room. Her long black hair hung in a braid down her back, and her plain dark gown of coarse linen dropped to her worn shoes. Her black eyes sparkled as she dipped an exaggerated curtsy. "Good evenin', yer grace."

"Good evening, Olga." The duke strode toward the woman and took her hand. "Have you had anything to eat today?"

"Oh, I had a bit of bread and cheese earlier."

He nodded. "I will have a bundle of food made up for you after you are done with my mother."

"Ye are a kind man, yer grace."

The gypsy curtsied to the other two women before swiveling to stare at Amora. "So, ye are the Earl of Hargrove's sister." Her gaze roamed over her face, and she dipped a small curtsy. "Ye have an interesting glow about ye. Give me your hand, girl."

Amora glanced at the duke and then at his mother, unsure if she wanted her "reading."

"She means well. Do not be frightened." Esme glanced up from her needlepoint to smile her encouragement. "Olga would not hurt a gnat."

"Unless it bit me." The old woman cackled until her laugh turned to a cough.

The dowager duchess signaled for a glass of water and offered the gypsy a drink and a chair.

While the women were distracted, Amora glanced at the duke and raised a questioning eyebrow indicating the gypsy.

He gave a slight nod and resumed his stance by the mantel.

Rising, she took a seat in a chair next to the gypsy

and offered her palm.

The woman's leathery hands warmed hers, and a tingle spread up her arms at the old woman's touch. Leaning close, Olga murmured unintelligible words as she traced the lines on Amora's palm.

The dowager duchess leaned forward as the gypsy muttered, her eyes bright with anticipation. "Is she the one?"

The gypsy swayed back and forth with her eyes closed and then stopped. She blinked three times at Amora and released her hand. "Aye, but there is darkness."

"And my son?"

The duke turned, giving his mother a questioning look. "What about me?"

"Let her see your palm, Alexander. Humor me."

Rising, the gypsy walked to the duke and asked for his hand. Taking a quick look and running her hand over his palm, she smiled. "Your heart beats with loneliness. Though surrounded by friends and acquaintances, you are withdrawn and empty inside. Your missing soul-half is nearby and seeks to join with you, but you shall not realize your true love's desire until you are dealt the gamble of hearts." With those cryptic words, she dropped his hand. Dipping another curtsy, she bid them "good night" and left, turning toward the kitchen and the promised meal.

Silence filled the room.

"What did you mean 'Is she the right one'? Who do you and the gypsy think Amora is? And what does this have to do with me?"

His mother smiled up at him. "Never mind, darling. All will be revealed before long. Thank you for allowing me my small idiosyncrasies."

"I do not like these intrigues you enjoy with Olga. If any harm befalls Amora, I shall cast her and her caravan off my property."

A shadow passed over his mother's face. "No harm shall come to your ward. I asked the gypsy about a particular problem, and Olga revealed the answer came in the form of a girl. When you spoke of your new ward on your last visit, I suspected she would be the one to solve this problem. Now, I have my answer. Do not fear for Amora. There is naught wrong, and I, too, shall say good night."

The dowager rose to her feet and walked away, leaving the other three staring after her.

"Do you know what this problem is only Amora can solve?" The duke sat opposite his sister and studied her face.

"I have no idea, but it cannot be too bad. Doctor Oliver visited the day before yesterday and assured me mother is in good health. I would think the problem superficial rather than physical. Mother does like to read tarot cards and study the stars. Allowing her these small pleasures has improved her health."

The duke sighed. "I do not like her relationship with Olga, and I would have demanded she leave our land save the effect she has on mother."

"I know. I have the same thought."

Amora rose to her feet. She had no time to worry about a gypsy and her cryptic words. Her thoughts were on her promise to help Antony and then her own future. The duke warned her they left for London in the wee hours, and she intended to get her sleep. "Good night."

The duke rose to his feet, setting his glass on the

marble table at their knees. "Do you wish for me to escort you?"

She shook her head. "No. I can find my way. Thank you, my lady, for a delightful dinner and interesting evening." She dipped a curtsy at the marchioness and left, thinking of ways to help Antony sneak a message to Lady Sarah before her mother's soirée.

****

They arrived back in London in time for tea.

Changing into a tea gown of peach-colored silk, Amora descended the stairs to take her place in the red salon to pour tea for the duke, should he entertain visitors.

William set a salver containing a note bearing her name beside the tea tray. "This came for you while you were absent."

Frowning, Amora broke the seal and froze.

The note read:

"I had the most interesting conversation with a lord of our mutual acquaintance. This friend revealed your false identity and your lies to me. You are Madame Pari, who played for the Earl of Hargrove the night I lost my inheritance at the tables. Despite your protestations of innocence and lack of knowledge, 'twas you who relieved me of my wealth, and I will have satisfaction. I do not require your hand in marriage, for the duke has made his opinion clear in this regard. I do, however, require you to play for me at the same tavern on Pudding Lane where you robbed me of my future. If you do not appear, I shall go to the newspaper as well as every hostess in town and let your indiscretions be known. Think what the Duke of Ravencroft will say when he learns the sister is as guilty as her brother. Be in Pudding

Lane Tuesday at nine o'clock in the evening sharp prepared to win, or all is lost."

The missive had no signature, but she knew who sent it. The Earl of Pembsy. God, what a mess. Bile rose in her throat. The earl understood the position he put her in, and he had one thing correct. The duke would never forgive her if he discovered the truth about her. He would toss her out in the street or, worse, have her arrested, too.

Biting her lip, she paced and thought. She had no choice but to give in to the earl's demands. If she could sneak out, play the game, and return before anyone noticed, all would be well. One night and she would be free of this nightmare. Clasping her hands together, she considered telling Antony of her plight but changed her mind the second he arrived.

He blew in the door, wreathed in smiles and joviality, swinging Amora into his arms and twirling her around the room. "She loves me. She loves me. She loves me."

"Stop, Antony, you make me dizzy." She held her head until the room quit spinning,

"As I am dizzy in love, my beautiful Amora. I have waited for ages and ages for you to return so I can tell you the crazy things which occurred in your absence. Sit beside me, for you must not stand while I relate the story. There is so much excitement." Without waiting for her reply, he led her to the settee and sat beside her. "One cannot imagine the time my Sarah has endured of late.

"Saturday at tea, the Earl of Chauncey came calling at Winchester House. After one bite of lemon cake, the babbling idiot fell to his knees, proclaiming his love and asking for Sarah's hand in marriage. My Sarah, knowing full well the earl courts her father's favor and a better place in court, rejected his suit, right there in the blue salon with her mother in attendance.

"The duchess swooned, and her maid tipped over the tea tray spilling hot tea onto the earl as she scurried for the smelling salts. The earl rose to his feet and demanded Sarah apologize for her rude behavior and called for a servant to bring him a towel to soak the tea from his white breeches." A smile tugged at Antony's mouth, and a twinkle shone from his overbright eyes. "I wish I could have been a servant dusting behind the door so I could witness the scene. My Sarah faced the earl, tea and all, holding her ground like a true blood. Concerned her parents might consider the earl's offer, she informed Chauncey she loved another and refused his suit. The cur called my Sarah a harlot, and several other expletives, not realizing the Duke of Winchester overheard the entire commotion from his office.

"Angry does not describe the rage boiling from the duke as he strode into the blue parlor and had Chauncey removed from his home."

"Did you say the Earl of Chauncey?"

"Yes." Antony stopped. "Why?"

"He is the man who bought me from my brother. The man who attempted to abduct me at the theater."

A frown passed over his face. "I cannot believe this! I heard the rumors, but I did not connect him with the scum who attacked you! Such a man has no business asking for Sarah's hand."

"I agree."

His solemnity lasted for a full minute. "After the earl left, the duke and duchess demanded Sarah send her answer to the Duke of Huntington. They want to announce the wedding this Sunday, and Sarah is in a panic. She told them she is in love with another and asked for their blessing, which they denied. After her parents forbade her to marry me, they informed her they will announce her engagement to Huntington in the Banns this weekend with or without her consent. In a terrible panic, Sarah sent me a note, and when we met, she agreed to run away to Scotland with me. We have no time to waste, or she will be the new Duchess of Huntington. Even though I am but a lord, she loves me. We will be so much better off together, and I intend to make her the happiest woman in the world."

"They know you love Lady Sarah, and she you?" Amora could not believe her ears.

"Nay. They know she loves a lord, but she did not give them a name for fear they would stop us. After their reaction to my title, she refused to say more, although they were quite strict with her. She swears she cannot live without me, and I feel the same. I fear my heart would stop if she were to wed another."

"Then she shall not. We will produce a plan so you may have the love you desire." She meant every word. Antony deserved happiness, and so did Lady Sarah.

Jumping to his feet in a return of good humor, he tugged Amora with him, where he proceeded to twirl her around the room. "I cannot wait until the night of the soirée. I have such plans for an elopement like you have never seen. Picture this. A carriage waiting in the shadows. Me in my evening attire, exiting Winchester House, making my way through the gardens where my love awaits. Together we leave London under cover of night and travel for Gretna Green, taking first the high road to make time and then switching to back roads so we are not found. Think, Amora, by this time next week,

I will be a married man if all goes well."

He left her on a settee and wandered to the window, still glowing from his exertion. "This week cannot pass fast enough for me."

"Why so?" The duke's deep voice made Amora jump.

He walked into the room and took a seat across from her, studying her face with intense regard, "And how do you feel about the coming week, Amora?"

How much did he overhear? She peeked at him from beneath her lashes. If he suspected Antony's elopement with Lady Sarah, all would be lost. Swallowing, she shrugged. "I have no need for it to slow or hurry. Although I am a bit anxious on my plight and what Thursday will bring. By this time next week, I could be scrubbing floors for my brother."

"Not ever again, Amora. I shall not allow such a thing."

"He is my blood, and if the magistrate releases him, I have no choice. There will be nothing you can do."

A little black cloud hovered over the salon, and she shivered in its shadow, thinking of what Nathan's release would mean for her.

Antony took a seat and cleared his throat. "Is your grace aware the Duchess of Winchester invited Lady Amora to sing for her on Thursday evening?"

Amora handed the duke a cup of tea and a slice of cake.

"Dante informed me. Amora has the voice of an angel, and I am sure her grace's guests will be entranced."

Antony took the tea she handed him. "You have heard her sing, then." He cast a sideways glance at

Amora. "Does your grace plan to attend her grace's soirée?"

She glanced at him while she poured another cup of tea. How clever of him to ask. If the duke attended the soirée, their plans must allow for his presence and any repercussions.

The duke shook his head. "The magistrate will give his decision Thursday, and I will be busy with the court." Setting his cup down, he rose to his feet. "I do not get many breaks from the courtroom. Today happened to be such a day, and I thought it would be nice to take tea in my own drawing room." His gaze searched Amora's. "Take care to stay close to Dante the next couple of days."

"Yes, your grace."

He stared at her as if he said farewell for the last time. "I wish you every happiness."

The door closed behind him and the two of them exchanged glances.

Antony stared into his teacup. "Did he hear me plan my elopement?"

"Why did he wish us happiness?" Amora set hers down and stared at the closed door.

She wished she were eloping, then she would not be here to gamble for the Earl of Pembsy. Understanding Antony's conviction of not wanting to live without love, she sighed. If the duke discovered her secret, she would lose him forever, and there would be no happiness for her.

"Maybe he thinks we are eloping?"

She smiled. "Why would he do so? He knows I think of you as a friend and nothing more."

Antony shook his head. "Nay, I do not think he does.

When he wished us well, he possessed the half-crazed expression of a man leaving his love forever. I recognize the look."

"Love makes you see everything through the glass of happiness." Unwilling to give his comment any of her attention in case her heart eavesdropped and took hope, she changed the subject. "Now, about Thursday night...

They planned to park Antony's carriage in the trees outside the main gate. Amora would visit Lady Sarah for tea on the morrow and pass her a note with her instructions. On the night of the soirée, Antony would pack his bags and load them in the carriage situated in the trees.

Amora would request the duke's carriage for the night and come to pick up Antony. Together they would arrive at Winchester House and mingle until time for Amora to perform.

According to instruction, Lady Sarah would pack her valise and leave it outside the kitchen door. Sometime after they arrived, Antony would sneak it to the carriage. Then while the guests gathered to hear Amora sing, the two would slip out the garden door and make their way to the carriage. From there, they raced for Gretna Green.

"Send me a letter later and let me know where you live. I shall pray for you in your travels and hope you find the happiness you deserve." Amora swallowed the lump losing his friendship created in her throat

"I hope you find yours, as well. I can never thank you enough for helping me. Without you I would never have had the nerve or the opportunity to slip Sarah the first note, and because of this, I would have lost the love of my life." He bent and kissed her cheek before taking his leave.

Amora followed him out and stood on the stoop until his carriage could no longer be seen. Stepping back, she spotted a movement out of the corner of her eye and froze. A quick vision of purple and black flashed through the bushes, and then nothing. Turning her head, she scanned the area on either side of the townhouse, but everything remained still.

Hurrying back inside, she closed the door and leaned against it, sucking in a deep breath to calm her racing heart. Anxiety and lack of sleep were to blame for her paranoia.

"My lady?" The butler strode toward her, concern furrowing his brow. "Are you ill?"

She shook her head. "Nay, just tired. Thank you, William."

Chapter Eleven

Tuesday dawned before she wanted, and the evening arrived even faster. Pleading a headache, Amora retired early to her chamber with instructions to cancel her engagements. When Mary hurried in to help her undress, she sent her to the kitchen for chicken broth to settle her stomach. Donning her night rail over her corset, stockings, and other undergarments, she climbed into bed and dismissed the maid as soon as her tray of food arrived. Dressing would require little effort since she took nothing off but her underskirts and bodice.

"Is there anything else, my lady? I would have helped ye undress for bed."

"I know, Mary. I appreciate all you do, but I wanted to lie down. My brother did not employ a lady's maid, and I became accustomed to dressing and undressing on my own. However, I will allow you to brush and plait my hair."

When she finished, Mary bobbed and disappeared.

Waiting for cover of darkness, Amora slid from her bed, padded over to the wardrobe, and lifted her battered valise from its hiding place behind all her new gowns. Stroking the rich fabric of her red velvet dress, she shivered. When Nathan presented the dress to her, she thought the fabric fine and soft. Compared to the ones she now owned from Bond Street, the dress felt gaudy and cheap. Dressing fast, she coiled her braid on top her head and pinned it in place. Then she threw a long, black velvet cloak over her shoulders and secured it in place. Tucking the domino mask into her pocket, she slipped from her room and down the back staircase. The servants took their dinner at seven and the stairs were empty. With a sigh of relief, Amora exited the townhouse through the kitchen door into the garden. Staying in the shadows, she made her way to the gate and out into the lane.

A brisk walk down two lanes of houses and she arrived at Hyde Park, where she hired a hackney carriage to Pudding Lane.

Thinking of her plight if the duke ever discovered the truth, twisted her insides. She understood too well Lord Antony's comment on his heart not handling rejection from Lady Sarah. If the Duke of Ravencroft ever discovered the truth about her, he would gaze at her with the same revulsion he did her brother the night of his arrest. This she would never survive and cringed at the mere thought. A shiver ran down her spine as the carriage drew to a stop, rocking as if a man jumped from the back. She hoped this night passed quickly so she could get back to worrying over regular things like if her stocking had a run, or if her hair stayed in place.

Counting coins from her reticule, she paid the driver and donned the domino mask before crossing the street to the tavern. Thank the gods the duke gave her pin money, or this would have been much more difficult.

Emotions and memories flooded her as she stood outside the large paned window and gazed inside at the scene of her misery and stiffened her spine. "One game. All I must play is one game." She did not know she said the words aloud until a whiny voice behind her answered.

"Not one game. You must play until I am satisfied. I want my hundred thousand pounds back."

Anxiety settled like a rock in her stomach. "A hundred *thousand* pounds? Are you daft? I did not agree to such an amount." Amora turned on her heel, but his next words stopped her.

"First thing tomorrow the gossip rags will scream everything I know if you do not do as I say."

She stopped. "I will play for you for one night and no more. I have broken my word to be here as it is, and I will not come again."

The earl's thin face grew more grotesque by the minute. His eyes narrowed, and his lips thinned, but she did not back down.

"Sure, I may be ruined, and the gossip will be highly exaggerated. I may get kicked out of the duke's townhouse or even arrested. But I know two things. One, I never cheat, ever. I do not have to. I play by the rules and am very good at it. And two, if I do not play for you, even though all hell breaks loose for me, and I languish in prison, or am cast from England, *you will not be one farthing richer*. If my name is dragged through the rags, so will yours. For I will ensure all England knows how you lost your inheritance. Think what your relatives will say then."

They stared at each other for several heart-pounding minutes.

Right when Amora decided she had enough and turned to go, the earl capitulated. "Okay. One night."

She stopped and, against her better judgment, strolled into the tavern, followed by the earl and his two men.

****

Lady Amora won hand after hand to the consternation of her victims but the elation of the earl. "A few more nights of this, and I will be a rich man once more."

Glancing around at the dwindling customers, she guessed the time to be around midnight. Rising to her feet, she shook her head at the earl. "We agreed on one night, and now I am done."

The Earl of Pembsy jumped to his feet with a roar of anger, spilling his tankard of ale on his fawn-colored breeches. A string of curse words poured from his mouth as he dabbed at the soaked wool with his kerchief. "God damn it! Every time I meet up with you, I ruin another set of clothes. These articles cost me a good deal of money! Now get your ass back here and play another game to make up for what you did!"

"I did not spill the ale, sir. You did, and I am done playing. Any man who cannot curb his tongue in the presence of a lady deserves to be left to his own fate. One more thing, call me an ass again, and I will knock you on yours."

She exited the tavern with her head held high and whistled for a hackney.

"Hyde Park, please." Climbing in, she closed the door and leaned back with a sigh.

The ride back took longer than the ride over, and she concluded her nerves were at fault. When they neared the park, the carriage rocked again as if someone had stepped from the back. Many carriages discarded by nobility became hackney carriages. This one needed a new spring to stop the violent rocking when the vehicle stopped. There were no footmen in attendance on hackney carriages, although the step remained, as did the handles the footmen held on to.

Ten minutes later, she slipped into her room with a sigh of relief and bolted her chamber door.

No sooner did she remove her corset and silk stockings; than a knock came at the door.

"Lady Amora? Dante sent me to check on ye. He caught some movement by the gate and wants to make sure you are all right."

Movement by the gate? She froze. Then grabbed her night rail and tugged it over her head before unbolting the door, feigning grogginess.

"I am feeling fine, Mary, much better after the rest I have enjoyed. So much so, if cook has any dinner left, I would be grateful for some."

"I will see what I can find."

She turned to leave, and Amora caught sight of Dante standing in the corridor behind her

Mary's hands rested on her hips as she glared at the outrider. "Out with ye. Ye cannot stay without me here."

"Something did not feel right about tonight, and when the lady did not answer, I became concerned for her safety. Now I see she is well, I will leave." He stopped. "I found nothing outside to be concerned about, m'lady. But if you hear or see anything strange, ring the bell so Mary can fetch me. I will bid you both a good evening."

She murmured, "Good night," as he closed the door, and the heavy thump of his boots walked away.

There would be no more sneaking out. She could not afford to be caught gambling. With Dante keeping her in sight, the act of slipping away presented far more danger to her personal safety and wellbeing than the earl spilling some sensational story to the rags.

Wednesday passed without incident, and then Thursday came.

To her relief, no further message or communication came from the earl, and she breathed a sigh of satisfaction. If he blackmailed her again, she would slip a note to his overprotective, overbearing mother about his activities in the garden at various functions, as well as his appearance at several taverns on the west side. She doubted he would be allowed out of the house without his mama and several men servants following such tidings.

After a frantic afternoon of rehashing the plans for Lord Antony's big night, Amora climbed the stairs to her chamber to dress for the soirée. Her mind whirled with all the possibilities failure would offer in both scenarios. Shaking her head, she whispered, "One problem at a time, my girl."

The red satin of her new evening gown whispered against the polished wooden stairs as she descended to wait for Antony's carriage. In her arms, she carried her black satin cloak and her reticule. With her hair piled high atop her head and long white gloves coming to her shoulder, she felt like royalty.

Stopping at the bottom of the curved staircase, she threw her cloak around her shoulders, tying the satin ribbon into a bow at the base of her neck.

Her hands trembled, and her knees grew weak as she waited. Not sure she recovered from Tuesday night and all the drama; she stiffened her spine. Today the magistrate made his decision on her brother, The Earl of Hargrove. Not knowing what tomorrow or the next day would bring nearly drove her crazy.

Amora walked to the red salon, passing William in the corridor. "I shall be in the red salon. Let me know when Lord Antony arrives."

"Very good, my lady."

Ignoring the plush velvet chairs and satin settees arranged around a marble tea table, Amora peered out the large window facing the garden at the late afternoon sun and wondered if every case took this long to come to an end.

She hoped for a chance to see the duke before Antony arrived to whisk her away to the soirée. Her life and future hung on the magistrate's decision. How could she go to the Winchester's party and pretend to be merry and carefree for hours when her world teetered on the edge of disaster?

The quiet garden spoke peace to her soul. A bird fluttered in front of the window and disappeared. If only she could fly away and leave her problems behind. Closing her eyes, she pictured the blue sky above and the wind swirling around her. Down below, London bustled and glittered while Nathan languished in prison and the Earl of Pembsy left for exile in France or Spain. The Duke of Ravencroft would smile in admiration at her, and she would be free to live as she chose. The scent of wildflowers clung to the breeze as she circled high in the sky, relishing her freedom.

A knock sounded on the door, and Amora jumped.

"Lord Antony waits for you in the foyer, my lady." William bowed his head in her direction.

"Why did you not ask him inside?"

"He said he is in a hurry and cannot wait."

A wry smile twisted her lips. If she were bound for Scotland and wedded bliss with her lover, she would be in a hurry, too. As the words ran through her mind, a vision of the duke's face and muscular body accompanied the thought, and she frowned. *She loved the duke!*

Dazed, Amora stopped at the entrance to the foyer and swayed. How could such a thing be true? Such a man would never love her, not when he could have any woman in London, and especially not if he ever discovered her secret. *Yet, he kisses you with passion and confesses his desire for you*, her mind whispered.

Footsteps approached, and Antony caught her elbow, frowning down into her face. "Are you ill?"

"Nay. Just dizzy. I shall be fine, but we must leave, or we will not arrive in time to make the proper preparation."

Sarah's valise must be collected from the kitchen door and stuffed in Antony's carriage before anyone noticed it. Once the guests arrived and the soirée commenced, there would be no time to do anything but stick to the plan. If anything out of the ordinary occurred, Antony and Sarah's lives would be hell. The scandal following this night would be horrific. How could it be otherwise? For no one jilted a duke for the second son of a lord, and the two love birds must be well away from London before the news became known.

Frowning over her thoughts, she took her seat inside the carriage and smiled at the flush on his face. "I am excited for you, Antony, and want to wish you every happiness."

"Do not wish it too much in advance. I have the whole of England to traverse before we arrive in Gretna Green, and once the duchess realizes what happened, she will send an army of officers and men servants after us."

"Have you a plan?"

He nodded. "I have spent a good deal of time thinking things over and have decided my best course of action is to let my horses have their head as soon as we are free of the busy streets. I figure we have an hour or two of leeway before the duchess sends servants to find Lady Sarah. The house will then be searched, and when her grace connects my absence with Sarah's, there will be an all-out attempt made to stop us. By then, the night will provide cover for us, and I must get as far north as I can before the sun rises. After this, we plan to stick to back roads until we arrive in Scotland."

Amora nodded, thinking hard. "But will they not expect this to be your plan? If I were you, I would stay on the main road and run as far as I could each day. Traveling in the light of day on the more traveled roads will not be what they anticipate."

Antony stared at her. "Do you think it wise to expose our presence in such a manner?"

"Aye. But you will make better time, have a better journey, and be among the many instead of among the few and easily recognized."

"You make a good point." Leaning across the carriage, he took her hand in his. "I will not get another chance to tell you how much I appreciate all you have done to help me. I feel a scoundrel to leave you to your own problems without doing anything to help. If you ever need anything of me, you have but to ask. You have been a dear friend, and my wish is for you to find the same happiness I have."

"And I shall, but first you." Crossing her fingers when she said the words made them seem less like a lie.

Chapter Twelve

They arrived at Winchester Manor and could not speak of their plans again for fear they would be overheard. So, they mingled and laughed, acting for all the world as if nothing important would occur.

Antony disappeared while the duchess instructed them on the order of entertainment, and they learned, to their dismay, Amora would sing last.

"I want Amora's song to be the grand finale to my fabulous party. After tonight, the Ton shall know of your angelic voice, and you shall once again join the throng as an equal. All this messy nonsense over your brother will be forgotten, and you shall sail to the top of every hostess's guest list. With my help and influence, we shall find a suitable suitor and have you married off before the season ends."

She doubted such a thing were possible, especially if anyone suspected her in tonight's intrigue. Amora smiled and dipped a curtsy, murmuring her gratitude for the duchess's intervention. Her smile dimmed when she met the panic in Antony's eyes and motioned toward the terrace.

Five minutes later, they stood in the far corner out of view of any window.

"I cannot wait until midnight to leave! Half of London will be on my heels at first light, and I will not have made it far with the time I have."

"Then I shall have to create a distraction by spilling punch on us both. Sarah will be forced to change, and I will weep in one of the upstairs rooms while I keep the maids busy removing the stain for my performance."

Antony grimaced. "If the duchess suspects your involvement, all this will be for naught."

Amora gazed into his eyes. "Not for naught. You will have the happiness you both deserve, and this alone will make tonight's adventure worth the price." She meant every word she said.

As the guests arrived and found their seats, she made sure she had a full cup of punch in her hand when she sat down beside Sarah.

They whispered together while Amora related the change in plan. Halfway through the first pianoforte recital, she tipped her punch over them both, filling their laps with red juice.

Sarah jumped to her feet, crying out, and rushed from the room, calling for her lady's maid.

Amora rose and, with a sheepish expression, made her way to the back of the salon where the duchess sat, frowning.

Amora pointed at her skirt, and the duchess rose, motioning her toward the door.

Together they left the salon and the interested gazes of the guests.

"What happened?"

Amora held her skirt wide, revealing the wet spot on the front of her gown, and explained she spilled her punch in both her and Sarah's laps.

"Well, Sarah can change, and you may go to the chamber at the top of the stairs to the left. I shall send a housemaid to help you. Thank the gods your dress is red as the punch and shall go unnoticed."

"I am sorry." 'Twas the truth. She felt awful for deceiving the duchess, but not contrite enough to stop the elopement. Antony would take far better care of Lady Sarah than the duke ever could.

Half an hour later, Amora re-entered the salon and took her seat. She prayed with all her strength Antony and Sarah made it to Scotland before they were caught and stopped.

When her turn came, she rose to her feet and walked to the front of the room. Taking her seat at the pianoforte, she played the introduction and sang the first stanza.

In the middle of the refrain, all hell broke loose.

Sarah's lady's maid entered the salon and whispered in the duchess's ear, who rose to her feet with a cry and rushed from the room.

The guests swiveled in their chairs, gaping to see what excitement stirred the household.

Servants ran past the door in both directions while the duchess barked orders.

Amora continued her song, hoping to keep the guests in their seats and out of the frantic activity in the corridor.

At the end of the second stanza, the duchess returned and ordered everyone out of the parlor. "My daughter has been abducted. We do not know by whom or what method yet. I ask each of you to come forward if you know anything to help me locate her."

The guests froze in their chairs. A moment of silence followed as they digested the information before they shook their heads, expressing their sympathy.

"The last time I saw her, she left to change her gown. Amora, would you search the stairs and gates to see if you find any clues?"

Thinking it best to help and divert any unwanted attention or questions, she agreed and left the salon. Checking the stairs, Lady Sarah's chamber, and the back stairs, Amora wandered out to the garden gate and peered out, frowning in consternation.

A carriage stood in the lane! How could this be when Antony planned to be outside London by now? In the dark, she could not make out whether the carriage belonged to Antony or not. So, she crept closer.

Suddenly, a man dressed in black stepped from the shadows and struck her head before everything grew dark.

****

Her head ached, and her eyes stung. The fabric in her mouth made talking impossible and breathing nearly so. The heat of the area around her made her want to gag. Every so often, a whiff of fresh air would skim across her face, and she sucked in as much as she could each time, realizing with a sinking heart, the breeze carried the scent of sea, fish, and the docks. While the rough surface beneath her reeked of rotting wood and human stench. Her stomach rolled. How long had she been unconscious?

Blinking in the dim light, she shifted, discovering her hands were bound, as well as her feet. Disoriented and getting angrier by the second, she twisted to her right and met the terrified stare of another girl lying a few feet away. Terror gripped her chest as she squirmed her way around to her left and froze. Bound and gagged human bodies lay everywhere, all of them young and female.

She lay in the bottom of a ship!

The Duke of Ravencroft's words the night he

rescued her raced across her mind.

"He is the Earl of Chauncey and has long been suspected of being involved in a human slavery ring here in London with connections to Singapore and the Orient."

Her heart thundered in her ears, and her breath came fast. Panic coated her forehead in a fine mist. She would never let them make a slave of her, never. Once in a lifetime proved sufficient.

Some of the girls cried, some of them tried to scream, neither would do them any good. Amora dropped her head and thought hard. The duke knew she attended the Winchester's soirée, and no doubt realized she had not returned. He would come for her, unless… Her brother's trial concluded yesterday, and she had no idea whether Nathan received sentence or his freedom. When she asked, the duke promised her he would never let her return to the life she lived before they met, and she must believe he would keep his word. He had to.

Men's boots clumped overhead, and more girls cried out, wriggling to get free. A loud, deep voice shouted, and the boots ran in every direction. Something happened on deck

Amora followed the curve of the structure around them, noting how narrow the beams became. They must be in the front of the ship in some sort of cargo hold, and their presence masked by a larger hold closer to the middle of the ship.

Frantic to escape, she studied the area as best she could in the flickering light of a single lantern hanging on the wall. Beside it stood a ladder, with a trap door lying above. Amazed by the narrow opening, she wondered how they managed to get all the women down those stairs without harming them. Frowning, she had a vague recollection of hanging upside down over a broad shoulder and a man's voice telling her to mind her head. Her head pounded, and her mouth ached for water. She asked for a drink, and someone handed her a goblet with a sweet, nutty liquid. The cool beverage eased the fire in her throat, and she knew no more. Poppy. The men drugged them. Anger filled her chest, and she struggled anew with her bonds.

Men's boots approached, and then the trap door lifted, and a pair of feet appeared. Light pouring through the opening told her the morning passed and part of the afternoon while she slept.

The man turned and lifted the lantern from the wall, holding it high. "She is over there."

Amora froze.

Stocky, red-haired with a bushy beard, the man wore the rough clothes of a sailor. Another pair of boots descended the ladder, and her heart sank. She recognized the fine breeches and superior smirk on the man's face, as the Earl of Pembsy turned and followed the sailor toward her.

He stopped when he stood beside her and crouched down. "I told you there would be consequences if you did not play as long as I wanted." He waved a jeweled hand at the man beside him. "Meet Captain Larkin, owner of this fine vessel and the load of…cargo…she carries to Asia."

Her mouth grew dry, and the thundering of her heart in her ears grew unbearable. She did not reply but stared her contempt back at him.

"What?" The earl put a hand to his ear. "No vehement denial or threat?" Laughing, he rose to his feet and turned to the trap door. "Come on down. She is quite safe and wants to bid you farewell."

A sixth sense warned her before the next man came into view. Gulping back her terror, she lifted her gaze to the Earl of Chauncey's narrow blue eyes.

He wore velvet breeches and a silk shirt with a fine linen handkerchief to his nose as he tip-toed on his bejeweled buckled heels to her side. Moving his hand from his mouth, he grinned. "Hello, my dear. Are you surprised to see me? I paid good money for you, and if I cannot collect what is rightfully mine one way, I shall another. The man I sold you to likes his women young and fresh. He paid a pretty penny to add you to his stable." A laugh escaped him. "I wish I could see the look on Ravencroft's face when his outrider informs him of your absence. I wanted to keep you in London because of your...skill with the cards, but our partner thinks Singapore is the best place for you." Chuckling, he crouched beside her. "Hope and rebellion chase each other across your face, but I am afraid I will have to squash them both. You see, Ravencroft thinks you eloped with Lord Antony and will not be coming to rescue you. So, enjoy the ride and try not to get too sick in the hull as you rock side to side all the way to Singapore." Laughing at his own joke, he rose to his feet and snapped his fingers at the earl. "Let us go. I am quite famished and desire to take another tumble with the wench at the tavern."

The men turned and walked away, but not before Pembsy kicked her in the stomach. "This is for embarrassing me and ruining my best jacket."

Amora curled up and tucked her chin to her chest to hide the pain. How could men be so childish, so selfish, and so callous? Whatever they thought, she would find a way out, and take all these other girls with her. Then she would see who thought this whole thing funny or not.

A bell clanged up on deck, and the heavy metal chain clanked against the side as it rose out of the water. The ship pulled anchor!

The earl's words rang through her head. Dante. He would tell the duke of her disappearance.

Pushing up to a sitting position, Amora hummed the tune to "The True Lover's Farewell," uncertain of why she did. Panic raced through her as she channeled all her energy into the song, thinking of the duke and reliving the moments she spent in his arms. If he cared at all, he must feel her call to his heart.

****

Alexander left the court and returned home as the Ravencroft carriage trotted away down the cobblestone road to the Winchester's party.

His heart turned to stone in his chest. By this time tomorrow Amora and Antony would be well on their way to Scotland and their new life together. He overheard them making plans the day they arrived back in London from his country estate. The joy in her voice as they discussed their elopement stopped his heart in his chest. He never should have succumbed to the desire to kiss her. If he never tasted the sweet nectar of her mouth or sipped from the cup of desire with her, her marriage would not be so hard.

Strolling into his study, Alexander splashed a generous amount of whisky into a glass. Taking a sip, he wandered to the fireplace and stared into the flames, remembering the night at the theater when the two of them sat so close their heads touched and whispered throughout the performance. Watching her fall in love with another man had to be the most painful thing he endured his entire life. And now, without her graceful presence, the house echoed in the silence, empty and cold.

He could still feel the pain her answer induced when he asked if she loved Antony.

"Yes. I suppose I do." His heart turned to stone and dropped to the bottom of his stomach in the same instant.

He took a mouthful of the fiery liquid, relishing in the burn all the way down his throat to his belly. Amora need never worry about Nathan again. The judge sentenced him to hang in two days' time for his involvement with the deaths of the four young men he ruined. She was free.

"Your Grace?" Dante stood in the door, frowning.

"Come." The duke took another sip of whisky and waited.

"The Earl of Hargrove escaped."

"What?" Alexander froze. "When?"

"A constable stopped by just now with the report. The prison cart had three loose boards in the floor, and he slipped away. When they got to Newgate, they found the boards set to the side and the earl missing. He must have dug the nails out and shimmied through the opening, disappearing in the busy streets. The driver did not hear a thing over the heavy rumble of the cart. They are gathering men to hunt him down."

Alexander nodded. "I will help. At least Amora is out of the way. She and Antony should be well on their way to Scotland, and Nathan will not be able to get to her."

Dante shook his head. "Antony elopes with Lady

Sarah Winchester, not Lady Amora." He dropped his gaze. "I have more bad tidings, your grace. I come for you because I do not know where the lady is."

The duke narrowed his gaze, setting his glass down with care. "What do you mean you do not know where she is?" His chest tightened as he considered what would happen of the earl found his sister. "Tell me all you know."

Rage raced through his veins as he waited for Dante to explain. He gave her his word she need never worry about her brother again, and now she disappeared and could be in his clutches at this very moment.

"She left the salon with the duchess. I followed her to the upstairs chamber, but the duchess commanded I wait downstairs. Amora must have gone down the servants' stairs because she never returned, and when I went in search of her, I could not find her. The chamber she borrowed to fix the stain on her gown contained no clue as to her whereabouts. I searched the house and grounds and discovered Amora's footprints in the dirt by the garden gate. A plain black carriage waited in the alley beyond the gate, which I did not recognize."

His blood ran cold. "You have no other information to go on?" A million scenarios raced across his mind, and the band around his chest tightened. "We go back to the Winchesters and search again."

Racing through London's streets, they found Winchester Manor in an uproar, still searching for Lady Sarah.

The duke asked for a private moment alone with the Duke and Duchess of Winchester, where he informed them of their daughter's whereabouts and the abduction of Lady Amora.

"So, my Sarah is on her way to Scotland with the second son of a lord after refusing both the Earl of Chauncey and the Duke of Huntington's suit?

"Antony loves her." Alexander shrugged. "And she loves him enough to leave everything she has ever known behind to be with him." He studied their faces. "There is something you must know about the Earl of Chauncey." He then told them everything he learned about the earl's involvement with human trafficking.

Silence filled the duke's study. "This Antony, he is of good character?"

"The best. I know him, and he will take good care of your daughter." He then filled them in on Nathan's escape and his need to find Amora.

"He is not what we wanted for our daughter, and we shall stop them if we can." After calling for their men at arms, they gave Alexander permission to search the grounds.

Which he did with meticulous care, the whole time reminding his heart to slow down, so he did not make any mistakes. Twenty feet from the garden gate, they discovered a lace-edged linen handkerchief embroidered with an elaborate "P."

"Pembsy."

Dante took the kerchief in two fingers. "I can smell his ghastly cologne from here. The men reported he left his townhouse early yesterday morning and has not returned."

"There is nothing more to be gained by traipsing around in the dark. Let us return to my townhouse where I can think."

Chapter Thirteen

Back at the townhouse, the duke paced up and down his study. "I find it interesting Chauncey and Hargrove have both gone missing. The question remains. Which one abducted Amora? If Chauncey has her, we will find her at the docks, but if Hargrove took her, she could be anywhere. And the kerchief leads us to Pembsy. Did they abduct her together, or did someone else, and if so, why? Send for the footmen, Lord Antony's as well. Call all the servants together. Someone witnessed something, and I will have an answer."

Alexander understood his chances to recover Amora grew more faint with each passing hour. The problem came with knowing which direction to take and where to look. Running in circles would accomplish nothing.

One of his housemaids reported a man outside the garden gate one day wearing Pembsy's colors. He did not appear to be doing anything but smoking, so she did not give him her attention. The Earl of Chauncey's valet approached Lord Antony's youngest footman the day before and asked about Antony's plans for the night. Thinking the earl meant to join Antony, he informed the man of the entertainment at the Winchester's with Lady Amora singing.

Alexander dismissed them, ordering his phaeton brought around. "We waste time. Pembsy, Chauncey, and Hargrove all joined the same set at the club. If the two are involved, chances are the other is also. These men are not fools and will suspect I am aware of Amora's abduction by now. They will want her far away where I cannot find her, and the quickest way to ensure their success would be selling her in Asia. We go to the docks and investigate any ships leaving for Singapore. Hargrove and Chauncey will no doubt find a hole to crawl into or leave the country until the scandal dies down. I will send a note to the constable asking them to pay Pembsy a visit while we go to port."

Winding their way through the tight streets, they crossed London bridge and raced toward the waterfront. Several ships were docked along the wharf. Men of all color and race roamed the docks, looking for work or enjoying their time on land. Ships came from all over the world, many staying for months before returning to the sea.

The duke sought out the nearest constable and spoke of his concerns, requesting police help to find his ward. A group of sailors listening nearby caught his attention.

"How would you like to earn some coin?"

After taking note of his fine clothes and listening to his dilemma, they agreed to help. Soon, Alexander had a small army of men searching for Amora.

The duke and Dante walked down the left side of the port, asking about departures and destinations until they discovered one ship setting sail for Asia. The captain ordered the gangplank taken down and made ready to leave.

Alexander jumped the side of the railing and hurried up the gangplank before the sailors stowed it, but his heart grew heavier with each step. Glancing back, he noted another ship on the far end of the dock behind him, making the same preparation. Which boat held Amora captive? He felt her cry for help in every fiber of his body and stopped mid-way up the ramp.

Remembering the gypsy's cryptic words, he searched his feelings, and the haunting music of "True Lover's Farewell" filled his senses *from the other direction.*

Turning around, he called to Dante and raced back the way he came. His hired sailors filled the busy dock behind him as he hurried around to the other end. The heavy clink of the metal anchor lifting from the water filled the air as they approached the other ship, and the decks were busy with sailors making ready to depart.

The first boat sounded a horn as she sailed through the water for the open sea, and Alexander turned, shielding his eyes from the sun to stare after her.

Panic flared in his chest, and he hesitated. Then the melody came again, guiding him onto the ship before him. "She is here." Running up the gangplank, he encountered a man as tall as he with red hair and beard.

"Who are ye, and what do ye want." The sailor's hand fondled the butt of a revolver tucked in the front of his breeches.

"I seek my ward, Lady Amora Hargrove. I know she is on board. Give her to me."

The man laughed and withdrew the gun from his waistband. "I carry cargo for Asia. Get off my ship."

Alexander punched him in the face and took the gun before he had a chance to fire. His hired men swarmed on board behind him, grinning at the prospect of a good fight. Chaos reigned as the ship's crew realized they were being boarded by the duke's men, who in turn, tossed them off their own boat.

Turning, the duke got a glimpse of purple silk and black breeches crawling into a tarp-covered rowboat, and he dropped the man he held, striding forward.

With a flick of his wrist, he tossed the tarp back to reveal the Earl of Chauncey and the Earl of Pembsy cowering beneath, but not the Earl of Hargrove.

He frowned at the thought and whistled for Dante to send for the constable. "Over here. I found the rabble responsible."

Dante tossed him a rope and brought one of his own. Together they tied the pair to the main mast and helped subdue the crew.

When the constables arrived, they found the crew bound and gagged on the top deck, and the duke below deck ripping the ship apart.

The tune in his head tore at his heart. He sensed her presence but had no idea where she could be. The cargo holds were filled with opium, not women. He stilled and calculated the length of the ship minus the cargo holds and frowned. Something did not add up.

Studying the layout of the rooms, Alexander strode on deck to the captain's quarters and searched the floor for a hatch. Rolling a rug away, he caught the ring and lifted. What he witnessed beneath filled him with rage. At least two dozen young women of every station in life lay bound and gagged below the captain's cabin, terrified for their lives.

He climbed down the ladder and searched in the dim light for her face. The faint outline of her figure wearing a tattered red silk dress sent his heart tripping. Standing at the bottom of the ladder, he whistled for Dante. "I found them.'

Alexander picked the women up and handed them

through the trap door to Dante one at a time, comforting them with soothing words of encouragement. When he neared Amora and took inventory of her face, he had to suppress the desire to kill both the dandies tied to the mast above deck.

Her eyes were bright with tears, and the entire right side of her face sported bruising in vivid shades of purple and blue. Her body trembled as she stared up at him, and he dropped to his knees to remove her gag and bindings.

She opened her mouth to speak, but no words came out.

"My love." Cradling her in his arms, he kissed her long and deep, shaking with relief. Never again would he let her out of his sight.

****

Like a starving woman, she stared as he lifted girl after girl to the waiting men above deck, rescuing them all, as she prayed he would. Then he had her in his arms, kissing her and holding her close. Amora sighed as his scent and heat enveloped her in a cloud of security. All day she thought of nothing but this moment and the sweetness being in his arms would bring.

"I love you."

She did not realize she whispered the words until he lifted his head and gazed into her soul with his piercing blue eyes. "And I you, my love. Let us speak of this when we are alone." Lifting her as if she were a child, he carried her to the ladder of freedom and handed her up to Dante.

The deck swarmed with police and crying women relating the circumstances of their abductions.

The duke shielded her from the crowd until they came to the two earls tied to the center mast, and Amora

155

stopped.

The Earl of Pembsy cringed when she bent down as if he feared she would strike him. "I want you to know I do not hold anger in my heart toward you. The justice of the gods shall deliver more to both of you than I ever could." Turning to Chauncey, she stared into his soulless eyes. "Every day you rot in Newgate thinking of ways to escape, I shall praise the gods for your captivity. Women are not animals or property to be bought and sold. Your very life is a gift from the woman who suffered through her confinement to bear you, and you owe her everything. Someday men such as you will be forced to admit your wrongs, and women will be given the rights due them."

"You speak blasphemy, and I will see you in hell first. Women were meant to ease a man's loins and to breed, nothing more. You should tremble in the presence of your betters, not challenge them. If I were not tied, I would give you the comeuppance you deserve."

"Then thank the gods you *are* tied, or I would teach *you* some." With her head high, she tucked her trembling arm into the duke's and made her way to his waiting phaeton.

****

A constable waited for them in the blue salon, and after seeing Amora to her chamber, Alexander returned to speak with the man.

The officer twisted his cap around in his hands while he gave his report. A patrolling officer discovered the Earl of Hargrove's body face down in the Thames an hour previous. Disfigured and beaten, they identified the body by the clothes he wore and a handwritten letter in his pocket detailing the planned escape

Unconvinced, Alexander thanked the officer for his help and sent for a physician to give Amora a bit of poppy to help her rest while he paid a visit to the undertaker to see the body.

Same height, same weight, same coloring with the same cut above on eye from a constable's stick. "He is the Earl of Hargrove." Alexander signed the form giving his testimony of the body's identity and returned to his home.

After a quiet afternoon, he dressed with great care for dinner. Much rested on the outcome of the talk he intended to have with Amora. Though he put her through hell, the death of her brother would melt her soft heart and give her pain. Pain her brother did not deserve.

The duke discovered two things when he gazed down at the earl's body. The first, Amora had no one left in this world to call family. And the second, he loved her and wanted to make her his in every way possible.

She spoke of love when he held her in his arms, and he must know if she meant what she said, for his heart and peace of mind depended on it. Realizing through the long night he could not live without her, and the hopeless uncertainty on which way to search for her, convinced him to never let her out of his sight again. He could not take the stress.

Pacing back and forth in the blue salon as he recited his prepared speech, he gazed up and caught sight of the lady as she descended the stairs. Dressed in dark pink silk, with a low square neck etched with wine-colored lace and a ribbon of the same hue tied around her tiny waist echoed in the elaborate embroidery on the bodice sleeves and hem of her gown, she embodied his idea of an angel, and he could not breathe. Her glorious curls were piled high on her head and threaded with pink sapphires. Her eyes glittered with happiness, and her soft pink lips turned up in a smile when she met his gaze.

"Your grace."

Dipping into a deep curtsey, her neckline gave him full view of her ample breasts straining against the fabric and lace of her gown.

His mouth dried, and his hands itched to touch her, to rip the silk from her luscious body as he carried her to his chamber where he could taste every inch of her satin skin as he drove inside her, over and over.

His breath came quick, and his heart sped up. First, he must convince her to accept his suit despite the way they met and her assumption he wanted her out of his life. Nothing could be further from the truth, and as he opened his mouth to recite the words, his mind drew a blank.

Taking her arm, he escorted her to a settee and stared down at her. "How are you feeling after your rest?"

She glanced up at him and blushed. "Well, thank you."

"I hope you do not suffer from your ordeal." He searched her face for a clue on how to proceed.

"I am fine."

The nervous tick of her heart in the side of her neck gave him hope.

He cleared his throat, willing the words to come forth, but lost his thoughts the second he gazed back into her beautiful eyes.

"What did the constable want?" Her soft melodious voice tugged at his heartstrings.

A knot formed in his throat as he gazed down at her, knowing the pain his words would cause. "Nathan is dead. They found his body in the Thames." He told her all he knew about the situation.

She glanced up. "Are you sure the man is Nathan?" Her voice ended with a half-sob, and he searched her face for tears.

"I identified the body." He took her trembling hands in his and squeezed, knowing how difficult this must be for her.

A long silence filled the room as several expressions flashed across her face. Disbelief, pain, astonishment, and then peace. "Thank you for coming for me."

She astonished him with her ability to forgive, and he stared, unable to think of what to say next. And then the words poured from his heart. "I will always come for you, my sweet. These past weeks have been both a torment and a joy. I tasted the stars when I held you in my arms and kissed your sweet lips but drank the bitter potion as I watched you with Antony. I thought you intended to elope with him, having overheard part of your conversation one day when he came to tea. I reasoned if you loved him enough to cause a scandal, you had all you needed. He would keep you safe and give you the love you deserve."

He paused. "I have since changed my mind. You do not know the relief I experienced when I discovered Antony rode for Scotland with Lady Sarah and not with you. I made plans to come after you and challenge him for your hand because I alone can give you the love you deserve. No man will ever love you as I do. For you are in my thoughts all day and in my dreams at night. I breathe in and smell the sweet fragrance of your hair and the essence of your delightful body. The haunting music of your soul fills my heart and mind as the beauty of your voice fills my senses. I yearn to hold you naked in my arms and teach you the beauty of love between a man and a woman. Let me show you the joy of desire and the ecstasy of fulfillment as we join and ride the waves of exquisite pleasure I can give you. Marry me, my love, and be duchess of my heart, of my life, and of my home."

Silence filled the salon. Glancing down, he caught the lone tear rolling down her cheek with the pad of his thumb and got down on one knee, cupping her velvet cheek.

"Will you marry me, Amora Elizabeth Hargrove, and make me the happiest of men?"

"Yes." She choked on the word and threw her body against him with a cry of happiness, to which the duke responded the only way he could, by lowering his mouth to hers in a soul-consuming kiss.

Chapter Fourteen

They were married a month later.

The duke kept Amora close to his side, and the dowager duchess could not hide her smile of approval. Olga predicted this girl would be the one to touch her son's heart and give him the happiness he deserved.

Tossing aside her mourning clothes, she threw her heart into making her son's wedding perfect.

A French seamstress from Bond Street arrived on Monday to measure Amora for her wedding gown. They discussed fabrics and patterns until they decided on a simple dress of Venetian Lace with a figure-hugging bodice and a long full skirt with a small train. The Ravencroft veil and tiara would adorn her head, and she would hold a bouquet of magnolias and white roses. Her wedding slippers would be made of white satin with pale pink rosebuds embroidered around the tops, and the Ravencroft diamonds would glitter from her ears, neck, and fingers.

The king announced he would give them a reception at the palace following the ceremony, and the Ton went crazy with the news. Everyone who was someone would be there.

Musicians would accompany a sumptuous feast of pheasant, duck, and venison. There would be dancing and entertainment for all.

Amora walked around in a daze, unable to believe

her greatest dream had come true. Twisting the priceless diamond ring on her third finger, she strolled out to the garden to get a breath of fresh air.

A knot formed in her belly while she wandered through the flower garden at the townhouse in London, thinking of the past few weeks and the changes in her life. They buried Nathan two days after her and the other girls' rescue. Alexander attended the details of the quiet procession, placing him in the Hargrove family sepulcher on their country estate following a brief prayer by the family priest.

The Earl of Chauncey had been imprisoned in Newgate for human trafficking, and his sources were hunted down and stopped. The Earl of Pembsy languished in debtor's prison for the large amounts he owed various merchants and gentry, unable to keep them satisfied once news of his penniless state reached the rags. His family refused to bail him out or visit but left him to his fate as a lesson in humility.

Picking a rose and holding it to her nose, Amora sniffed the delicate floral scent. She should be overcome with happiness, but a niggling doubt remained in the back of her mind.

The earls mentioned a partner when they spoke to her on the boat.

Wondering if her brother sold her to this un-named partner as well as Chauncey and the duke kept her awake at night. Would he come for her like the last two did?

When she spoke of her concern to Alexander, he tilted her chin up and stared into her eyes. "You have no need to worry. I shall keep you safe, and nothing and no one shall come between us again."

Even as he said the words, a shiver of premonition

tingled over her. She knew without a doubt, something or someone would and worried each morning if today were the day he discovered the truth about her.

But nothing happened.

"My love."

Jerked back to the present by Alexander's deep voice, she turned to him with a smile. "Hello."

"Hello." He caught her to him and plundered her mouth in an openly carnal kiss, thrusting his tongue into her mouth and caressing her back with his large hands.

Caught up in a sea of emotion, she wrapped her arms around his neck and gave into his sensual onslaught, delighting in the security of his embrace.

Desire spread like quicksilver through her body, and she moaned into his mouth, wanting to get closer. "Alexander."

Lifting his head, the duke gazed down at her. "One more long torture-filled night, Amora, and you shall be mine. I have so much to show you, so much to do to you, and so much to teach you. I cannot sleep for thinking of you."

Fluttering filled her belly, and her knees grew weak. All this seemed like a dream. She would never get used to this handsome man taking her in his arms and kissing her senseless, nor the way he said her name as if it were a caress. Blushing over the images his words created, she hid her face in his shoulder.

"This time tomorrow, I shall sweep you into my arms and carry you to my chamber where I shall demonstrate all the ways a man makes love to his woman."

Her face grew hot, and she trembled against him, unable to stand. "I am most curious about this activity. I wonder if I should have a tutor to instruct me beforehand, so you are not displeased with my performance."

A growl rumbled beneath her cheek, and he caught her chin, lifting it to gaze deep into her soul. He knew she jested and returned in kind. "I am the only man or instructor you shall ever need. Already you quiver with eagerness for my possession, and I have given you but one kiss. Tomorrow night, I shall taste all of you, and then we shall see whether you require additional training or nay."

If mating were anything like his lessons on kissing, she would require additional lessons for the rest of her life and told him so.

"And I am eager to give them, my love, always and forever."

Forever sounded so secure and comforting, it warmed her through, and she reveled in the feeling. Hugging the word to her heart, she tucked it away within where it could grow and blossom. Content, she smiled up at him and lifted her face for another kiss.

The wedding day arrived in a burst of glorious color as the sun spread her sparkling rays over the myriad of flowers adorning the townhouse and gardens.

Amora awoke to Mary's gentle touch. "Happy wedding day, my lady. I have a tray of breakfast for ye before we begin yer bath and dress."

Fragrant tea with a splash of cream and freshly baked biscuits accompanied by fresh fruit were placed before her. She ate with relish and allowed Mary to help her undress for her bath.

Fragrant soap made with real cream and rose petals scented her skin and hair, after which the maid lifted a new silk chemise over her head. New silk drawers and a satin garter for her silk stockings came next, followed by the finest satin corset available. Two silk petticoats and a satin underskirt later, Mary tugged the laces on the back of her wedding gown tight. The Venetian lace gown fit her slender form to perfection, she noted as she turned side to side once finished. The small train draped in an elegant cascade to the floor and trailed behind, adding the right amount of style and grace to her silhouette.

Mary dressed her hair in high curls and wove a string of diamonds through them before stepping back to admire her handiwork. "Ye look like a princess, my lady. His grace will not be able to tear his gaze away from ye."

"I feel like royalty in this beautiful gown. My life has the mystical quality of a fairytale. I cannot believe this is real, and in a few hours, I shall marry the duke."

The maid chuckled. "Everything will be real enough when it comes time for the bedding. You mark my words."

Heat rose to her cheeks. "I suppose so."

Mary lifted the heavy Ravencroft veil over her hair and placed the heavy tiara on top. "There. Up ye get, his grace will no doubt be pacing in the cathedral waiting for ye."

Laughing, Amora agreed. Alexander had not wandered more than two feet from her side since the day he rescued her from the ship, except at night when he kissed her soundly and left her under the watchful eye of his men at arms stationed around the house and yard with Dante outside her door.

Picking up her full skirts, she descended the stairs and allowed Dante to escort her to the waiting carriage.

The wedding could not be more perfect. They said their vows and shared a chaste kiss before turning to their audience for congratulations. Twenty-five hundred guests filled the flower-adorned cathedral and surrounding gardens, anxious to offer their good wishes for a long and happy union.

Amora ducked as well-wishers threw rice and shouted greetings. Never in her most fanciful dreams did she imagine she would marry the Duke of Ravencroft in such a lavish ceremony. Glancing up at him, she caught his heated gaze and blushed. "Three more hours," he whispered in her ear, and she stumbled.

With a husky chuckle, he swept her away to the palace for their reception and audience with the king.

Nothing marred her beautiful day or diminished the magic of her new life until she turned in the ballroom at the palace and came face to chest with the gentleman from court with the inch-wide strip of white through his dark hair and a mutual acquaintance. Her heart leaped to her throat and threatened to choke her.

The gentleman by his side bowed. "Your grace, may I present the Duke of Huntington." Turning to the duke, he extended a hand toward Amora. "Your grace. I do not think it necessary to introduce the most breathtaking bride in England, Her Grace, the new Duchess of Ravencroft. Now, if you will excuse me, I must find the beautiful lady who promised me the next dance."

The Duke of Huntington! Lady Sarah's jilted suitor! Amora did not know what to say and bit her lip. This man could prove more dangerous to her existence than being all alone holding a bad hand in a smoky tavern surrounded by strangers in west London. He knew about Madame Pari, and if he shared his knowledge, her life would be over. Glancing up, she met his dark gaze, and his watchful expression gave her pause.

Dipping a curtsey, she rose. "Your grace." Ignoring the shaking in her knees, she swallowed and lifted her chin, refusing to show fear.

The duke's glowering eyes roamed her face. "I would congratulate you, duchess, on your advantageous marriage." Lifting her hand to his thin cold lips, he gazed into her eyes. "I planned to let past bygones remain so until I discovered you are the one behind Lady Sarah Winchester's rejection of my proposal. A lady as beautiful and vulnerable as you should not meddle in other's affairs."

"I know not of what you speak. Lady Sarah eloped with a man of her choosing. I had naught to do with the affair." Glancing around for Alexander, she caught sight of him standing beside the king in conversation and quelled the nervous flutter in her belly.

"I learned from our mutual acquaintance, you encouraged Lady Sarah to deny my suit and turned her against me with your lies. I am not to be made a fool of. Hargrove assured me you ached for my attention, or I would not have touched you the night we joined you in Pudding Lane. Any connection I have with a woman of low moral character has nothing to do with my would-be wife, and I resent your interference."

The heavy silence between them choked her. The glint in his eye told her he spoiled for a fight, so she ignored his insults. "I do not know what you mean. I never discussed that night or any other with Lady Sarah."

Huntington forced a kiss on her when he had to withdraw from the game at the tavern on Pudding Lane, and Nathan laughed. The duke's slobbery lips and thick tongue gagged her, and she dashed for the back door, where she lost her meager dinner on the cobblestones outside. The whole experience disgusted and upset her to the point she shoved the memory to the back of her mind behind a wall of solid ice where it could not escape and forgot it existed. Fresh on her mind now, she tilted her chin up to hide her nervousness.

"Does Lady Sarah know your part in all this, I wonder? Does anyone, including your new husband, know the identity of Madame Pari? I am curious to find the answer because if I were a betting man, I would say they know nothing. Be careful how you choose to play this game, duchess. I am not a man to anger."

Amora stiffened her spine to keep upright. "Whoever told you this story, lied."

Menace rolled off him in waves, tightening her stomach into a painful knot.

"Lord Antony and Lady Sarah love each other and planned their own elopement, and I had nothing to do with her denying anyone. You cannot blame me for something I had no part in." Choosing to ignore the rest of his statements, she lifted her chin and maintained her composure.

"On the contrary, I do blame you. Beware, duchess, for what you do to me, I shall return it to you twenty times over." Turning, the man walked away, leaving her alone, biting her lip with worry and fear.

The lump in her throat grew as she thought of the possibilities the duke could use against her. He spoke of revenge for losing Sarah, but the dark feeling in her belly told her he had other reasons, too. Did Nathan barter her to the Duke of Huntington, as well? Shaking her head to negate her own thoughts, she whispered, "Who has my brother *not* sold or bartered me to?"

Shifting her feet, she considered her options. If she

mentioned the conversation to Alexander, he would dig until he uncovered the truth. If the path of discovery led him to Madame Pari, her life with him would be over. Something she would not survive, and determination stiffened her resolve. The truth of her involvement on Pudding Lane must remain a secret, forever, never to be spoken of again, for Alexander would not deal well with her. After the time and money her husband spent to bring Nathan to justice, how could she face him knowing what he thought of gambling and cards? No, she would keep her secrets close to her chest and not reveal her hand to anyone.

"Are you ready to leave, my darling?" Alexander's deep voice rumbled behind her as he caught her about the waist. "I burn to have you in my bed."

Heat filled her stomach and spread to her face. Glancing side to side to make sure no one overheard his comment, she turned to face him. "I am prepared to go with you on one condition."

One eyebrow rose. "What is this condition?"

Twisting her fingers together, she ignored her quaking knees and trembling body. The Duke of Huntington's threat shook her more than she thought at first. "I will have your word you will love me forever no matter what happens or what anyone tells you."

His eyes darkened as he gazed deep into her soul, stroking her cheek. "I do solemnly swear on everything I hold righteous and dear, I shall love you to the end of time and beyond. My love increases with every breath I draw and every beat of my heart. My hands shall never stop reaching for you to give you comfort and aid, and my eyes shall never stop searching for ways to make you happy and content. All I have or hope to have is yours for all time. You are part of my very being, and I know, as sure as I stand here, I cannot live without you."

Swallowing, she nodded and kissed his cheek. His word meant everything, and she hoped when the truth became known, he would remember his vow and this moment.

Together they bowed before the king and took their leave.

They rode in silence for long minutes before the duke took her hand in his and removed her glove a finger at a time in slow, precise movements. "What could any man or woman tell me about you to cause you to doubt my love and devotion?"

The warmth of his hands and the heat in his eyes made her knees weak, and her breath come fast.

Her glove came off, and he dropped it on the floor of the carriage before lacing his fingers with hers. The skin-to-skin contact made her mouth go dry, and she could think of no easy answer for his question.

"I know nothing except my love for you and the pain I would endure if you stopped loving me. I have no one else. You are my family and my entire world."

He placed her hand in her lap and took her other hand to remove her other glove. "And I am all you will ever need, my darling. No man lives with half a heart, so never worry about such things again. What I have is yours and what you have is mine, entwined together forever."

Her glove joined its twin on the floor as he bent his head to kiss her hand.

Hard warm lips made their way over her knuckles sending shivers of awareness through her. Her quivering increased, as did the fluttering in her belly.

When he turned her hand over and kissed the sensitive skin on her wrist, she gasped, and he glanced up, pinning her to her seat with his searing gaze. "I have waited for days and weeks to be alone with you, and this carriage takes too damn long to get us back to my townhouse."

She understood his frustration, for the feel of his tongue on her wrist sent heat waves through her body and anticipation tripping through her heart. "How far away are we?" She glanced at the little window in the carriage as the duke drew the heavy curtains across it.

"Too far. Come sit beside me."

Rising to her feet, she hesitated, but he caught her around the waist and lifted her onto his lap.

His mouth came down on hers before she could make a sound, even as his hands tugged her close, gripping her against him. Sandalwood, teak, and mahogany surrounded her, along with his heat. She moaned when he thrust his tongue into her mouth and stroked along hers. His hands caressed her back in slow, easy circles before moving around front to cup her breasts through the heavy fabric of her gown.

"You have too many clothes on."

She agreed, tugging his mouth back to hers and wrapping her arms around his neck. He tugged at the laces on the back of her gown until it gave way, and he pushed her bodice down to stare at the tops of her breasts pushed high by her tight corset. The undergarment fell to the floor moments later as he tugged her chemise from her shoulders.

Amora gazed up into his slumberous eyes and trembled. He gazed at her like a starving man seeing food for the first time in weeks. Drugging desire burned in her veins as she stared back at him. He caressed one breast and then the other before moving down to cover her with his mouth. The feel of his heated breath on her bare breast made her go hot all over, and she squirmed against him, moaning. An ache grew between her legs, and moisture dampened her pantalets as he moved to her other breast sending shivers of carnal delight through her.

"Your mouth feels so good, I ache."

With a groan, Alexander laid her back and lifted her skirts to her thighs. Before she could formulate a protest, he rose over her nudging her legs apart with his knees and settling between her thighs. The hard hot length of him pressed into her belly, and the ache in her core grew. Amora closed her eyes as his mouth came down on hers. His hands were everywhere, caressing her breasts, gripping her waist, and cupping her buttocks beneath him. Anticipation beaded on her forehead as his tongue thrust into her mouth, and he rocked his hips against her. God, he felt good. Her breath came fast, and her chest heaved against him as she struggled to get closer. The moisture between her legs grew as his shaft rubbed up and down her quivering belly.

Amora's head thrashed side to side. "I cannot breathe, but I do not want you to stop touching me. I do not know what to do."

He growled low in his throat. "I do." One hand slid up her thigh, sending ripples of heat up the inside of her leg. Amora could not breathe when his fingers slid into the opening of her pantalets and probed the flesh of her womanhood. One long finger slid between her slick folds and rubbed against her sending her arcing against him, screaming with delight.

"Is this what you wanted?"

"Yes, Oh God, yes!" She opened her legs wider and lifted her hips to meet his hand, rubbing her nub against him and shaking with pleasure.

They hit a bump in the road, and his finger slid to her opening. Amora moaned and lifted her hips as he penetrated her and withdrew, once, twice, and then again. Her cry of delight filled the carriage as she rocked her hips in time with his hand.

The carriage turned a corner, slowing down before coming to a stop.

Amora stilled and gulped in huge breaths of air, opening her eyes to gaze up at the duke in concern. "What if someone sees us? My dress is unlaced, and my skirts—"

"Shhh, love." Alexander sat up and helped her right her skirts. Lifting her to a sitting position, he made quick work of her corset and laces. The footman opened the carriage door as he bent to retrieve her gloves.

Thick smoke rolled into the carriage, and the smell of burning wood permeated the air.

"Your grace, someone set your townhouse ablaze! We could not get any closer than Hyde Park." The footman stepped back, pointing into the distance.

"What?" Alexander jumped from the carriage, and Amora followed.

Black pillars of smoke rose from what remained of Ravencroft Townhouse. The servants stood under a tree in the park as the horse-drawn fire truck sprayed water on the remains. Acrid thick smoke filled the air and blocked the sun.

Amora gaped in amazement as flames licked the side of the duke's home. Who could do such a thing?

And on their wedding day, too.

William waved at them and hurried toward them with a note in his hand tied to a brick.

"How did this happen?" the duke asked as he drew near. "Is anyone hurt?"

"When I returned from your ceremony, the back of the house burst into flames. I ran round front to get the servants out and found this." He handed Alexander the note.

Mark how easy it is to get close to you despite your armed guards. Be warned, I intend to have satisfaction and regain what is mine by right.

Chapter Fifteen

Alexander whisked her away to his yacht and set sail for France as soon as he spoke to the police. He gave instructions on where to leave him messages while on honeymoon and hired extra men for protection.

"Who could do such a thing?" Amora sat in the elegant saloon in her wedding gown, now covered in ashes and reeking of smoke. "Could Pembsy or Chauncey hire someone from Newgate to set fire to our house?" A flash of Pembsy's face as she walked away from him on the ship filled her thoughts, and a knot formed in her belly. Both men were furious and threatened her on the boat when they were arrested.

"The note said they wanted satisfaction and planned to regain what is there's. I shall have my investigators look into both men at the prison."

Alexander removed his soiled topcoat and loosened his cravat. "Let us put all talk of this aside. Tonight is our wedding night, and I refuse to allow a madman to ruin our special day with his insolence. I have a bath being drawn for you, after which we will dine and retire for the night. I yearn to hold you in my arms and continue what we started in the carriage."

Heat rose to her cheeks. "A bath sounds like heaven. After all the fuss and the smoke, I could use a tub of warm water."

Her husband helped her to her feet and held her

against his chest. "If there were room for two, I would show you heaven."

Images of their naked bodies joined together in steaming water danced across her mind and she blushed. "Heaven sounds wonderful."

Smiling over her embarrassment, he kissed her neck and drew her across the salon to the master cabin, ushering her through the masculine cabin done in shades of navy and blue to a smaller room beyond. A shiny brass tub mounted to the wooden floor steamed with warm water, and Mary smiled in greeting from her position beside a dressing table and chair, both mounted to the floor.

"You have a special room for bathing?" She gaped at the beautiful cream walls and polished wooden floor covered with a thick wine-colored rug.

"Aye, I refitted this cabin after I bought the ship so I could bathe inside. Do not spend too much time in here or I shall come to fetch you."

She had not forgotten the enticing images his earlier words provoked and assured him; she would make haste.

Half an hour later, Mary wrapped her in a velvet dressing gown and cinched the belt. "The stove in the master chamber has a nice fire going so we can dry yer hair."

Amora opened the communicating door and froze. Alexander stood gazing out the window at the ocean, fresh from his own bath. The last rays of the sun outlined his magnificent form in light, from the top of his wet, slicked-back hair to the bottom of his bare feet. His black trousers accentuated his lean hips, and his flowing white shirt did little to cover his bulging arms and chest.

Turning, he smiled at her and held his hand out.

"Come, watch the sun set with me."

Heat rose high on her face. "I am afraid I am underdressed." She wore the dressing gown and nothing else, unprepared for him to be in the room when she returned.

His gaze roamed her body as a slow smile spread across his face. "I would say you are overdressed."

Amora did not know where to look. Her knees knocked together, and the way he stared made her heart beat faster. Liquid heat filled her belly, and her breath came fast.

Mary's knock saved her. "If ye will sit beside the stove. I will brush yer hair, your grace."

"Hand me the brush. I shall attend your mistress, and you may have the evening off." Alexander strode to her side and drew her arm in his. Leading her to a velvet chair beside the stove, he took the brush from Mary and bolted the door behind her.

Alone, the air crackled with expectancy, and Amora gave a nervous little laugh. "If you will hand me the brush, I shall tend to my own hair."

"And deprive me of the opportunity? Nay, the pleasure is mine."

The fluttering in her belly increased a hundredfold as he neared and ran his hand over her hair.

"Such luxurious black curly locks, they remind me of mink, shiny, thick, and so tempting I want to run my hands through your silky tendrils."

"I would say they are unruly, undesirable, and a test to my soul." She gritted her teeth and waited for the first strokes of the brush.

The movement came as a surprise, gentle and delicate, he ran the brush the length of her hair as if caressing her, and she shivered in response. The scent of musk, teak, and mahogany surrounded her, as did the heat of his body, and she tingled with awareness.

Leaning back as he stroked her hair time and again, she thought of his large warm hands and the gentle way he touched her.

"You smell of roses." His hand dipped into her hair and held a length to his nose, inhaling. "So sweet, so fresh, and so mine."

Her breath caught in her throat when his hands caught her breasts and squeezed before sliding into the opening of her robe to cup them.

"I want you, Amora, under me and around me while I teach you the pleasure I can give you." His thumbs rubbed across her stiffening nipples, and she cried out, leaning back to allow him better access.

Her mouth dried, and her heart beat in her ears as his hand dropped to untie her belt. Her robe gave way, and his hand dropped to caress her quivering belly. Desire raced through her veins like liquid silver, and she moaned. "Alexander."

His mouth dropped to her neck, and he kissed and licked his way to her ear before tugging her lobe into his mouth.

Her breath came fast, and she squirmed as he rolled her nipples between his thumb and forefinger. Her core throbbed with every tug of her nipple, and she shifted in her seat, oblivious to everything but the tug of his fingers and his hot mouth devouring her neck.

Still standing behind her, his hands dropped to her belly and slid to the apex of her thighs.

"Open your legs for me."

They spread of their own accord, and he dipped his

hand between her trembling thighs to the molten lava of her core. Leaning back against the velvet chair, she cried out when his finger slid between the lips of her mound to stroke her. "God, yes! Right there! Oh God!"

Gasping and shaking with anticipation and pleasure, she widened her legs, hooking her knees on the sides of the chair.

His finger penetrated her, and she moaned with delight as he moved in and out of her slick opening.

She rocked her hips against his hand, clutching the arms of the chair in a death grip. "Oh God! Oh God!" Her litany filled the room, along with their labored breathing. Her core quivered and jumped with every stroke of his hand until he inserted two fingers.

Every nerve in her body focused on the fullness within her, and she could not breathe. His fingers worked in and out until the universe spun around, and she panted with anticipation over every thrust of his fingers.

Then, he plucked her from the chair, removed her dressing gown with a flick of his wrist, and carried her to the large bed, throwing the coverlet back before setting her in the middle.

Before she could blink, he slid naked into the bed beside her, rolling on top of her and spreading her thighs with his knee. "Alexander."

His hot, hard shaft pressed against her belly, and she blinked up at him. Large, throbbing, and hard as metal, his member pulsed against her as liquid heat pooled between her legs.

Before she had a chance to speak, he bent his head and tugged her straining nipple into his mouth to suckle. She gave a little cry coming off the bed and spreading her thighs wider in invitation.

179

Groaning, he centered the head of his shaft at the entrance of her slick opening and tugged her other nipple into his mouth.

His hands caressed her arms, belly, and sides, molding her to him and cupping her breast to tug more of her into his mouth.

She thought she would die if he did not touch her again. "Please, Alexander."

He pushed inside her an inch and then another. Delirious with lust, she rocked her hips against him and moaned as he slid in another inch. "I want all of you inside me. Please, Alexander."

Incoherent, her head thrashed side-to-side as he suckled one nipple and then the other, cupping her breast to draw more in as he slid inside her more and more.

When he felt the barrier of her virginity, he caught her mouth with his and stroked her with his tongue while his fingers flicked her nub. He thrust forward in one powerful motion, seating his pulsing member deep inside the slick glove of her sheath. She gripped his shaft, sending convulsions of pleasure through him. He stilled, giving her time to adjust to his invasion, and searched her face for signs of pain. Some women experienced cramping with the tearing of their virginal membrane, and he had no wish to hurt her.

Oblivious to his concern and in no apparent discomfort, Amora rocked against him, moaning and quivering with each thrust.

Alexander rolled onto his back, taking her with him. "Straddle me and ride me as you please."

Dazed, she gazed at him with slumberous, sensual eyes and pushed to a sitting position atop him.

Her eyes widened with the increase of depth his

shaft penetrated her. "Oh my God!" Her belly quivered, and her thighs trembled against his hips. Propping her hands on his chest, she lifted off him and sank back down, screaming with delight. "I never thought, never supposed..."

Tilting her head back, she lifted and lowered her body onto his pulsing shaft while propping her hands on either side of him for leverage. "Balls you feel good."

Higher and higher the excitement grew until she shook in violent spasms above him and around his aching shaft, unable to breathe.

Laughing, he rolled in one quick motion laying her back and rising above her. "My balls are not what is pleasuring you." Wrapping her legs high around his waist, he pumped into her with hard, fast thrusts carrying them both to the peak of orgasm. They came at the same time, crying out as wave after wave of soul-shattering satisfaction washed over them, sending them spinning out of control into a void of blinding gratification.

Trembling, naked, and dripping with sweat and fulfillment, Alexander propped his body up on his elbows and gazed down into her flushed face. A smile teased his lips as he ran a finger down her cheek. "Lesson one."

Breathless and flushed with pleasure, Amora smiled back. "I had no idea a woman could straddle a man while mating. My maids always started their tales with 'There I lay, flat on me back.' "

Alexander chuckled. "After dinner and a little rest, I shall demonstrate other positions we can use to give each other satisfaction."

Amora's lips parted as she recalled his fullness thrusting into her, and heat spiraled in her belly. "I cannot wait." No one told her having a man moving inside her would give her such mind-numbing delight. Stretching, she smiled up at him. "Can we eat? I have worked up an appetite and need food before the next lesson."

"Of course. I cannot have you fainting from lack of sustenance. I have so much to teach you."

Sucking in a shaky breath, she clasped her knees together. She would be an apt pupil, for he made her feel things she never thought possible and trembled in anticipation for more.

Alexander slid from the bed and tossed her discarded robe onto the coverlet beside her.

Lifting the silver domes from the platters of food left on the small table within the cabin, they discovered a selection of breads, cheeses, thin-sliced meats, and fruit. Three bottles of wine chilled in a silver bucket.

Alexander shook his head. "I thought we would have to send dinner back to be reheated. Thank God for a valet who understands the essentials of a honeymoon."

They ate until they could hold no more.

Amora took a sip of her wine, and a drop spilled onto her chin.

Her husband swooped over and caught the drop of wine with his tongue before she could wipe her mouth with her napkin. Awareness tightened the air between them. The heat of his mouth and the closeness of his naked body made her heart trip. She gazed up at him with longing, and he responded by swinging her into his arms and striding toward the bed.

This time he made love to her with gentle, deliberate motions until she clung to him and cried her fulfillment over and over. Perspiration dampened her brow, and passion glowed from her beautiful, flushed face.

He caught her cries of pleasure with his mouth and rocked into her until every ripple of satisfaction evaporated. "Roll to your belly."

Opening her eyes, she complied and waited.

He entered her from behind with one swift thrust, and she cried out. "Alexander!" Gripping the sheets with both hands, she lifted her hips for deeper penetration.

"I have waited for this for so long!" Thrusting hard and fast, he held her still and plunged into her slick folds time and again. Riding the wave of desire and lust, they crested the peak together until it rose over them both and sent them spinning in a world of blinding fulfillment, falling through wave after wave of delight.

When they fell apart, he turned her in his arms and tucked her beneath his chin. "I love you, my darling, and have yearned to make you mine for what seemed an eon of time. You will never know the self-control I had to exercise when I woke to find you in my bed in the middle of the night. First, I thought you were a dream, a fantasy lover, playing with my affections. When I discovered you were real and not the figment of my feverish imagination, I could not resist the sweet temptation of your soft lips and luscious body. Now you are mine, and here in my bed, all I can think about are ways to love you and bring you pleasure."

Amora stretched like a cat in front of the hearth and snuggled into his chest, content in the circle of his arms. "I am ever a willing pupil, but first, I need rest. This…exercise…we participated in has left me weak and breathless. All I want to do right now is sleep." Laughing, she ran her fingers through the dark hair on his chest. "Had I known the joys of sleeping in your bed,

I would not have left no matter what you said. And bugger to anyone who thought aught about it."

Sublime fulfillment dragged at her limbs and senses as the warmth of his body lulled her to sleep with a satisfied smile on her face.

They made love often over the next month and a half as they sailed to France, Spain, Italy, and Greece, sometimes three times a night.

Every magical day of their honeymoon, Amora thanked the gods for bringing Alexander into her life, and though she did not condone the sins of her brother, she thanked him in her heart for catching the duke's attention enough to bring him knocking on their door.

They loved, laughed, and reveled in the glorious enchantment of their love for each other. The sights and luxuries of the world she experienced during the day did little to rival the bliss and excitement of the duke's bed at night. Never had her heart been so full of love and contentment, nor her soul so well fed.

As the last days of their honeymoon slipped away, Amora leaned on the rail of his yacht, gazing out over the aqua waters of the Aegean Sea. From their position in port, crystal blue ocean rolled for miles before her eyes, and she breathed a deep sigh. Tomorrow they would sail for England and all the uncertainty which awaited her.

She did not know Alexander approached until his arms slid around her waist, and he tugged her back into his embrace. "What are you thinking?"

She smiled. "I do not want our time together to end. These past few weeks have been the happiest of my life, and for the first time since my parents' death, I have been loved and safe."

His chin dropped down beside hers, and he kissed the side of her neck, sending tremors of awareness through her. "Nothing shall change when we return home, except the scenery, of course." His chuckle rumbled behind her back, and he hugged her to him.

"You have responsibilities, and there shall be times I will be home alone. Have you heard any word on who burned your lovely home to the ground the day of our wedding?"

Amora knew Alexander had his men investigating the incident, for she stood by as half a dozen missives were passed back and forth through his valet and steward.

He stilled behind her. "Nay. Nothing. But do not worry. I purchased a townhouse closer to Hyde Park with a bigger yard and hired more men. You shall be as safe there as you are here."

She doubted such a thing was possible but said nothing. Leaning back, she rested her head on his broad chest and closed her eyes, committing the security of his embrace and this moment to her memory in case she required them in the future.

Chapter Sixteen

Alexander returned to the deck to think after Amora drifted off to sleep following an energetic and soul-satisfying coupling. Every time he took her in his arms, the experience grew richer and more profound. He never would have imagined it possible to love a woman as much as he loved her, and the feeling grew deeper by the day. Concern for her safety once they returned to England dominated his thoughts. The Earl of Pembsy made mention of a partner and the duke focused on finding the man's identity. In their search, his investigators uncovered a tavern on Pudding Lane where Hargrove and Pembsy spent their evenings. Rumors of a woman gambler circulated among the regular customers, stating she never lost a hand and Hargrove used her to relieve half a dozen younger lords of their wealth.

Alexander flipped open Dante's report.

Thorough and accurate, he wrote every conversation and gave details. When the duke read the report, it was as if he stood in the room as the conversation took place.

The proprietor knew nothing except she came and left with Hargrove. When questioned about her identity, the man shook his head. "Ain't no tellin' She wears black mask across her face, but I will say, she is a fine built woman. The red gown she wears dips low in the front, and when she plays, if stand behind my counter right here, I get a show." The man leaned on the end of his wooden counter and pointed at a round table in the corner. "She's a tiny thing, standing a 'ead shorter than Hargrove with the kind of body a man dreams about. I never seen a woman play cards like she does. Many a young lord came and left his fortune and his heart behind on the table. I cannot say I blame 'em. I would not mind having a go with the lady." He scratched his groin and shifted feet. "Last time she was 'ere it were a month or so ago. She came with Pembsy. They got in a tiff, and she left on her own. I have not seen 'er since."

No other leads. The house is ready for you return.

He would find this woman if he had to turn London upside down to do so. Alexander shook his head, unsure why his investigation of Hargrove omitted his sister and this mysterious woman gambler. Either way, Amora belonged to him now, and he would do everything in his power to make up for her past and secure her future.

Tucking the note back into his pocket, he padded to the master's cabin, latching the door behind him. Stripping his clothes off, he slid between the cool sheets and tugged his naked wife into his arms, lifting the covers over them both.

Sighing with contentment, he kissed the top of her head. No matter what happened, she belonged to him, and he would never let her go. If this mysterious woman had anything to do with the fire or frightening his wife, he would see her in prison for the rest of her life. As a gentleman and a duke, he considered women the weaker sex and vowed to protect them, but as a husband and lover, this one would rot in Newgate. What low-bred woman stooped to play cards and gamble with men? He could not fathom.

****

They returned to England around the first part of August, breezing into port with a brisk tailwind.

The duke's carriage waited at the dock as well as a dozen outriders for security.

Amora raised an eyebrow but said nothing. England meant danger if their unknown assailant roamed free.

The new townhouse proved to be more elegant than the last, and when she commented to Alexander, he squeezed her hand and replied, "I have had workmen refinishing the place while we were gone. Most of the plaster needed to be replaced as well as the floors. The new furniture arrived the day before yesterday, I am told, as well as new gowns for you. I count us fortunate we purchased a trousseau before leaving on our honeymoon, or you should have gone naked. I would not have minded, for we would have stayed in the cabin for the entire honeymoon." His gaze wandered over her, and a lustful smile curved his mouth. "While we are on the subject. Allow me to show you the master chamber."

Laughing, she gave him her arm and allowed him to lead her up the curved staircase to the large, overstuffed bed in the duke's room.

He drew the heavy navy velvet drapes closed and latched the door before turning toward her. "Let us get you out of your traveling gown, so you are more comfortable."

"Of course. While I do the same for you."

Two hours later, they emerged laughing and flushed with satisfaction.

"And now the grand tour." Alexander held his arm toward her and gave a stiff bow.

The rooms smelled of new plaster, paint, and lemon polish. The floors gleamed in the afternoon sunlight, dancing in the large windows overlooking Hyde Park. Fresh cut flowers in crystal vases filled the townhouse with their sweet perfume, and a new pianoforte stood in the freshly painted blue salon in front of the tall paned window.

Amora gave a cry of delight and hurried over to run her fingers over the shiny ivory keys. "How wonderful. Did you buy this for me?"

"I did. I want the love of my life to be happy, and any way I can add to her joy, I will. Your smiles please me."

"You please me, as well." She grinned and sat on the red velvet stool in front of the instrument.

Soon the haunting notes of "A True Lover's Farewell" filled the salon and echoed down the hall. Amora gave her whole attention to the song as her fingers danced over the glistening keys. Somewhere above, her mother must hear the tune and know she found happiness, at last.

When the last notes died away, she sat with her hands in her lap, surprised when a tear splashed onto her hand.

Swiping her eyes, she rose and wandered to the window. Her mother felt farther away and closer at the same time. She wished with all her heart she could have been to her wedding and met the duke. Mama would be shocked someone of the duke's importance would stoop to marry the daughter of an earl but overjoyed for her happiness.

Alexander stood behind her. "What is wrong?"

She sniffed. "I thought of my mother and how much I miss her."

"Ahh." He slid his arms around her waist and kissed

her hair.

Suddenly the heat of the sun through the glass and the weight of his arms on her belly made her nauseous. She just made it outside before she lost her dinner in the shrubs bordering the fence. Leaning over to avoid getting any on her beautiful gown, she heaved until she supposed her stockings would come out of her mouth. Weak and shaky, Amora fumbled in her pocket for a kerchief to wipe her face.

One appeared in the grip of her husband's hand. The last thing she knew, he wiped her face, and everything went black.

When Amora awoke, she lay in the master chamber in her silk night rail.

Alexander stood at the foot of the bed frowning, Mary wrung her hands from her position by the hearth, and an elderly man stood beside her.

He picked up her wrist and consulted a gold watch hanging from his vest by a gold chain.

"What happened?" She glanced at the man and then at her husband. "We were in the blue salon, and I do not remember anything afterward. How did I get here?"

"You swooned, darling. Let the doctor do his assessment."

She nodded and waited as he tucked his watch away and listened to her chest.

After a few questions regarding her general health, he tucked his instruments away in his black bag and studied her face.

"I can find nothing wrong. You are in good health and have an attentive husband. There is no reason this pregnancy should not go to term. Swooning sometimes occurs in the first few months, and nausea is to be expected in the mornings, but neither are signs of any abnormal condition." He turned to the duke. "Women can be victims of their emotions in the early months, so be warned. A sudden burst of tears is not unexpected. Patience is the best advice I can give. I have two of my own, grown now and both married. I do not envy you the next few months. If you have any further concerns, contact my office. I will return in a week to check on you."

Her mouth dropped open. "I am with child?" She stared at the doctor in disbelief before glancing at her husband. "How could this be?" She never considered the prospects of being a mother.

The doctor gave her a long look over the rims of his spectacles. "You understand how babies are created?"

Heat rose to her cheeks. "Aye, of course."

The duke walked round to her other side, facing the doctor. "When shall we expect the babe?"

Good question. Amora placed a hand on her lower belly, marveling at the miracle within her while she waited for the answer.

He did some calculations. "I calculate the little one will arrive in the middle of March. The midwife will be more specific. If you feel sick in the mornings, try a little tea with biscuits and make sure you get your rest." He left the chamber, escorted by Mary, closing the door behind them.

"A babe." She caressed her stomach and smiled up at Alexander.

He placed his hand over hers. "I apologize if I was too rough with you earlier. I did not consider you in a delicate condition and allowed my passion to rule my head."

"Do not apologize. You did not hurt me, and if truth were told, I participated with as much vigor as you. I enjoy what we do together, and there is naught wrong."

He sat on the side of the bed and held her in his arms, kissing her with tenderness. "I love you, my darling. Together we created a life, and together we will bring the babe into the world. Never again will you be alone, for now, you have us both."

Those words would comfort her a great deal in the future though she knew it not but tucked them into the empty space her parents left in her heart. No one could replace a lost loved one, but the promise of a new family and future filled the void in her life.

The next day, a handwritten note appeared by her elbow at breakfast.

Antony and Lady Sarah made it to Gretna Green and were married. They lived in Cumbria and were expecting their first child. When they learned the news, Lady Sarah wrote her mother and informed her of her condition, inviting them to share in their joy. The Duke and Duchess of Winchester paid them a visit a month prior and were reconciled.

Though I am aware I am not what the duke and duchess wanted for their daughter, they were cordial, and for this, I am grateful. Sarah has been quite sick, and I have spent a good deal of time taking care of her. The duchess shared her remedies for morning sickness, and we are doing better than at first. We would both love for you to pay us a visit at your convenience. I, for one, would never have found the nerve to approach Sarah if not for your prodding. I am the happiest man in the world, and I have you to thank. You have my deepest gratitude forever.

Lord Antony

She remembered his words about them both finding their happiness and smiled. They did and with both babies on the way, life took on a golden glow. Thoughts of her wedding and the Duke of Huntington surfaced, and she examined her feelings. No word and no sighting of him made her wonder if he traveled abroad or languished in the country. Either way, he posed no threat. So, she put him out of her mind.

As her pregnancy progressed, so did her peace. With Nathan in the ground, the Earl of Pembsy in debtor's prison, and the Earl of Chauncey locked away, her inhibitions left her one by one.

The days of gambling, smoky taverns, and lewd, boisterous men became a distant memory, a fog in the back of her mind best left alone.

She focused on the pleasure of each day as the child grew inside her belly and the love she shared with Alexander as they anticipated the birth.

She took short walks in Hyde Park after tea with Alexander beside her when the Ton rested in preparation for the evening's entertainment, and they were left alone to their musings.

The air turned crisp, and often, snow kept them from their daily walks, making the time go slower.

When the weather permitted, they strolled twice around the green, discussing politics, the weather, and popular baby names.

Dante stayed ten paces behind as they chatted.

"There are common names to consider, such as Mary, Elizbeth, Margret, Anne, or Francis, but I prefer something more original." Amora held her skirt up as she stepped over a small puddle created when the sun melted ice on the walkway.

"Why do you think the babe is a girl? My heart tells me you carry my son. There are enough John, William, Thomas, Richard, and James's in England. I think we should consider Matthew, Maurice, Nigel, or Maddock."

Gazing up at his handsome face, she grinned. "Hyacinth it is. Such a beautiful name. I cannot wait to hold her in my arms."

The baby kicked, and she chuckled, catching Alexander's hand, and placing it over her stomach. "Our daughter agrees with my choice of name."

He cast her a sidelong gaze. "Maurice signals his displeasure in being thought a daughter when he has such masculine qualities to share."

Glancing up to disagree, Amora caught the glint of metal across the way. It took her a moment or two to realize a man stood on the path facing them, pointing a pistol! She opened her mouth to scream as Alexander caught her to him and dove behind a tree!

The crack of a pistol rent the air, followed by the thud of a bullet hitting the tree in front of them.

"What the hell!" The duke tucked her face into his chest, wrapping both arms tight around her.

Terror gripped her chest, and his reaction made her knees weak. Their tumble to the ground knocked the breath from her. Alexander took the brunt of the fall, and Amora lifted her head from his chest to gaze down at him. "Who is he? Why would he want to shoot us?" Trembling in his arms, she wrapped both arms around him. "What do we do?"

"You stay here while I see who this bastard is and where he hides." His shrill whistle rent the air. "Swear to me you will wait here."

"I promise." She shook with terror as he rolled to his side, setting her against the side of the tree. Rising to his feet, he peeked around the tree and disappeared.

Silence followed his departure, and Amora leaned back, too terrified to breathe.

Heavy footsteps pounded the cobblestones behind her, and Dante appeared.

She explained the situation, and he nodded, withdrawing a pistol from his waistband before leaning around the tree for a better view.

Another shot rang out, and running footsteps crossed the street. A constable appeared, blowing his whistle and shouting for everyone to stay back as the area filled with curious onlookers. The inhabitants of nearby houses flooded into the street and park, all asking questions and voicing their opinions.

Dante helped Amora to her feet. "Let me check the area. If we can escape in the crowd, we will."

Carriages stopped, and horsemen appeared as the Ton commented on the impropriety of such a thing in Hyde Park, giving the two behind the tree the opportunity to leave the area undetected.

Alexander appeared beside them before they took three steps, tucking his wife's arm through his.

Dante dropped behind to protect their backs as they retraced their earlier steps to the townhouse.

Once the door closed behind them, the duke scooped her up in his arms and carried her up to their chamber. Depositing her on their large soft bed, he kissed her. "Ring for Mary. I must speak to the constable about the incident. Promise me you will rest until I return."

"You have my word." She had no need to be anywhere but here and relished the security of their chamber. Shivering with remembered terror when she gazed into the barrel of the gun, she wrapped her arms around her swollen stomach and sang to the child to calm them both down.

Four long hours later, Alexander sat on the feather mattress beside her and took her hand. Amora read the worry on his face.

"We found the area where our assailant waited for us but were unable to find him. Several people gave reports of seeing a man with a pistol running from Hyde Park. From their accounts, we were able to track him to a tavern where the constable placed him under arrest. We questioned the man, and he said a toff gave him a gold coin to shoot the ground in front of us to cause a scare. He never intended to shoot us and took the job to feed his family." Alexander shook his head. "His description of the nobleman who hired him fit more than half my acquaintances. Without a name, I will not know where the next attack will come from." He placed a hand on her protruding belly. "I spent all afternoon thinking of a solution and decided we shall move to my country estate until I find the bastard who hired the gunman. I cannot risk something happening to you or our child, and at my country estate, you shall have the company of my mother and sister."

She digested his comments in silence. The baby kicked, and Amora rubbed the spot as anguish filled her heart. If something happened to her child, she would never be the same again. "All right. I will go." Alexander made a good point. If they did not know the identity of the man who hired their attacker, how would they know if he rubbed elbows with them at the next ball or soirée?

"Nothing matters but the safety of our child, and I can think of no safer place to be."

Chapter Seventeen

Country life agreed with her.

Though the weather grew cold and frosty, she would take small walks in the garden for fresh air. The peacefulness of the familiar paths brought a sense of security, and she escaped there often to be alone with her thoughts. All would be perfect if they knew the man's identity who hired the gunman, but so far, they had no new leads.

Christmas arrived with all the festivities and excitement possible. Amora lounged on a velvet settee, sipping warmed milk and eating roasted nuts as the others opened gifts. And then Alexander carried in the most beautiful hand-carved cradle she ever saw with the Ravencroft crest carved into the head.

"Merry Christmas, my darlings." He kissed her upturned face and set the cradle beside her.

Amora ran her hand over the satin wood and smiled with delight. "Thank you, Alexander." Esme presented her with a hand-stitched baby gown for the christening, and the dowager duchess gave her a luxurious coverlet for the cradle embroidered with both blue and pink against a wine-colored background. "They are beautiful. Thank you."

Amora gazed at her companions as she stroked the intricate design on the coverlet, realizing she had more family and love here at Ravencroft than she had her whole life and prayed her mama could see her here with Alexander and the two women safe, warm, and loved.

The dowager duchess and Alexander's sister, Esme, did all they could to make her welcome and comfortable. The three grew close through the long winter months, but the terror of the attack in Hyde Park never ventured far from her thoughts.

Alexander hired more men to patrol the grounds and house, but no threat appeared.

As her belly grew, so did her nightmares.

First, she dreamed of her life with Nathan and the unpleasant company he kept. Then, she dreamed of Pudding Lane and Nathan's arrest. Alexander would knock on the door and gaze at her with the same coldness he directed at her brother. She woke covered in a fine sheen of terror, trembling like a newborn lamb.

She would not survive the heartache such a situation would produce and poured her heart and soul into their lovemaking when her husband took her in his arms to comfort her. Her mind wandered again to the identity of the man who hired their attacker and wondered if he was connected with Nathan or the two earls. Remembering the time movement in the bushes caught her eye at their London townhouse, she wished she would have demanded the men search the property rather than brushing the incident away as an overactive imagination. A shiver ran down her spine as she relived the moment, and later, tucked in the secure circle of her husband's arms, she spoke of the incident.

"Why did you not alert William or Dante if I were not at home?"

"I wanted to believe no threat existed and chose to ignore the signs. For this, I am sorry."

"How could we know what either earl intended? One would have to think as they do to predict the future, but they are behind bars and shall remain so for a long time. As for the real reason you lie awake at night, I have men searching for the culprit of the shooting in the park." He smoothed her hair as he spoke. "I will find him, but for now, get some rest. The babe requires your strength to grow, and I require your smile to breathe. Neither of us shall get what we desire if you do not get the proper amount of sleep."

Alexander never ventured far after their conversation, and his presence brought peace to her troubled heart.

The new year enveloped them in a blanket of snow and another long month of freezing temperatures. The warmth of the thick stone walls and the constant fires throughout the two-story home kept the chill out as Amora walked the corridors for exercise.

One day, as she sat in the red salon beside the fire doing needlework on a baby cap, the men delivered news of a horseman on the south property.

Fear and panic lit inside her like fire on dry kindling. Her hand trembled as she knotted and snapped her thread. "Are there often riders on Ravencroft?" Her voice wobbled and rose in pitch against her wishes, revealing her agitation.

"Travelers seeking shelter wander into my property from time to time." Alexander gave her a quick smile and rose to his feet. After bending to kiss her cheek, he followed Dante and the guard out the door. "Do not worry. You are safe here."

Shaking with anxiety, she smiled, and he left with the promise of a quick return.

Esme sat on the facing settee, reading a book from the library, and silence filled the room.

Footsteps approached, and Amora glanced up to see the gypsy, Olga, enter the room followed by the dowager duchess.

"There you are, my dear." She sat on one side of Amora and waved the gypsy to the other. "I wondered if you would allow Olga to do a reading."

Thinking the old woman might tell her the reason for her nightmares and distract her from her husband and his search, Amora agreed. Setting her needlework aside, she extended her hand palm up and waited.

Olga took her hand in her leathery one, muttering strange words and swaying for long minutes with her eyes squeezed shut. Stillness followed, and she opened her eyes, staring into Amora's soul. "There are tears of joy and tears of sorrow, freedom, and captivity. You shall have both a full heart and an empty one. The child you carry is a son, and the birth will be traumatic."

Frowning, she held Amora's hand up and followed a line across her palm. "The child will learn to live without you for a time, but—"

Amora snatched her hand away before the old woman could tell her more, her agitation over the intruder getting the best of her tongue. "No! My babe will be strong, healthy, and tall like his father. My heart is full and shall remain so, and any tears I shed shall be for happiness. I shall never let my son out of my sight, nor shall either of us be captive, proving your malediction false. Take her away." Turning away, she swallowed the knot of fear in her throat. "Do not bring the old woman to me again. I have no wish to hear more of her lies." She dismissed the gypsy with a wave of her hand.

But Olga did not budge. "Heed my warning. Evil comes for you, and you must play the hand dealt you. You are very talented when you play, but soon, your heart will be too broken to care which one to discard and which one to keep. The last game you play will reveal all your secrets and give you the answers you desire, but first, you must take a gamble on your heart."

Amora took a quick peek at the other two women's faces and swallowed. Did they catch the gypsy's reference to gambling and cards? "Take her away! I do not wish to hear more!"

The men escorted her from the house, and later at dinner, Alexander informed her he had the gypsy escorted from his property for good. "I cannot have the woman upsetting you with her dark predictions. I do not believe in fortune tellers and magic, for it is my belief we create our own destiny."

He then gave details of their search for the stranger. They found the area where he camped and followed his tracks for two miles until he left Ravencroft land, to the relief of all.

Nothing new occurred for days, and the house, once more, settled down to a regular rhythm.

After the first initial shock of losing the gypsy woman's tea, companionship, and advice, the dowager duchess agreed with her son. Every effort must be made to keep Amora calm while she anticipated the birth of her babe.

As January gave way to February, the midwife, an older lady named Gertrude, came once a week to check on her progress. Her swollen belly kept her from moving as quickly as she would like, and oft times, she sat to catch her breath. As her stomach grew heavy with her unborn baby, so did her thoughts, and her nightmares returned.

Pacing the floor for hours, unable to lie down and rest, she rounded on her husband. "Who do you think hired the man to shoot me?"

Alexander sat his glass on the marble mantel in front of him and turned to study her face. "We believe the man responsible left England right after our attack to evade capture. As far as my men have been able to determine, there is no more threat. You have nothing to fear."

Amora wished with all her heart she believed his words, but something lay heavy as a stone in her chest, and deep down she knew whoever sought her dead waited for another chance.

Then, one night in March, when she rose to relieve her bladder, a sharp pain caught her off guard. Crying out, she caught the end of the bed to steady her trembling body and waited for the agony to subside. Wetness gushed down the inside of her thighs as another pain tore her apart, and her knees buckled.

Her husband caught her before she hit the floor and scooped her off her feet. "What is wrong?"

"I think the baby is coming." Wiping the perspiration from her brow, she gazed up at him. "I am frightened."

"There is no need to be. I will be right here the whole time holding your hand." He sat her on the bed and rang for Mary.

The maid tapped on their chamber door before peeking inside. "Did you call for me?"

"Send for the midwife. Amora's time has come."

"Aye, your grace." She closed the door behind her,

and her shoes clicked along the wooden floor as she walked away.

Pain caught Amora around the middle taking her off guard as she listened to Mary's retreat. Leaning over, she cried out as the fierceness threatened to rip her apart. Sweat beaded on her forehead, and panic tightened her chest. No one prepared her for this torture. Panting against the agony, she swung her feet over the side of the large mattress and rocked back and forth with her arms wrapped tight around her belly.

"What if there is something wrong? Is bearing a babe supposed to hurt this much?" Her blurry eyes stared at Mary as she fought for control.

"Aye, mistress. The midwife can tell ye if something is amiss, but having a babe is the worst."

Amora had to agree. Never had she fought so hard to control her body as she did now.

More than an hour passed as pain after pain tore through her shaking body, and perspiration dampened her dark curls to her head. Too hot, then too cold, she could not hold still but then complained she desired to sit. Another pain would come, and she would lie back down, rolling to her side and hugging her taut belly."

At last, Gertrude arrived and ordered towels boiled and clean linen made ready. She commanded Alexander to leave the room but after the glare they both gave her, she relented.

Servants carried the birthing chair in, and the midwife settled Amora on it.

As her contractions grew stronger and closer together, she refused to make eye contact with anyone and focused on the joints in the wooden floor at her feet to keep panic at bay.

Then everything changed and the midwife bent between her open thighs demanding she push. "I can feel the babe."

Every cell in her body tightened as she bore down with all her strength but still the midwife wanted more.

Hour after faint hour passed until Amora became so overcome with fatigue, she could not lift her own head. Mary, and another housemaid held her upright on the chair while Alexander held her hand and spoke encouraging words in her ear.

With a sigh of regret, Gertrude walked away to the small table holding her bag and withdrew a sharp blade.

"What do you plan to do with the blade?" Alexander rose to his feet and stood between her and the midwife. Anger flashed from his eyes as he folded his arms over his chest.

"Lady Amora grows too weary. We must cut her open and take the babe out, or she will die."

The thin voice drifted across Amora's mind, and alarm filled her chest.

"No!" The word rang out, and she struggled to open her eyes, unsure if she gave voice to her thoughts or if someone else did.

The voice came again. "No, you do not." The gypsy woman, Olga, stood in the door beside the dowager duchess. "My guess is her grace needs to change position."

Gertrude drew her withered body up to her full height of five foot two and glanced up her nose at the gypsy. "What do ye know of birthing? Get out of my chamber."

"If I do, they will both die. The child is not in the correct position. If I turn him, he will come."

The sentence echoed around and around inside Amora's head. She turned to gaze at her husband, too weak to form a sentence but begging for help with her eyes. She sent the gypsy away because she did not care for her or her fortune, and now when her life hung by a hair, the woman returned with the offer of help. Nothing the midwife did changed the situation. If the gypsy knew what to do, she would allow her.

Alexander read her plea and faced the door, inviting the gypsy in. "Come. See what you can do."

Gertrude rounded the birthing chair in a flash. Challenging his decision. "If you let her in, I will leave, and your wife and child will spend an eternity in hell. Do not give them into the hands of this witch."

"She stays." The muscle along his jaw twitched.

The urge to push overcame Amora, and with a groan, she bore down until blackness claimed her.

"Roll to your hands and knees." Olga's gentle voice spoke beside her, and several pairs of hands lifted her, rolling her over onto all fours. Her hands and knees flattened against the polished wooden floor, and Alexander held her up.

"Stay like this, and when the next pain comes, push. I will help you. Do not be frightened."

When the urge came, she cried out, uncertain of what to do next.

Olga checked the progress of the baby's head and said something in a foreign tongue. Sliding her arm inside Amora to her elbow, she turned the baby and commanded her to push.

In shock and bone weary, she gave the last bit of strength she possessed. With a woosh and a cry, the baby slipped into Olga's waiting arms, screaming at the indignity of leaving his warm haven.

"You have a son." The gypsy massaged the infant's tiny chest as his cry filled the silent chamber.

Alexander caught her as she sank to the floor, crying tears of joy. She stared at the tiny black head and smiled, relieved by the lusty power of his cries.

Her husband scooped her up in his arms and sat her against the mountain of pillows on their bed, as the gypsy swaddled their newborn son.

"He will need to sit beside the fire for warmth." She gathered linen and instructed Alexander to put it beneath Amora. "We are not done yet. Go hold your babe while I finish with her grace."

When the old gypsy had the bleeding under control and a fresh night rail buttoned beneath her chin, she gathered soiled linen in her arms and walked toward the door.

"Thank you." Though Amora's voice drifted from her mouth as a whisper, the gypsy understood and nodded in return.

"Ye are welcome, your grace."

"Olga." Alexander's deep voice vibrated through the chamber, along with the cries of the newborn. He rose from his seat beside the fire.

The woman stopped and turned toward the duke. "Yes?"

"You may stay anywhere on Ravencroft land you desire as long as you like."

The two stared at each other for a full minute before the gypsy dipped her head in acknowledgment and left the chamber.

When the door closed, Amora discovered the dowager duchess beside her. She had no idea

Alexander's mother witnessed the birth and did not know what to say to cover her embarrassment.

"We shall call him Gerald Maurice Remington after both his grandfathers. What say you, mother?" He approached the bed and placed the babe in Amora's arms.

The duchess stroked the baby's soft cheek with one finger. "The perfect name for your son and heir. Do not be angry with me, Alex. Olga arrived a few minutes before I showed her to your chamber. She claimed she witnessed the birth of your child in a dream and came to preserve two lives. I believed her story and allowed her inside."

"Thank you, Mother. Without the gypsy's help, I am afraid of what would have happened. Thank the gods they saw fit to send Olga back to us."

Amora would have answered the same were she not sound asleep with her black-haired son held tight against her heart.

Chapter Eighteen

The man stood under a pine tree near Ravencroft's grand country estate and surveyed the happy scene through large paned windows of the red salon. Evening fell, and stars glittered overhead as the man shifted feet. The light of the candlelit chandelier highlighted the smiles on the inhabitants' faces as they gathered close to the hearth. Family, food, wine, and happiness tied together with the golden thread of wealth. Heartwarming scenes made him sick to his stomach. He spat on the ground in annoyance and leaned against the tree trunk.

The old duchess held a tiny infant swaddled in blue and smiled as she rocked back and forth. The duke stood beside the hearth with a glass of whisky in his hand while his sister, the marchioness, did needlework on the facing settee.

The man's gaze swiveled to the infant's mother, and his eyes narrowed. She grew stronger as the days turned to weeks. Tonight, she entered the salon without the duke's aid but sank down onto the satin settee with a pale face. His boss wanted to know when the duchess could walk unaccompanied from room to room. Nearing a month since the infant made his appearance, the boss grew tired of waiting.

Once the toffs had the duchess where they wanted her and made the announcement, he would get paid for all the God-awful time he spent looking in windows from outside in the cold.

A man had to have dreams, and his included a chateau in France with two or three fine-looking whores to keep him busy and a barrel of wine to pass the time in style.

The crunch of boots on snow sent a chill through his thin frame. Time to leave. The duke's men patrolled the grounds around the estate as if it were the palace with the king in residence.

The man picked up a small tree branch which lay on the ground at his feet and swept his tracks away as he retreated to the nearby village. The place he chose to hide had easy access from the nearby property, and with all the trees and wildlife between, he could traverse the area under the duke's nose without being detected. Another week or so, and they could make their move on their graces, the Duke and Duchess of Ravencroft. His boss planned to destroy their happy lives as they destroyed the boss's.

****

Gerald grew like a weed as Amora's strength returned.

They hired a wet nurse from a nearby farm for the boy to suckle while she recovered from the difficult birth.

Weeks melted together in one long dream as she grew more and more in love with her son. Though she could not provide the milk he craved for physical growth, she gave him all the love and security she never had and spent hour after hour cuddling him beside the fire.

As the spring flew by, May arrived with her bounty of new wildflowers, and the days grew longer.

Alexander strolled into the red salon late one

afternoon as she read Gerald a story from one of the leather-bound books taken from their extensive library and poured a glass of port. "I think we should discuss moving back to London for the coming season. What are your thoughts on the subject?"

Amora marked her place in the book and smiled up at him, wondering how she managed to marry the most wonderful man in the world. Most men of noble birth commanded their wives as if they were vassals. Very few asked for their thoughts. "I like it here. Do you think it wise to return to London after what happened last winter?"

"I would not consider such a move if I thought there might be the least bit of danger for you or our son." He spoke the truth, and she nodded her assent. "Then I leave for London in an hour's time. I have a meeting with my private investigators first thing in the morning, and I want to check on the townhouse before I move you back to the city."

"We shall make ready to return whenever you decide." Picking up her book, she glanced up through her lashes. If he left in an hour, he would not be there later to warm her bed. Disappointed, she opened to the appropriate page and lifted her gaze to his. "Did you require anything else? We are at a most exciting part and must continue."

He chuckled and bent to kiss her, sliding his lips over hers and stroking her tongue until her breath came fast between her parted lips. "I require you and will not leave without it. Give the babe to his nurse and come with me. I have one or two things I would like to discuss with you before my departure."

She knew what those things were. He required her

naked in his bed while he plundered her heart and body until she cried out in fulfillment. Her heart sped up, and her palms grew moist. Every time they came together, their lovemaking grew more exciting. No man would ever satisfy her the way this one did. Licking her dry lips and setting the book aside with a trembling hand, she motioned for the footman to leave his post outside the door and come to her.

"Send for Master Gerald's nurse. Please."

When the woman disappeared to the nursery with the baby in her arms, Alexander tucked her arm in his and escorted her to their chamber.

Thank the gods Esme had a dinner party to attend and took the dowager duchess with her, leaving them alone to their own devices, or this interlude would never happen.

Alexander closed the chamber door behind them and caught her to him, tugging at the strings on her gown. She sidestepped and laughed at his expression. "Sit there and let me entertain you."

The midwife commanded they refrain from coupling until the bleeding from Gerald's birth ceased. Six long weeks of no intimate contact made their coming together sweeter and more satisfying. Now, two weeks later, they joined whenever the opportunity arose.

The first time she removed her clothes for her husband following the birth of their son, she cringed. What if he did not admire the fullness of her breasts or the roundness of her hips? Her body changed while carrying the child, and she worried he would not approve of the changes.

When she glanced at him through her lashes to determine his reaction, a knot formed in her stomach.

She need not have worried, for admiration and lust chased across his face like a fox before the hounds.

"My god, you are beautiful. Come closer, and let me love you."

She did, and he worshipped her with his mouth and body, forever dispelling the notion he found her less than at first.

Now, she sought to give him something to think on until he returned to their bed. "Sit there."

Tugging his arm, she led him to the velvet chair before the fire and removed his jacket. His lids dropped over his eyes, shielding his expression as she worked to remove his tunic and breeches, leaving him in his small clothes. His muscular chest gleamed in the afternoon light, and her mouth grew dry. Pushing him into the chair, she trailed her fingertips down the front of his bare chest. "Now, watch."

He did.

Stepping away, she unlaced her gown and turned her back to him, letting the garment slip from her shoulders a bit at a time while swiveling her hips in slow seductive circles. She hummed a familiar tune, keeping time with her hips and swaying back and forth. Her belly fluttered with anticipation.

"What are you doing?" His words dripped with sexual interest.

When the gown pooled at her feet, she hitched her thumbs through the waist of her underskirts and twirled to face him. "Undressing for you."

The hungry expression he wore tightened her belly. He would fill her until she cried out in ecstasy. Liquid heat pooled between her legs as she envisioned the moment. Glancing at him, she bit back a moan.

His heated gaze focused on her breasts, held high by her corset, and dropped to her undulating hips. "You think to drive me mad with lust and have accomplished your design. Come here and straddle me. I will show you what your dancing does to me."

"Not yet. I will give you something to think about while you are in London and not in my bed. Anticipation makes the moment memorable."

His eyes glittered with desire as they roamed her body. "You are all I will ever want. Come, I have anticipated enough."

"Nay." She laughed, removing her skirts one at a time in slow motion, rotating her hips to the right and then to the left, resuming her song. When her skirts lay at her feet, Amira bent from the waist to the floor, gazing at her husband through the space between her thighs with her backside pointed up at the ceiling. He took her from behind often enough to tell her this view would get to him, and it did.

A groan came from his lips, and his knuckles turned white against the arms of the wine-colored velvet chair. "Come here, wife."

"Not yet." Quivering with need, she rose and sauntered to the stool beside the bed. Stepping out of her slippers, she lifted one foot to the stool and turned to gaze at him. Starting from her foot, she ran her fingers up her leg to her garter and stretched it away from her silk stocking.

His gaze never wavered as she rolled the stocking an inch at a time down her leg.

He rose to his feet, but she shook her head, stopping him from taking a step.

"Stay there, or I refrain from undressing." She

anticipated this very moment while carrying their child, planning how to tease him when she no longer grew heavy with his seed. Mating with him grew complicated the larger her belly grew, and she could not wait until she could move about with ease. Now the moment she envisioned arrived, and she would play the part.

Alexander stared at her and sat down with a groan, his dark gaze hot and focused.

Leaning, so he got the top view of her ample cleavage, she unrolled her other silk stocking before tossing it at him.

The garment fell to the floor in front of her. "Somehow, in my mind, when I stripped off the stocking and threw it, it landed farther out." Every part of her yearned for him to burn as she did.

"You have my full attention. What now?" His raspy voice filled the silence between them while his eyes burned with lust. "I have an idea. Come closer."

"Oh, I plan to, but you cannot touch me until I say." Satisfied her teasing drew the reaction she hoped for, she grinned.

"What manner of torture is this? I burn to fill you and carry us both to the pinnacle of sensual delight and soul-shattering satisfaction we find when we join our bodies together. I cannot do so without touching you."

"Not torture. Fantasy. Have you ever wanted to be violated by a woman? I am here to seduce you. Afterward, you can do whatever comes to mind."

His gaze sharpened. "Anything?"

A small sigh escaped her wishful lips. "Anything."

Wearing her corset, chemise, and drawers, she walked in slow, exaggerated movements, swinging her hips in provocation as she approached and circled him, running her hands over his head and shoulders before facing him. Bending, she ran her hand from his face down his warm muscled chest to his thigh before straddling him. "I want you." She whispered the words in his ear as she circled her hips on his rock-hard shaft beneath her.

"God, you make me burn, and I yearn to show you how much. Take your drawers off." He gasped as she rocked back and forth on his lap, brushing her breasts against his chest.

"Nay, not yet."

Catching her to him in an open-mouth kiss, stroking her tongue with his, and clasping her hips in his large hands, he groaned. "I have suffered enough. Let me love you."

"You cannot touch." Sliding from his lap, Amora faced him, placing both hands on his knees.

Lifting one leg, she brushed his crotch before lowering her foot to the ground.

"Amora, let me taste you." His hot gaze rested on her breasts as she brushed them against him.

"Nay." She had a couple more things planned before she gave into the lust pounding through her veins like wildfire. Turning, she lowered her backside onto his lap and rotated her hips against his hard shaft. Her belly jumped at first contact, and her knees shook. Leaning back, she wrapped her arm around his neck and kissed the line of his jaw. The memory of the last time they mated played in her head, and she quivered as she rubbed against him. "I have no more planned and burn for you inside me. You can touch me now."

Before the words left her mouth, his hands tugged the laces of her corset and threw it to the floor.

"It is about damned time." Scooping her up in his arms, he carried her to their feather bed and stripped her of her chemise and drawers. "You tease me beyond my ability to endure." His mouth descended on hers while he tossed the coverlet aside and laid her back against the cool linen of the bed.

She shook with desire, anticipating the moment when he slid into her pulsing sheath, and they became one. "I want you inside me, husband."

With one tug, he dropped his drawers to the floor and joined her on the bed. "You promised to violate me." Rolling to his back, he stacked his hands behind his head and devoured her with his heated gaze. "I am ready for you to carry out your evil plans. Shall I protest and cry out or guide you in the proper manner to ravish another?"

"You can do whatever pleases you most." Rising to her knees, she straddled his hips and gave him a stern look. "But do not cry out, or I will have to gag you. And tell no one what I do, or I will find you and punish you." The ache between her legs grew as she stared down at his swollen shaft and lowered her hips little by little until they both panted with excitement.

Alexander coughed. "I shall tell everyone if you promise to punish me like this often."

Amora could no longer think of anything but the heat of his possession and rode him up and down, moaning with pleasure.

He caught her hips and thrust up every time she came down, sending them both spinning through a world of brilliant carnal delight.

Her orgasm shimmered a breath away as she trembled above him. "Alexander." Her heart beat like a drum, and her breath came fast. Every nerve in her body centered around his thick manhood and the friction created by their combined movement. Grasping his forearms, she moaned, throwing her head back as he lifted his hips into hers.

In one quick movement, he flipped her onto her back and wrapped her legs high around his waist. Thrusting hard and fast, he carried her to the edge of the world and sent her falling over the top into a blinding abyss of earth-shattering delight, crying out as he joined her in the fall.

Wave after wave of satisfaction rolled over them as they lay twisted together in the aftermath of their loving. Their sweat-soaked bodies glistened in the afternoon sun coming in the window, and soon the air around them cooled.

"Must you leave tonight? You will not arrive in London until the wee hours of the morning."

"I thought to be in the city tonight to have a rest before going to my appointment, but you have convinced me to stay here with you and leave early in the morning."

They dined in their chamber and made love once more before falling asleep in each other's arms.

Amora marveled at the love and happiness the duke brought her and drifted off, thinking she was the luckiest woman in the world.

A scream of fear woke her with a start.

She touched the pillow beside her and discovered Alexander gone and his pillow cold. Frowning in alarm, she sat up.

The screaming grew louder as a woman approached down the long corridor.

Slipping from her bed and grabbing her dressing gown, she hurried to the door of her chamber and discovered Gerald's nurse outside the door.

"He is gone! I woke to give him his feeding, and his crib is empty. The window is open, and there is a ladder against the side of the house. Someone stole the babe!"

Terror gripped her in its iron hold as she gaped at the woman. "Dante!"

Her cry echoed down the long corridor as hurried boots thumped along the wooden floor, and then he stood before her. "What is wrong?"

She explained, wrapping her arms tight around her middle in anguish. "We must send a rider to his grace with the news." God, she needed Alexander. Her heart ached with terror and uncertainty. How could this be real? She would walk down the corridor like she did every morning to discover the boy in his nurse's arms smiling.

Dante's voice brought her back to reality. "We found the ladder against the side of the house and tracks leading away a few moments ago. I sent a patrol to follow them and came inside to see what occurred. I hoped for a robbery and not something of this nature. Do not worry, your grace. We will find the babe."

Shaking her head in amazement, she stared at him. "Someone came in the night and took my baby while we slept." Oh God! How could she not know her son needed her? And all the while, she lay in Alexander's arms delighting in the pleasure he gave her.

Dante flushed. "From the look of the tracks, I would guess they took him not long ago after the duke left for London. We would have noticed the ladder on our last patrol. So sometime in between is when the villains struck. I sent a rider after his grace, but I do not know if they will catch him before he arrives in the city."

219

Swiveling to the nurse, she caught the woman's shoulders. "Where were you? You were under orders to stay by his side. How can someone enter my home and take my son without alerting us to their presence?"

The nurse stepped back, flushing a bright red and stammering incoherent sentences.

"She and the stable master have been keeping company in the barn." Dante's lips twisted in disapproval.

"And you knew?" She could not fathom how her baby could be missing. Who could it be after all this time? They had not seen tracks in months.

"I found out about an hour ago, your grace. If I knew she left the babe alone, I would have done something about the situation."

Reality hit her like a galloping carriage. Her whole world collapsed, and she trembled with fear and outrage. "I will get dressed and see these tracks. I want to know who dares to touch my son and when I find them, may God have mercy because I will not."

"Nay. His grace will not like you outside the safety of the house. You should stay here and let us search the grounds."

Her happiness vanished like mist in the sun as she dressed. How could she lie in Alexander's arms safe and secure while some unknown evil planned to take her child? Pressing her lips into a grim line, she threw her cloak over her shoulders and left the house. No way in hell would she stay safe and warm when heaven and the gods alone knew where her babe had been taken and who had him.

Chapter Nineteen

Tracks led from the back of the house to a set of carriage wheels in the dirt.

Time stood still as Amora stared at them. An unknown villain took her son into the equipage which waited here, climbing inside and driving away, shattering her world.

A picture of Gerald's innocent blue eyes and chubby cheeks swam in the tears dripping unheeded down her face. Her heart thudded hard in her chest as if to burst free of her body and go winging away to her child. He must be frightened without her, and whoever took him would die a miserable death if they touched one curly black hair on his small head.

She swallowed the lump in her throat and commanded her mind to think of a plan to get her babe back. Numbness consumed her, and her head may as well be stuffed with wool, for the grief consuming her prevented any thought to form.

Birds sang, and the nip in the breeze chilled Amora's face, as the morning sun warmed the countryside, but nothing permeated the cold icy fear consuming her heart.

"There are tears of joy and tears of sorrow, freedom, and captivity. You shall have both a full heart and an empty one. The child will learn to live without you for a time..." The gypsy's words played in her head

as she stared at the empty cobblestone drive and denial filled her being. This could not be happening. The dowager duchess and Esme appeared beside her, giving bits of encouragement and suggesting she go back to her chamber and lie down.

"The men will find Master Gerald, and Alexander will return as soon as the rider gives him the message." Esme laid a gentle hand on her arm. "I know the grief of a lost son. Come with me, and I will order you refreshment."

Turning, Amora took two steps before the reality of the situation hit her again. How could she sit beside the fire and drink tea as if nothing happened when her child's life might be in danger? Something must be done, for every second, Gerald moved farther away from her. With a cry of despair, she turned and ran away through the trees lining the drive in front of the house. Grief and terror tore at her chest as she circled around and dashed into the trees separating Ravencroft from the neighboring estate. If she ran hard enough and fast enough, maybe she could run away from the horror of her life. Going farther away than she planned, Amora collapsed against a giant pine tree to catch her breath. Black spots danced before her eyes as she struggled to breathe in against the tautness of her corset. And then she saw them. Boot tracks in the trees circled around and came back toward her. Glancing up, she realized the guards were too far away to hear her call, and as she turned the other way to avoid whoever crept upon her, an ugly little man stepped from behind a tree.

"Your grace."

His whiny voice made her squint as something hit her over the head and her world turned black.

****

She awoke to the heat.

Sweat ran down her face and back as she jostled up and down on the rock-hard surface beneath her. The air reverberated with the rumble of carriage wheels on cobblestone. Turning her head, she gazed up. Thin strips of sunlight slanted through the sides of the cramped area where she lay. The smell of leather, horses, and dust told her she rode in the boot of a carriage.

Men's muffled voices spoke behind her from the interior as she wiggled, assessing the binding around her hands and feet. Her jaw ached from the width of fabric stuffed between them and the sides of her mouth were raw from the tightness of the cloth tied behind her head. Amora tucked her chin against her chest to relieve the pressure of her gag.

"Evil comes for you, and you must play the hand dealt you. You are very talented when you play, but soon, your heart will be too broken to care which one to discard and which one to keep..."

Her breath quickened as she considered what the prediction meant and terror dampened her brow. Someone evil took Gerald, and now they abducted her, too. She wondered if the same villain were responsible for both crimes and a flicker of hope filled the emptiness inside her. If they were both taken by the same person, the chances of seeing her babe again were higher then she anticipated since the news of his abduction.

Amora had no doubt, Dante would get word to Alexander, and he would come for her. If she were wrong and Gerald traveled with one villain and she another, Alexander would be forced to choose which to follow first. Their son must be his choice, for she would not accept any other. Survival until he came for her would be the hard part. Groaning under the weight of loss, she closed her eyes and wondered how her happy life turned into this hell so fast. One minute she lay in Alexander's arms, her heart swelling with love and passion, and the next, she lay here desolate, alone, and heartbroken.

The carriage turned left off the cobblestone road, and dust filled the little space around her, making her cough. Amora's senses perked up as she made mental notes for the future. They must be in the country, for the rumble of their carriage wheels were the only ones present.

They traveled for an hour up the dirt road until the rumble of cobblestones once more filled her ears. Her right side ached from bouncing up and down for hours on the hard, flat surface, and she wondered if she would be able to stand when they took her out. Gritting her teeth against the pain, she listened and waited.

The men's voices stopped with the carriage, and quiet filled the boot.

Straining to hear or see anything of their destination, she wiggled her hands against their binding.

Terror tightened around her throat when the carriage rocked back and forth as the passengers alighted.

"Go get the girl." The deep voice came from outside, close to her head, and shivers traveled down her spine as she waited.

Boots approached, and the leather cover lifted, filling the cramped area with bright sunlight. Amora squinted to allow her eyes time to adjust to the sudden brightness before glancing up at her captor.

The thin little man she met under the trees gazed

down at her. " 'ello, your worshipness. Did ye 'ave a nice ride?" A wheezy laugh rasped up his throat and ended in a hacking cough. "Come on out. The boss wants to get a good look at ye."

She narrowed her eyes on the man's face wanting to tell him what she thought of his cowardice in attacking a lone woman and a lady. Realizing the words would be muffled because of the gag in her mouth, she remained silent, glaring at him with all the venom she could muster.

Another pair of boots approached.

Her knees shook as the ugly little man and the newcomer, a blond-haired man wearing a purple and black uniform, caught her arms and dragged her from the boot.

Dizziness hit her, and she dropped her chin. *The man spying on her through the bushes at the townhouse before it burnt wore the same colors!*

Panic tightened her chest, and she took a deep breath to prepare her emotions for the confrontation with the nobleman who commanded this man, for the feeling in her belly told her he waited close by.

The blond man bent, cutting the binding around her feet, before catching her none to gently by the arms and extracting her from her cramped space.

Her knees gave way the second she put weight on them, and the wiry little man caught her other arm before she crumpled to the ground. She hung between the two men sucking in deep breaths of courage and biting her lip as the blood flow returned to her aching limbs.

A walkway of cobblestones lay at her feet. Lifting her head and struggling to stand on her own, she gaped up at a large two-story stone home with acres of green grass and immaculate flower gardens. Long paned windows faced her, and two more men dressed in purple and black uniforms waited on the walkway in front of them.

Amora took a step and then another. Pinpricks of pain shot through her feet, and she stumbled, biting back her moan of pain.

"We ain't carrying ye. Now, walk." The ugly little man jerked her arm.

"Give her a minute." The blond man helped steady her before taking her arm. "You can lean on me if you want."

The ugly man gave a snort. "She ain't worth yer time, Sanders. If ye coddle 'er now, next thing ye know, ye will be bringing 'er ladyship tea and biscuits. Just because she is pretty don't mean she's innocent. Mark my words, if she had a knife, she'd cut the smile off yer face."

The blond man glanced at her and continued holding her steady as she walked, ignoring his companion. "As soon as we get inside, I will cut the cloth in your mouth."

"His grace will kill ye if ye do." The ugly little man's wheezy laugh shot out from behind them as they walked along the cobblestone walkway.

Up three steps and they stood before a large wooden door with an intricate brass knocker.

The other men in uniform opened the door and ushered her inside.

Gray and white marble tile lay at her feet, and cream plaster walls adorned with tapestries and paintings met her gaze. A massive gold chandelier hung from an ornately painted ceiling with gold scroll work.

Sanders stopped and stepped behind her to untie her

gag.

Amora's gaze rose to a life-size painting on the opposite wall, and trepidation gripped her. She knew whose house she stood in even as his voice spoke behind her. *The Duke of Huntington abducted her!*

"Welcome to my home, duchess. I trust you had a pleasant ride?"

Her gag came free, and she dropped her head to work the stiffness from her jaws so she could give voice to the fury pounding through her veins.

Taking a deep breath, she gazed up and met the duke's cold stare. "Your grace." Anger rose high in her throat and her hands fisted at her side. "Where am I, and why have you brought me here? This is intolerable, and when my husband discovers what you have done, he will kill you."

A thin smile touched his lips. "This is my remote country estate. As for why? All will be revealed in time. Come, this way."

Holding out an arm, he raised an eyebrow when she refused to accept his offer.

"Have it your way, but if your weakened knees give way, do not expect me to help you up."

Furious with her lack of stability, she took his arm, holding her body as far away from his as she could as he led her down a long corridor and through the first door on the right.

Leading her to a red velvet settee, he let go of her and stepped back, motioning for the two guards to close the door.

They did and assumed a position in front, making known her position as prisoner.

She would not be intimidated by a man such as the

duke, a villain, a crook, and a scoundrel. Lifting her chin, she stared at him. "I cannot think what you could want with me when you know my husband will tear you apart for what you have done. Your days are numbered once my absence is noted."

The duke clucked his tongue as he strolled to a drink trolley and poured a glass of port. "And if I have what you want most?"

Her eyes narrowed. "Which is?"

A crafty smile played around the corners of his mouth. "Do not tell me you have forgotten the lad so soon. I cannot in all conscience take a babe without his mother. I am not a monster."

"Which remains to be seen as I see no evidence to the contrary." Her gaze never wavered from his.

The corner of his eye twitched at her barb, but he did not comment. Holding up a hand, he snapped his fingers, and dropped his gaze as he moved away from the liquor trolley, swirling the amber liquid in the crystal cut glass.

One of the guards stepped out the door and spoke with an unseen person before returning to resume his position.

Amora's lips twisted in response. "How many men does it take to keep a lady prisoner against her will?" One eyebrow rose in defiance. "If you are to be believed, one duke and two guards plus whoever waits on the other side of the door are required against a woman half your weight. I must be truly terrifying."

The duke stiffened. "They are not for you but your husband. I am not a fool. His expertise with the sword and pistol is well known. I know he will search for you, and this is the reason you are here. How else would I lure him to my trap?"

Lace dripped from the edge of his immaculate jacket sleeve, and the sun pouring through the large window outlined his bulky form resplendent in black jacket and breeches with buckled heels. His deep-set eyes and narrow gaze sent a shiver of revulsion through her. What a horrible, twisted mind the man possessed. Amora resisted the urge to be sick all over the thick Persian rug at her feet.

The human version of a snake before her masquerading as a duke abducted Gerald as well. He better pray the child remained in good health, or there would be hell to pay. She stared at the revolting man and thought of various ways she'd like to hurt him when an infant's cry drifted down the long corridor toward her.

Her heart jumped to her throat and did double time when soft footfalls approached and a knock sounded at the wooden door.

With a cry, she rose to her feet and stumbled forward.

The two guards stopped her, grasping the hilts of their swords.

"Come in." The duke swirled the amber liquid in his glass and waved a hand at the guards.

They sheathed their swords and stepped aside.

The door opened from without, and a small brown-haired woman in a severe black uniform and starched white apron entered, carrying her son in her arms.

"Gerald!" The cry of joy flew from her lips as she lunged for the pair. Snatching the baby from the woman, she hugged him to her heart and wept with joy. He lived! She could not believe the comfort his small body brought her heart as she clasped him against her.

Tears of relief poured from her eyes as she buried

her head in his blankets to breathe in the sweet, innocent scent of her child. For long minutes she clutched him to her, trembling with emotion until the silence of the room deafened her. Glancing up, she noted every eye on her and Gerald.

"Thank you for returning my son. Now, move out of my way before my fury get the best of me. You cannot keep me here." She took a step toward the door, but one of the guards moved in front of her and glowered, fondling the hilt of his sword.

Her predicament took the happiness from her soul. She could not risk her son getting injured or killed in a bid for freedom. Hate and anger filled her soul as she turned to face the duke. "Why have you brought us here? What do you want? You refused to answer the last time I asked, and yet you know Alexander will kill you for this."

A smile twitched the duke's mouth. "Perhaps. But very few know where I am, and even fewer have any idea where my country estate is located. You see, I acquired this property from an eccentric old baron who lost his family to smallpox. No one knows this estate belongs to me except the king and a few locals, so Ravencroft and his men will not think to look for you here. And should you get the inclination to run away, there are three miles of forest to the main road and fewer travelers. Any hope of rescue you may entertain would be futile."

Gulping back her exclamation of dismay, she bent to kiss Gerald's soft cheek. "Once again, you avoid my question."

One eyebrow quirked up. "On why you are my guests? It is quite simple. You owe me, both you and Ravencroft. I purchased you from Hargrove to play cards for me, and Ravencroft swept you out from under me before I could collect my prize just like you did with Lady Sarah."

Amora glared. How many more men did Nathan sell her to? If he were not in the grave already, she would put him there. "What difference does Lady Sarah make? You are wealthy and do not need her dowry. London is full of empty-headed debutantes anxious to wed and willing to put up with your grotesque form and personality for the privilege of being a duchess. One denial does not break a man such as you."

Anger shot from his eyes. "Be careful, duchess. Ravencroft is not here, and you remain my prisoner. I may decide to punish your sharp tongue for the slights you deliver." He took a sip of port. "In answer to your question, I did need a wife, and the situation is urgent. My paramour is with child, and I plan to claim the babe legally. At my age, I cannot risk waiting for some nervous virgin to accept my seed and give me an heir. I must take advantage of the opportunity before me. To make my coming child my heir, I must be wed, and I have no time to pander to the silly whims of some virginal debutante to appease her family until they agree to the marriage. I planned to take Sarah, but you destroyed my chances by encouraging Lord Antony to court her and lying about my character to her. Had we wed when I planned, I would have swept her away to the country, away from the curious gaze of the Ton until the birth of my child. Everyone would assume the babe came early, and no one would be suspicious about the child's mother. But now, such a thing is impossible. My child is due in four months, and I do not have time to follow through with my plan. My chance to make this babe my

231

successor has passed. I warned you the day of your wedding I would take from you what you took from me. You took my one hope to make my child legitimate, Lady Sarah, and I took yours, Master Gerald."

"How do you know his name?" Blackness surrounded her, and she hurried to the settee to sit.

A hollow laugh escaped him. "My men kept you in sight all winter. There is very little I do not know about you."

Amora digested his comments. The man in the bushes at the townhouse, the times the hair on her neck stood on end as she sat in the red salon at their country estate, and times she wandered the gardens and her belly told her someone followed came to mind. How could the duke know so much and escape Alexander's guards? "My husband shall search for me."

"And he will find you, but only when I am ready. Ravencroft must also pay the price. Now, take the child, Miryam. Lady Amora must practice."

An uneasy feeling swirled in her stomach as evil surrounded her like a mist, and she struggled to breathe. They would never take Gerald from her again. In desperation, she stalled for time, hoping a solution would come to mind.

"What am I practicing?" Her gaze swiveled around the room, searching for a means of escape or a weapon.

The brown-haired woman the duke called Miryam, held her hands toward Gerald, but Amora refused to give him up.

"Cards, games of chance, those sorts of things. You see, I plan to have a grand party, and the finale will be you, the Duchess of Ravencroft, playing for your life against the best card players in England. If I were you, I would practice because you will not like what will happen if you lose."

He snapped his fingers, and a butler entered the salon. "Take the duchess to her chamber."

"I will do nothing for you or anyone else unless I am allowed to keep my son." Her chin lifted as she bit the words out, glaring with all the pent-up anxiety and fury pounding inside her.

The duke's frown sent chills down her spine. "Give Miryam the child, or I swear I will kill you both here and now."

One woman against five men. The odds were not in her favor. Terror choked her, and she blinked back tears, furious with her inability to hold the winning hand. "How do I know you will not kill us anyway?" The bitter words spilled out even as she thought them.

"You do not. But, if you submit and do not give me any problems, I will allow you one hour a day with your son. Otherwise, you will not see him again until the night you play the big game against five of the best I can find. Afterward, I will return you both to your husband and your home."

Something in his tone told her he did not think she would win.

"And if I lose?" Her whispered words vibrated between them.

"You lose everything. The pain will be fitting for what you did to me. If I must force the child from your arms, this will be the last time you see him."

Trembling with emotion, she kissed her babe's cheek and handed him to Miryam.

"I will look after him, m'lady. Just do as he says, and no harm will come to ye." The servant took the baby in her arms and snuggled him close before turning toward the door.

Choked with sadness, Amora struggled with her feelings as the woman walked away with a piece of her heart wrapped in a tiny blue blanket. Loneliness and emptiness surrounded her like a bad dream, and she resisted the urge to scream her fury and frustration. Hiding behind her gaming face, she studied her captor with watchful eyes.

The duke nodded his head at the butler hovering nearby. "Daniel will take you to your chamber. I ordered a bath and clothes prepared. Once you are dressed, we will dine, and you shall play cards."

Chapter Twenty

Alexander rode hard all the way from London the second he got Dante's message. How could such a thing be possible? Did not the guards patrol the grounds? How could a man hide beneath the trees, and how could Amora and his child be gone?

He arrived at midnight the following night hungry and furious, demanding the staff meet him in the red salon.

His mother and Esme sat together on a settee, comforting each other while he questioned every member of the household.

Nurse confessed to leaving the babe unattended while she visited the stable master, and he fired her in the same instant. She had one job and failed to do it.

The guards had no excuse for not seeing the tracks of an intruder on the west end of the estate. The land bordered the neighbor along the west property line grew wild with trees, brush, and other native foliage. Animals often made the strip of land their home until they met the neighboring lord's pack of large hunting dogs. Because of them, no threat ever came from the west, and therefore the area remained unpatrolled.

When the men used such logic as an excuse, the duke turned. "Well, danger has come today, and my wife is gone."

"Her grace should not have gone so far from the

house. I thought she ran into the woods to gain privacy and give rein to her emotions. Lady Amora does not cry if others are present, so I gave her a little time to be alone. When she did not return, I realized my mistake." Dante shook his head. "We were so focused on finding the child no one followed her grace when she ran down the drive. I had no idea she would run as far and as fast as she did. I apologize for my negligence, your grace. Anything could happen in those woods."

The duke shook his head. "Tomorrow, as soon as there is light, we will scour the grounds. Hire as many men as you can. We will find out who took my family, and they will pay for their mistake."

A week passed with no new leads and no new information. Alexander grew thin and dark circles formed under his eyes. He paced at night, calling out to Amora with his heart and listening for the strains of A True Lover's Farewell, but nothing responded. She had to know he would come for her and their son. Nothing could keep him from them.

After another week with no appetite and no sleep, the dowager duchess had enough and sent for Olga.

The duke said nothing when she took his hand and traced the line in his palm. "Her grace lives, and so does the boy. They are well but unhappy. The duchess is being held in a place where there are ornate flower gardens and many servants. The dwelling is two-story and made of stone with a long cobblestone drive. She cries out for you, but something holds her to the place where she is. Something...selfish and evil." The gypsy's eyes widened, and she leaned forward, gasping. "This cannot be."

"What do you see?" The news Amora lived lifted a

weight from his chest, and hope surged in his veins. If there were gardens and servants, a man of noble birth held her hostage. His eyes narrowed. The rest of her description matched any number of country estates, his among them. A new thought made him frown. The mysterious partner must have abducted her for some unknown reason, for no other noble would dare touch his duchess. The duke's gaze sharpened on the old gypsy's face. "Tell me."

Olga's blue eyes gazed up at him as she studied his expression. "The duchess is frightened. She dreads each day and lives to free your son from the clutches of her captor. She has one chance of escape but fears her next meeting with…"

He waited for long minutes before asking. "She fears her next meeting with who?"

The gypsy's wrinkled brown hands covered his. "You."

He swallowed the lump in his throat but said nothing while he searched for a reason she would be frightened of him. He could think of nothing and told Olga so.

Shaking her head with regret, she traced another line on his palm. "Your gamble of hearts has begun. You must bide your time and play the game. If you do not, your duchess will suffer. Trust your heart…and hers." Olga let go of his hands and dipped a curtsy before slipping from the room.

Alexander stared out the long paned window as the gypsy's words replayed in his mind. He must bide his time and play the game.

"Your Grace?" William stood at the door. "There is a messenger here from the palace."

Alexander blinked and rose to his feet. "Show him

237

to my study." Nodding at his mother and sister, he strode from the room.

The messenger handed him a scroll bearing the king's seal.

"Your presence is required by His Majesty the king forthwith. The woman gambler known as Madame Pari has been found, and His Majesty requires your counsel as to how to proceed in a delicate situation."

He could not disobey a summons and sent the messenger back with his acquiescence.

Striding from the study, he wondered if going to London was part of his assigned role or if leaving would mean the death of his wife and son. He must find them but could not spare more time to search for them until he answered the king.

"They shall not come to harm while you are in the service of the king. You must have patience and play the game if you are to win." Olga smiled as she passed him on her way out the front door with a cloth filled with food from Cook.

He stopped mid-stride and stared after the gypsy. Her words brought a breath of relief, but he turned away with a troubled heart. Why would Amora be frightened of him?

****

"We have located Madame Pari, and she has an interesting challenge for us. The Duke of Huntington approached me two days ago with a proposal I find exhilarating and very interesting."

"What is this proposal?" Alexander knew of Madame Pari and sought her out on his own, determined to end the predatory card players preying on unsuspecting young lords new to their titles. The Earl of

Hargrove and those like him were responsible for the needless deaths of hundreds of young men drawn to games of chance.

"The duke invited us to a secret location to watch the woman play. If she loses, she must reveal her identity. No one knows who the lady is because she wears a domino mask when she plays. We have been informed this woman is one of the best players in England. We would enjoy witnessing such a spectacle. Imagine a woman outthinking a man." He laughed aloud, wiping tears of mirth from his eyes as he considered the notion. "We want to discover if she cheats or if she is, indeed, the best player in England. Who could guess such a thing possible? And we must admit we are quite intrigued by the prospect. Imagine a woman in Parliament." He laughed for a minute and then stopped. "On the other hand, think of the information we could obtain from unsuspecting dignitaries used to losing their tongues around the fairer sex." The king stroked his beard for a moment as he contemplated the idea. "At any rate, we know you studied cards and games and thought you might enjoy joining us in this endeavor."

Alexander nodded. "I would. When does this game take place?"

"In a fortnight. We are invited to spend the weekend at the duke's country estate. We hear the gardens are fabulous there."

Alexander stiffened, and hope rose in his chest. "Then I shall be delighted to accompany you, Sire."

"We thought you might."

Bowing low, the duke took the steps two at a time on his way out. He would spend the next few days exploring London for clues of the duke's whereabouts.

When the king mentioned the Duke of Huntington's gardens, his heart leaped to his throat.

Olga mentioned gardens, and everyone had one, especially country estates. But for unknown reasons, Huntington's gardens caught his attention. Whatever else happened, he would find Amora if doing so took his last breath.

The first place to poke around at would be a certain tavern on Pudding Lane, but after several nights of drinking stale ale with no new information and no news of Huntington, he crossed the tavern off his list. Wherever Madame Pari played now, Pudding Lane no longer suited her.

The Duke and Duchess of Winchester invited Alexander to dinner the minute they discovered him back in London.

When they learned of his wife's abduction, they were shocked and offered whatever help they could. "Is not this the second time?"

Alexander nodded and related the incident on the ship when Chauncey and Pembsy were arrested.

"I am certain a titled gentleman is responsible for Amora and Gerald's abduction. Both earls spoke of a partner." Alexander picked at the meat on his plate, more concerned with finding his wife and child than eating.

"Alexander, dear boy. Eat something. You will be no help to Amora if you faint for lack of food and sleep when you find her." The duchess laid a gentle hand on his sleeve. "I understand how the emotions of your missing child affect your appetite, for I suffered a great deal when my Sarah eloped, but you must keep your strength up. Her grace needs you to be in top form for her rescue."

"I agree, Ravencroft. No woman admires a man who swoons before she does."

Alexander nodded but knew sleeping would be impossible until he held his family in his arms once more. "What do you know of the Duke of Huntington? He is the man you betrothed Lady Sarah to, I believe."

"He is, and I cannot say I blame the girl for eloping. We assumed he would come at the first of her season and escort her to the various functions as part of his courtship, but he did not. We wondered at his lack of interest, for although we did not have a signed wedding contract, we had a gentleman's agreement." The duke sighed. "Sarah made her views on our arrangement quite clear. If the duke would not pay her court, she would not accept his suit. The chap never showed up until the week before Sarah ran off. He walked into the salon, told Sarah they would be wed in two days' time, and turned to go. No engagement ring, no pretty words, nothing. He never even asked for her hand. He just strolled in as if he had a right. When the duchess commented we could not make wedding preparations in such a hurried fashion, he got upset and made two or three rude comments on my wife's role as a mother."

"What happened?" Mild curiosity made him ask.

"I kicked him out and told him never to come back. When we made the agreement to affiance Sarah to him, he seemed quite keen on the idea. We never anticipated a situation such as the one we experienced. Any man would be lucky to have my daughter as wife, and Huntington is no exception."

"I have reason to believe he may be the partner and the nobleman behind Amora's abduction. Have you ever been to his country estate?"

The Duke of Winchester wrinkled his brow. "The one, yes, but not the other."

Alexander perked up. He noticed Huntington speaking to his wife at their wedding, and although she never told him what they discussed, he knew the talk had not been pleasant. Curious, he had his man keep an eye on Huntington's country estate, but nothing out of the ordinary occurred. "He has two estates?"

"Aye. He owns the Duke of Shelby's estate in Watford. I am told there are the most fantastic gardens there."

His gut told him Amora would be there. And his son.

"Thank you for the information." Alexander's mind ran rampant with possible outcomes as he considered the king's request and who he suspected abducted his family.

"Of course." Then they turned the conversation to Lord Antony, Sarah, and their new granddaughter, Rose. Pride and happiness glowed from both their faces, and Alexander nodded with satisfaction.

Time healed the wounds, and a bond formed with the birth of their granddaughter.

When dinner finally ended, he rode away with renewed hope and purpose. Amora and Gerald were in Watford. He knew it in his gut, and his heart sang with joy. At last, A true Lover's Farewell tripped through his head, and he knew what direction to take.

Once he vanquished this woman gambler and satisfied his king's command; he would rescue Amora and take her home where she belonged. Determination tightened his mouth as he trotted up to his townhouse and dismounted. Tonight, he would visit the club and see what new information he could find.

At White's, two hours later, the game of chance with Madame Pari and the king's interest in the event had everyone's attention. No one spoke of anything else and laughed at the idea a woman could outthink a man. They gave odds of fifty to one against the woman, and Alexander shook his head.

No one could be so good and not cheat on some level.

The more he listened to the talk about this woman, the more he disliked her. From all accounts, one would believe she cheated on the same level as Hargrove. Many young lords claimed to be the victims of her callous disregard, and Alexander joined the tables to hone his skills. If the woman had the same predatory attitude as Hargrove, female or nay, she would go to Newgate.

No week ever passed so slow as the one he endured waiting to accompany the king to Huntington's game. The one redeeming factor he kept close to his chest was the old gypsy woman's words the night he left for London. At least Amora and Gerald were well and being watched after.

As the eventful day arrived, the king announced they would journey to Watford at noon and commanded Alexander to ride with him. Several other influential lords were invited, including the Duke of Winchester.

Alexander packed his bags with care and turned in the door as Dante appeared.

"Your grace, there is something you should know. A man is at the door claiming the Earl of Hargrove faked his death. He is alive."

The duke froze. Olga said Amora feared her next meeting with him, and the only reason she would, had to be connected to Nathan.

"Show him into the study. I will be right there."

****

"Hello, sister. Did you miss me?"

Her blood froze in her veins, and her breath caught in her throat when the deep voice broke the silence of the room. *This could not be! Nathan drowned in the Thames!*

Amora glanced up from her game, and all the blood in her face dropped to her red-heeled slippers. Disbelief flickered through her.

"Surprised to see me? You should not be. I told you I would be back.'

Masking her reaction and studying the cards in her hand, she willed her voice to be steady. "No, I did not miss you, brother. Go away." Her hand trembled. Dropping it to her lap to hide the telling sign of her emotional state, she stared at the king of hearts painted on the card before her.

"Now, do not be so unkind. I should think a few months of believing your brother dead would make you more amenable."

"You thought wrong. I care not where you are or what you do. When the police gave the news you perished, not a tear spilled, and I slept like the dead. I have given you no thought at all and would it remain so." Flipping the card over, she dealt two cards and tucked them under the first.

Nathan approached with a smug smile, undeterred by her indifference. "You should thank me for putting all this together." He waved his arms around at the room.

"All of what?" Her heart pounded loudly in her ears, and her body grew weak with fear. Forcible will and years of masking her reaction kept her from flinching as he approached.

"Well, this. It is no accident I allowed the Duke of Ravencroft to capture me. Nor is it a coincidence you ended up in his lap." He chuckled. "Figuratively and realistically."

Amora discarded two cards and drew two more. "My marriage has nothing to do with you." Tilting her chin, she willed her nervous tremor away. Flipping her two cards over, she revealed the queen and jack of hearts, and a sigh escaped her. She won again.

A satisfied smile curved her brother's thin lips. "Oh, no? If I had not been arrested, you would not have married Ravencroft. Such a powerful man would never look twice at you under normal conditions, and I am the reason he did. No one wanted you as you were, fat, ugly, and dumb."

She forgot how cruel Nathan could be. "And yet you managed to sell and barter to me to four different men, two of them dukes and the other two earls."

"So, you know about all of them. I imagine Ravencroft does, too, the bastard. Well, I made do with what I had under the circumstances."

Amora stilled. "I am not yours to make do with, Nathan. I never was. You cannot sell another living person. Such a thing is immoral and evil." She sucked in a deep calming breath and flexed her shoulders to shake off the anger consuming her. She required a cool temperament to deal with her brother.

"Yet somehow, as you pointed out, I managed to sell you to four men, two of them dukes and the other two earls. And one of the dukes made you his duchess. Although after the big game we have planned, your marriage and title will no longer matter."

A shiver worked down her spine. "What do you

mean? Why will my marriage not matter?" The familiar tingle of fear she experienced when dealing with Nathan compounded in her stomach.

"Now I have your attention. I want what is mine, Amora, and I mean to take it." He stood at her elbow, glaring down at her. "Your protestations mean nothing. I see your fear and note how your hand trembles."

She trembled no more, for white-hot anger ignited inside her. "What is yours, Nathan? You lost everything, even my dowry, and left me with nothing. No one owes you a thing, least of all me." Her voice rang strong in the silence of the room as she glared up at him.

Repercussion came on wings of lightning.

He slapped her so hard that she fell from her chair. "Never speak to me in such a manner again." Catching her by the hair, he lifted her from the floor and drew his other fist back to strike again.

"Hargrove!" A sharp voice called from the door. "I said you could talk to her, not mar her. I want her to be at her best for the game."

"She is impudent and made me mad." Nathan's whiny voice grated on her nerves

"I do not care if she makes you froth at the mouth. Do not strike her again. For our plan to have the maximum effect, she must be unmarked. We cannot afford for anyone to be sympathetic toward her."

Nathan glared at Amora as he stalked past. "Stay out of my way."

"You may count on it, and you stay out of mine." She resisted the urge to trip him as he staked off.

"Now then." The duke turned to Amora when the salon door slammed closed. "Go get changed. We have guests coming for dinner."

She frowned. "When I arrived, you mentioned one game. Is this the game?"

He laughed as he strolled away. "Nay. I said one *important* game. This one is a practice game. Now go."

"So, you lie as easy as Nathan does. Where are your honor and family pride?"

The duke's gaze narrowed on her face. "Do not bait me with barbs. If I strike, you will not waken for days, if ever. Honor is valued between men, not women. Now go, or I shall not allow your visit today."

Biting her lip, she kept her sharp words at bay. She could not refuse while he held her babe hostage, and they both knew it.

Rising to her feet, Amora sailed away with her head high.

Chapter Twenty-One

The gown Huntington provided had a lower neckline than the other, allowing a full view of the valley between her breasts. Figure-hugging and a rich deep red in color, she grimaced at her reflection in the mirror before going down the stairs. Anyone would be forgiven for thinking her a trollop in this gown.

The butler waited for her at the bottom of the stairs. "You are to put this on." He handed her a black domino mask and waited until she tied the strings behind her head. "In here, your grace." Opening the door to the blue salon, he ushered her into the room.

Amora lifted her chin and resisted the urge to fold her arms over her near bare chest as she strolled inside, where a large round table stood.

Her gaze roamed the faces of the men already seated and stopped on Lord Antony's. Tripping in surprise, she froze to calm the frantic beat of her heart and regain her balance.

How the hell did he get mixed up in this? Her hand rose to adjust her mask in a self-conscious gesture. *Dear god, do not let him recognize me!*

Her gaze swung around the table for any more surprises.

Nathan sat on a chair near the hearth and gave her his evil "I got you" grin. So, Antony's presence meant one thing. They knew of her friendship with him and planned to destroy him because of it.

"God, help me." Her gaze met Antony's as she approached, but indifference stared back, not the recognition she feared, and a breath of relief escaped her.

"We need no introductions. Gentlemen meet Madame Pari. She is the best card player in England. Prepare your hearts and your billfolds, for she will take them both."

Everyone laughed but her. Swallowing the tight ache in her throat, she sat and picked up the deck of cards. With one word, Antony would leap to her defense, but in so doing, he would lose his life, for guards stood beside each door, and Nathan withdrew a dagger to show her what would happen if she sought help. Terror and hope both warred inside her the entire game.

Two hours later, one man sat before her shaking his head. "There is no way you could hold four kings unless you cheated."

"I do not cheat, sir." Masking her voice as best she could, her chin came up in challenge.

"I want to pat you to see if there are any cards hidden in your gown." His gaze roamed the tops of her exposed breasts with a lustful expression.

"And where pray tell, would I tuck them away?" The sleeves on her gown were long and skintight, and her bodice just covered the essential part of her bosom. "Any card hidden within would not remain so but would fall out to everyone's view."

The Duke of Huntington laughed. "Go ahead. Search her."

Amora's head swiveled. "Nay. This is not part of the—"

"I will search her." Lord Antony jumped to his feet

and rounded the table before any of the others had a chance to offer. "I am not in the game, so I have no reason to take sides. I will search the lady."

"If he discovers who you are, I will kill him." The duke's whispered words stiffened her spine as he ran a hand over the back of her neck.

"I understand." Staring straight ahead, Amora avoided eye contact and held still as a statue as Antony approached and stopped before her.

Her breath left her body. He would recognize her at this range, and she fought the terror rising in her chest. *Do not say a word, dear friend. Both our lives depend on your actions.* Dropping her gaze as he gripped down each arm and patted her bosom, she blinked back tears of frustration. God, she missed him. To have a friend so close yet so far created a special torture to her soul. She had not been this close to him since the night he eloped with Lady Sarah, and the scent of his cologne warmed her heart. Yearning to whisper her plight in his ear, she caught a glimpse of Nathan taking a step forward with the dagger in one hand.

Trembling with emotion, she prayed Antony would not find anything familiar about her, and if he did, he would say nothing for both their sakes.

"She has nothing. The cards she holds are real, and she has not cheated."

As Antony walked away without a backward glance, she let out a slow breath of relief.

"You may go, Madame Pari. We have no further use for you." The duke tilted his head toward the door, and Amora all but ran to get away. Flying up the stairs, she sped down the corridor dashing the tell-tale wetness from her cheeks as she ran.

In her chamber, she ripped the domino from her face and paced, crying furious tears of frustration. Running her damp hands down the side of her gown, she clasped both arms around her waist and wept. Enraged with Huntington, Nathan, and her own stupidity for getting caught, she tightened her hands to fists and called for Alexander in her heart with every ounce of strength she possessed. Somewhere, he must feel the call of her heart.

Hour after hour of the long, dark night passed as she tossed and turned, too upset to sleep.

The next morning at breakfast, she rounded on the duke the second he strolled into the room. "You said one game. And now you hold my child's life over my head and force me to play at your command. I am not a marionette for your pleasure. Neither is my son." Seething with rage, she shot him a glare of pure hatred.

"Do not be so angry, duchess. The fault lies with you. Had you not angered your brother, he would not have struck you. Because he did, we must wait an extra day or two for the swelling to go down before we play our final hand."

Her gaze narrowed on the duke. "I know he works for you. If you kept him under control, I would not have to. Do not allow him in the same room alone with me again, or I will not play one more game."

The duke did not look up. "I grow weary of your threats, Amora. We both know you will do nothing except what I ask of you."

Fatigue and the hopelessness of her situation made her bite her tongue. She could always slip a cutlery knife into her lap and cut the duke's throat while he slept.

"The servants count the cutlery after every meal, so none go missing."

Amora refused to allow her frustration to show. "For me or for my brother? If he is willing to sell his sister, think what he will do with your things when you are not looking."

Her brother strolled in as she spoke. "If you open your mouth about me again, I will split your lip, and you then will have to play extra games for us for a month." His evil smile sent a shiver down her spine.

"You shall do nothing of the sort. I postponed the game for one week and will not do so again. Both of you will do as you are told or else."

Nathan dropped to his seat with a scowl and tucked into his meal with an angry growl.

Amora rose to her feet and sailed away to the security of her own chamber where she could think.

Five more games were set up and five more times the duke forced her to play, all the while threatening Gerald's life.

When she questioned Huntington about the repetition, he shrugged. "The more you win, the higher the stakes. You will play until I destroy the one man I hate more than any other. All of this," he waved his hands around to encompass the table and empty chairs, "leads me to him. When I have accomplished my goal, then you will have your freedom."

Six weeks to the day of her abduction, the evil duo announced the final game would be played in two days' time, and the king would be in attendance.

****

"God's teeth. If Huntington postpones this game one more time, I shall have him beheaded." The king frowned at Alexander. "I am beginning to think Madame Pari is a figment of his imagination and not real."

"She is real and very good with cards. Some think she counts as she plays to know which card will be dealt next. Others say she cheats. I have an associate who played with her at the duke's estate in Waterford a week ago, and he is impressed with her skill. She beat Travis and Baker."

"Then we shall give our command. There will be no more postponement. Either we play, or he loses the chance to have our royal presence in his home."

When gossip circulated, the king planned to watch Madame Pari play. Obtaining an invitation to the big game became an obsession for many. Everyone whispered about the mysterious woman who beat men at a game of chance.

Friday dawned in brilliant shades of orange, yellow, and red, and none too soon for Alexander.

The Duke of Ravencroft rose before the sun and dressed with care. Six weeks without seeing his beautiful wife and her brilliant smile made his heart ache. He prayed to the gods this day would go according to plan, for he could not live without her, and waiting proved more torture than anything he had known.

Starting with black breeches and a snow-white cravat tied in an impossible knot, he added a gold and black waistcoat with heavy embroidery around the wide cuffs, neck, and hem. Topping off his costume with shiny black boots and a black top hat, he took his black cane with the gold claw on the top from the rack beside the door and drove to the palace.

The king would not rise for another couple of hours, but he could not bear to look at the same walls of his townhouse any longer.

Eating an assortment of small fish, sausage, fruit,

and breads in the dining hall and sipping a hot cup of black coffee, he waited in the dining hall. This day could not go fast enough to please him, for he had many questions and prayed he found the answers before the sun set. After today, Madame Pari would be no more, and he would be reunited with his family. His heart sped up at the thought, and he rose to pace the long corridors and think.

At noon, the royal carriage rolled from the palace toward Watford, surrounded by an entire platoon of soldiers on horseback. Five other carriages followed along behind, filled with the king's servants, clothing, and guests. They made quite a procession as they rolled through the narrow streets of London, and many stopped to view the spectacle. The big day had arrived, and everyone waited with curiosity for the outcome.

As soon as they left the narrow streets and crowds behind, the king leaned back on his velvet seat. "Now, Ravencroft, tell me what you know of Madame Pari. We know you know more than you say, and while we are alone, we would hear the truth."

****

Amora rose and dressed, hurrying with the task so she could hold Gerald for a few minutes before going down to breakfast.

Miryam proved to be quite sympathetic to her cause and allowed Amora into the nursery when she had a few extra minutes. Now, handing the babe to his mother, she smiled. "Yesterday, when he heard your voice, he turned to gaze at you as you opened the door."

Catching the baby close, Amora kissed his downy black curls and stroked his tender cheek. "He is a smart lad and shall grow to be a strong man like his father. I cannot wait to see Alexander's face when he sees how much the baby has grown."

"He will not be seeing his father or anyone else for some time. Why do you disobey my orders?" A deep voice caused her heart to lodge in her throat. She swiveled as the Duke of Huntington strode into the room, followed by a servant.

"See. I told ye she snuck in here when she was not supposed to." The servant pointed a dirty finger at Amora and grinned, revealing her missing teeth and crooked smile.

The duke growled. "Get back to work." His angry gaze swung to Miryam. "I trusted you to do your job, and you betrayed me. I am disappointed in you, and for your disobedience, you shall be locked in the east wing until I determine what is to be done about you."

Snatching the baby from Amora, he handed the child to a soldier. "Take them to the east wing. You know the place, and see she is secured."

Crying out, Amora lunged for the baby, and the duke tripped her, sending her sprawling to the floor in a furious heap. Jumping to her feet, she shoved the duke aside screaming, "Give me my son!"

The duke withdrew a knife from his waistband and gripped her arm hard. "Do not say another word, or I shall slit your throat. You know I will."

Her chin came up and white-hot anger filled her soul. "Do it then. But if you do, how shall you get revenge, I wonder? This plan of yours includes me winning a game, and to do so, I must breathe."

The muscle along his jaw twitched as he took a menacing step toward her. "Make one more mistake today, and I will not slit your throat but the babe's. Do you understand? Do not test me further."

Swallowing, she nodded her head, and he flung her arm from him. "Go to your chamber and stay there until I send for you. You have already cost the nurse her life."

Turning on her heel, she hurried away, thinking if she ran, she could see where to turn for the east wing. If she knew where to go, there might be a chance to rescue Miryam and Gerald.

Soldiers caught up to her in the next corridor and marched her to her chamber, where the housekeeper waited with a look of disgust. "Get in there."

Shoving her through the door, she fell to the floor as the heavy door slammed shut and the key turned in the lock.

Amora stared at the door, fighting back her tears. This could not be the end, not for her and not for her child. Rising, she wandered to the window to gaze out with unseeing eyes. Long minutes passed as she struggled with her tears. Why did Alexander not find her? Six weeks seemed like a lifetime ago with no word and no hope. Leaning against the side of the large panes, her gaze wandered over the acres of gardens, and she sighed. Her arms felt so empty and her heart equally so. Somehow, she must find a way out of this on her own. Alexander may not know where to look, so the burden of her escape lay with her.

Studying the parts of the house she could see from her window, an idea came to her. What if she drew the part she did know? Could she figure out the part she did not and discover where they imprisoned Miryam and Gerald?

Putting her theory to the test, she took a pen and dipped the end in the ink pot. Taking a new paper from the secretary, she drew what she knew and stared at the missing section.

There had to be stairs and a corridor like the west wing, and she drew them in. Now to decide which room held her baby and Miryam...

The lock clicked, and Amora flipped her paper upside down and slid it beneath the top of the writing desk. Turning, she faced the door and took a giant step back toward the window.

The housekeeper entered, followed by the servant who tattled on them. "Here is yer breakfast. I think ye should go hungry for disobeying his grace, but he said ye need yer strength. The duke wants ye to get dressed, so yer maid will be in in a few minutes. Eat yer food while it's hot."

The housemaid set the tray on the small table, grinning at Amora before turning away. The housekeeper waited until the maid walked out before she closed the door, and the key clicked in the lock.

Amora gazed at the tray, and her stomach rumbled. The food smelled delicious. Her usual fare would be hot grits and toast. Today she had sausage, eggs, and tea. Surprised, Amora poured a cup and added sweetener. She took a bite of sausage and eggs, thinking this food resembled the last supper. An uneasy feeling clutched at her chest, for no sooner did the thought cross her mind than the room darkened and spun around. Too late, she realized they added herbs to her food to make her sleepy. Her legs weighed at least twenty stone and were impossible to move. Darkness hovered at the corner of her mind, threatening to envelope her in a black numbing cloud of forgetfulness. Crossing to the bed, she sat and slumped over, oblivious to all else.

When she woke, the sun peeked low in the sky, telling her the morning and afternoon had passed by while she slept. The late afternoon light danced across the wooden floor of her chamber.

Sitting, she rubbed the sleep away and rose to her feet.

"So, yer awake." The housekeeper swung the door open and strolled inside, laughing. "Next time, do as yer told, and we won't have to drug ye with poppy."

Shaking the fog from her head, Amora said nothing.

"His grace wants ye downstairs in an hour. The big game is tonight, and I have to say it will be a real treat not to have to see ye anymore."

Her maid brought in her gown, and men servants carried in a brass tub and steaming hot water.

"Rose scented soap." Her maid held it up with a smile. "His grace bought this in London last time he returned with orders ye were to bathe with it tonight."

Amora frowned. How odd he bought her favorite soap. He did not buy the soap out of kindness, so why? Shrugging when nothing came to mind, she stepped into the steaming water and lay back.

Chapter Twenty-Two

An hour later, Amora stood outside the salon door and waited. Her side ached where she hit the floor, and a large bruise developed, making the simple act of walking most painful. Shrugging away her discomfort, she entered the room when the guards signaled her and came to a dead stop. Anxiety and fear twisted in her belly like a dagger.

Every lord of note except Alexander waited in the salon along with the king!

Glancing down, she swallowed the lump in her throat and strove for a serene expression, but nervousness hit her like a runaway carriage, and all the emotion of the past six weeks welled up inside her. Help lay a cry away, but she would have to reveal her identity to receive any. Teetering between the knowledge of utter desolation such a revelation would create and her need to protect her life, the duke's good name, and her babe, she eyed the men staring at her.

The king would make Huntington give her baby back, but at what price? An intelligent man like the duke would never leave such a thing to chance.

The object of her thoughts stepped to her side, whispering in her ear as he took her arm. "My man waits with the child and the nurse. One wrong word or look, and my housekeeper will give the order to kill them."

She turned her head to the right and met the evil

delight on the housekeeper's face from her position against the door. Swallowing the tightness in her throat, she nodded and allowed the duke to escort her to the king.

Dipping into a deep curtsy, she rose and kissed the royal hand.

"How delightful. You are Madame Pari? We must confess to being curious as to your identity, but Huntington assures me all will be revealed tonight."

Her head whipped around to the spear the duke with a questioning look. "This is not our agreement." She gritted the words between clenched teeth when he shrugged. No one could know her real identity, or Alexander would suffer the consequences. Even the purity of his blood and title would not stop the scandal of marrying Madame Pari while destroying her brother for the same reason.

The tightness in her chest grew, and her resolve vanished. The Duke of Huntington had no plan to act with honor, not for her, not for her son, and not for Alexander. No way would she play another game if he planned to destroy them all in any event. Turning toward the door, she took one step before he stopped her.

"The agreement is, you shall remove your mask and reveal your identity *if you lose*." Turning to the king, he bowed. "This is the arrangement is it not, Sire?"

"Of course, of course."

"Now, my dear, I have a special surprise for you." Taking her by the shoulders, he turned her around as *Alexander* strolled into the salon to stand beside the king!

Her heart thumped so hard she wondered how it stayed in her chest and her knees knocked together. Her entire body shook like a leaf in the wind as she stared.

God, he looked good. Her gaze swept over his dear face and beautiful body as her mouth grew dry. Three giant steps, and she would be in his arms. Those same three steps would also end their son's life. Her heart grew heavy as the weight of her situation settled over her. This night and this game required every skill she possessed both to play and to maintain her composure. One wrong turn of the cards and she lost everything she cared for in life.

"Do you forfeit, Madame Pari?" The king leaned forward. "If you do, take off your mask, and we shall enjoy the wonderful dinner we were told awaits us and go home. I admit being most curious about the manner of woman bold enough to frequent taverns and play cards with men. Are you foreign? You must be, for no decent Englishwoman would lower her standards so far."

The king's comment hit Amora like a lightning bolt. Any Englishwoman worth her salt would do whatever necessary to protect her family. Her chin rose, and determination stiffened her spine. "Nay, I do not forfeit." She would play, win, and take her baby far away. To hell with the lot of them. Nothing, not even her love for her husband, would keep her from protecting her son, whatever the cost.

Serenity settled over her like a warm blanket on a chilly winter's eve. Squaring her shoulders for the ordeal ahead, she strolled over to her seat at the table and lifted her gaze to the king. "Whom do I play?"

"Me." Alexander took a seat directly across from her.

Amora tucked her heart inside a suit of armor and tossed the key into the moat of fortune. She would win for Gerald whatever the ante, whatever the price.

Four other noblemen joined, and every eye in the room bore down on her as they waited for her to begin.

Nathan never ventured into the salon while she played during previous days for fear of being recognized. But tonight, he stood behind the open door, out of Alexander's view, grinning like a child on Christmas morning, his eyes on her husband. The gleam in his expression answered her questions. He came here for one purpose, revenge.

Understanding dawned, and her hand trembled as she counted the coins before her on the table.

Her brother and Huntington planned all of this, from stealing her baby, abducting her, drugging her, and inviting the king to see her play to destroy Alexander and her both. Even the rose soap scenting her skin played a part. They hoped to tease her husband in front of the king as the realization of her identity came to him. An elaborate plan put into motion for some imagined slight with devastating consequences.

Dishonor and disfavor would be her reward if she failed. For no scandal past, present, or future would compete with the Duke of Ravencroft and his pursuit to end gaming while married to the sister of the man who destroyed his nephew. A sister who lowered her standards to gambling in smoky taverns with the wretches of society. The image brought cold sweat to her forehead as she anticipated such a future.

The Duke of Huntington brought her back to the present by slapping a stack of cards onto the table beside her. "Deal."

She always checked the stack before she shuffled to ensure a full deck. Flipping the cards, she counted two missing. Her gaze snapped to the duke, and he gave her an evil smile.

Her heart pounded so loud she assumed everyone could hear. They meant to cheat any way possible, and if she walked away from this ordeal unscathed, it would be because of her wit and a heaping pile of pure luck.

Taking a deep breath, she dealt. Her mind worked the possibilities on which two cards the duke withdrew from the stack to be most detrimental to her game. Both cards must be a higher ranking, or their loss would have little effect on the game. Lifting her gaze, she noted every nuance of the men surrounding her, making a note of their expressions and mannerisms. Both were crucial if she were to gain victory.

These lords were the best in England, and she used every skill she possessed to keep up. Two dropped out, and then Alexander, and she dealt again. The men waited on the side standing around the table in a large circle, whispering and betting against her, but she did not care. Nothing and no one would deter her from her course of action. Her babe's life depended on her keeping her emotions under control and mentally keeping count of the cards.

On the last hand, after the last draw, the unthinkable happened. In her hand, she held the winning combination, but her coins were gone. She counted before the game started and calculated she should have twenty thousand pounds left to play, but somehow, they were not where they should be. Then she remembered the spill. The man to her left spilled his port, and the butler brought in several men servants and a flurry of linen to clean up the mess. An entire stack of coins disappeared with the servants. Her gaze shifted to her left, where the Baron of Weldonshire raised an eyebrow at her regard. Did he play for the duke, or were the servants acting under the duke's orders alone? The salon appeared innocent enough but crawled with human vermin.

Dropping her gaze to her cards, she thought hard as a lump formed in her throat. She never lost before and could not afford to do so now. Perspiration broke out on her forehead as she anticipated defeat. She had nothing to ante up with, and cold, hard, heart-pounding terror covered her in a fine sheen of hysteria. Within minutes Alexander would know her secret and kick her out of his life or imprison her. Her days of being the duchess of his dreams were over, and her heart shattered into a million jagged pieces at the thought. She would never spend another night in his arms as he whispered words of love in her ear. After tonight, Amora doubted she would see him again except through the bars of the prison. Everyone would know of her shame and the dishonor she brought down on him and his good name. Disbelief and the hopelessness of her plight filled her with despair.

Nathan and the duke would go free and unpunished for their crimes while her life ended. The Ton would never forgive her for stepping outside the bounds of normalcy and never forgive her husband because of the scandal such a situation created.

Swallowing the tightness in her throat, she gazed at the Duke of Huntington and met his knowing smile. Glancing toward the door, Nathan's victory grin covered his face, and her body shook. They waited like wolves on the hunt to move in for the kill, anticipating the moment of her demise in their evil little hearts.

She pictured Gerald's tiny face, and her heart cracked with grief. He had only her to fight for him, and she would never concede.

"Soon, your heart will be too broken to care which one to discard and which one to keep. The last game you play will reveal all your secrets and give you the answers you desire, but first, you must take a gamble on your heart."

Fire burned through her, and her chin came up.

Such vile men would not get the best of her nor destroy the man she loved. She would not give them the satisfaction. Closing her eyes, she strove to regain her composure as a plan formed in her head.

"If you cannot even the bet, you lose. Take off your mask, Madame Pari. We will know your identity." The king's voice echoed in the hushed silence of the salon.

"I need a moment to consider my options." Her voice shook despite her command to remain steady.

"Very well. You have one minute." The king folded his hands across his chest and waited.

Hysteria rose in her throat. Alexander stood four feet away, and yet after she revealed her face, they might as well be two million miles away, for he would never want her again. She thought of every possible solution, and her mind settled on the king. He might be persuaded to be lenient and allow her to keep her secret if she could think of something to entice him. What could she offer him? A game with the *dauphin* of France?

"Would Your Majesty be willing to negotiate the terms of my unmasking?"

"Nay Madame, Huntington set the terms, and we agreed. You played well, but we have waited long enough. Remove your mask."

Taking a deep breath of resignation, Amora closed her eyes in defeat and caught the edge of her domino.

At the same moment, the unthinkable happened.

A warm hand closed over hers, and Alexander's cologne filled her senses. She choked at the touch of his hand and his nearness made her giddy with longing. The heat of his body told her he stood beside her and faced the king.

"I give Madame Pari twenty thousand pounds to win. She holds the winning hand and does not lack skill but the funds to continue the play. If Your Highness will allow me to gift this remarkable woman these coins, the game can continue."

The king coughed. "Trust you, Ravencroft, to play knight errant. We had our heart set on finding out who she is, but in all fairness, she deserves to continue. We will allow you to gift her the gold."

Her heart stopped for a full ten seconds, and she wanted to weep with relief. Sucking in a deep breath, she shook the stiffness from her hands and fought to control the emotions surging through her. But what of her two tormentors? Lifting her gaze from her lap, she met the fury in the Duke of Huntington's eyes.

Tilting her head in defiance, she accepted her husband's marker and placed it in the center of the table. Alexander's closeness warmed the chill in her body, and she smiled for the first time in six weeks. "Thank you, your grace."

He nodded and stepped to the side, never taking his gaze from her.

She won the game.

As she laid the winning hand face up on the table for all to see, she glanced toward the door and met Nathan's glare.

The housekeeper stood beside him, frowning like

someone stole her last biscuit, and the band around her chest tightened. She won, and now Huntington could keep his word to release her and Gerald. If either one budged from the door toward the east wing of the house, she would tear them apart.

Her chin came up as she turned to stare at the duke. "As you can see, I have won and demand you honor our agreement."

The duke narrowed his gaze and snapped his fingers toward the door. "Of course. You shall both receive what you deserve."

Everything happened at once.

The gentlemen present rose to their feet, clapping their hands. "Well done. Well done."

"I stood behind her the whole time, and she does not cheat. I do not know how she knows when to pass and when to hold, but she is the best I have ever seen." The men's voices floated around her as she rose to her feet, wondering what the duke's comment meant.

Turning, she froze. Movement out of the corner of her eye made her gaze back at Nathan. With a scowl, he withdrew a pistol from his waistcoat and aimed it at Alexander.

She cried out in alarm and threw her body across the space between them. "Watch out! He has a gun!"

Large arms closed around her as they fell to the floor and rolled together, coming to rest with her quivering body tucked into his chest and both his arms clasping her to his bosom.

The report of a pistol filled the shocked room, sending the men scurrying for safety.

"Seize him! Arrest them both!" The king's roar filled the room, and his guard erupted into a flurry of activity, whisking their liege away to safety. The guards in front cocked their revolvers and took aim at the door while the others tackled the Duke of Huntington to the floor.

Nobility ran in every direction as chaos erupted, followed by the report of a second pistol.

Dazed, Amora stared into her husband's face, relief coursing through her until she remembered. "My babe!" Jumping to her feet, she tore through the side door, past a crumpled Nathan and several guards, before racing up the stairs to the east. She must beat the housekeeper to Gerald, or all would be lost. Frantic with fear, she took the steps two at a time.

"Amora!" The deep voice called behind her, but she did not slow down. The housekeeper outweighed her by several stones and if she ran hard enough, she could catch her before she had a chance to order her son's death.

Alexander caught her as she stepped from the top stair and tugged her into his arms, pinning her heaving body against him. "Dante has our son and the nurse. Their rescue is the reason I came late to the game. I told Huntington I went to retrieve something for the king and found where they were being held. The servants were more than willing to point out the right direction to take with the right persuasion." He lifted the corner of his jacket to reveal a revolver tucked inside his breeches. "The king commanded I accompany him armed. Do not worry, my darling. Gerald is well, but we must get you to safety so I can return to help the king."

"This way!" a deep voice called from the bottom of the staircase.

Amora glanced down to see the Duke of Winchester

standing beside the railing at the bottom of the stairs. His powdered wig tipped sideways on his gray head, and fury shot from his eyes. "No man brandishes a weapon in the king's presence, and if your brother is not dead, he soon will be. How dare Huntington endanger our king! The fool should be hung!" He waved a hand at Amora, beckoning her to come to him. "Come along, my dear. I have a carriage ready."

When she stared and moved not a limb in his direction, he turned to Alexander.

"Bring her to me, Ravencroft, the girl has been through too much to understand the danger she is in. I will see she gets to safety while you deal with the bastards responsible."

Confused, and shocked by this sudden turn of events, she gaped at the older man. "You know?" She could not believe her eyes and ears as her husband scooped her into his arms and raced down the stairs to deposit her outside in the Duke of Winchester's carriage. The heat of his body and the strength of his arms around her brought a lump to her throat. She thought she would never be this close to him again, "And you love me still?" Forcing the question past the lump, she stared up at him in wonder. Though her words were a bare whisper past the dryness of her throat, he heard.

"Yes, my love. Go with the duke while I tend to the king. Dante will bring the babe to the crossroads. He left with Gerald and his nurse before you dealt the first round. My soldiers accompany them. I will see you back in London so do not fear. Winchester's soldiers travel with him so you will be quite safe. Now, go!"

"Wait!" Her heart ached to be with him, but first, she must get to Gerald and ensure with her own eyes he lived.

Alexander turned, and she blew him a kiss. "Thank you!" He would never know the terror she endured the last few weeks, but his timely interception saved both her and their son.

"We will discuss this later." With a grin, he shut the door after the Duke of Winchester, and they were off.

Five whole minutes passed as she digested the current events. Shaking her head, she asked the question burning in her mind. "Where is my babe?" Leaning forward to gaze out the little window, anxious for the sight of her son, she allowed the breeze to cool her heated cheeks. God, how she ached to hold her son close so she could believe the terror had ended. Glancing behind the racing carriage every few minutes for fear the Duke of Huntington's men followed, she fought to convince her suspicious heart her ordeal had ended.

"You can take off the mask, Lady Amora. Alexander's outrider will meet us on the main road with your son. Settle back, your grace. We have this in hand." The Duke of Winchester's quiet voice penetrated the haze of fear clouding her thoughts.

Taking a deep breath, she tugged off her mask. "Does everyone know?" She gazed at the duke as she thought of the duchess, Antony, and Sarah.

"Nay. Only a select few are privy to this sensitive information. I am sure after the way you flirted with your husband out there, more will figure you out."

Red filled her face. "I cannot help how I feel. I have missed you all more than I can say."

Alexander knew her secret and loved her still. Awe and wonder danced inside her chest causing her heart to peek out in surprise, struggling to grasp her nightmare had ended.

The drive toward the main road took forever, and when she thought for sure they missed a turn, the carriage stopped.

Dante's face appeared in the window a few long minutes later. "It is good to see you, your grace. I imagine you will be wanting this little lad." Opening the door, he handed her a blue bundle.

Profound relief and happiness filled her bosom as she took her son in her arms. "Where is Miryam, his nurse?" Amora clutched the warm, wiggling bundle to her chest, burying her face in his sweet warmth and covering his chubby little face with tender kisses.

"Here, your grace." Her head appeared beside Dante's. "We are well. Although I cannot say as much for the chamber they put us in. Ye should have seen the mess the Duke of Ravencroft made when he kicked the door open and rescued us. He took the babe from my arms as if he were the most precious thing he ever touched and escorted us out of the house as if we were royalty. The servants stood to the side and said not a word. No one dared touch us or stop us."

Tears pricked Amora's eyes. "I am so happy you are all right, and thank you for protecting my son. I owe you my deepest gratitude for making an intolerable situation bearable. If you have need of anything, you have but to ask."

"We must leave, your grace. Do not worry for Miss Conrad. She will ride back with me. See you back at the townhouse. The duke has fifty outriders with you, so I will escort the nurse home."

Amora nodded, too caught up in the joy of holding her babe to notice the blush highlighting the nurse's cheeks as she stepped back beside the outrider so the carriage could pass.

Chapter Twenty-Three

Midnight brought the thump of boots on the wooden floor outside her chamber that she'd waited all night to hear. With a cry of joy, she flung the door wide and threw her body against his. "Alexander. I have missed you."

"And I, you, my love." He crushed her against his chest as he kicked the door shut and caught her to him. "We have much to talk over, but first, I need to hold you close."

She could not agree more and led him to their bed, where their clothes fell off in a heap on the floor.

His lips, hands, and tongue worshipped her body, and she worshipped his until they both panted with the need to meld together. Nudging her thighs apart, he entered her slick opening with one powerful thrust, and they both moaned with pure delight.

"God, how I have missed you." His deep voice heated the side of her neck as he plunged into her softness and withdrew time and again.

Wrapping her legs high around his waist, she held him in her tight embrace, crying out as he rocked against her in a rhythm as old as time. She would never get enough of his loving.

"And I, you. I cannot believe I am here with you, and you know. I love you more than you know." Her breath came fast as she rode the waves of ecstasy he created. His fullness sent her to a place only he could, and she cried with delight over every thrust of his body.

"God, you feel good." She wrapped her legs tighter around his waist and clung to him as he took her higher and higher into the blinding storm of passion and lust.

The friction between them grew brighter and more intense with each thrust of his hips. Amora's cries of delight turned to moans of pleasure as she rode the wave of rapture and satisfaction until it sent her over the edge into the sensual sea of fulfillment and sexual gratification.

Once she fell over the edge, he caught her hips and thrust hard and deep until his own climax sent him spinning out of control into the same sensual sea.

They lay twisted up, gasping for breath, as the last waves of pleasure ebbed away. Their sweat-soaked bodies gleamed in the glowing embers of the fire, and Amora shivered when the night air cooled her heated flesh.

"I missed you." His deep voice whispered in her ear.

"I missed you more." She flashed him a grin and kissed his cheek. "I want you to know I never played of my own will or choice. Huntington forced my obedience by threatening the life of our son."

"I am aware, and I want to throttle the coward with my bare hands."

Snuggling against him, she sighed. "Tell me how you knew about my...skill with cards."

Her husband's deep voice vibrated beneath her ear as he spoke. "Not long after you came to stay, we spoke following Chauncey's attempted abduction at the opera. A stack of cards lay on a side table, and you picked them up. You were quite upset and shuffled the cards several times before setting them down. I recognize an expert when I see one. I practiced for weeks to shuffle the way you did, and your skill surprised me. Not long after, as we spoke in the conservatory, you shuffled note cards taken from the flowers of your many admirers, as well. I puzzled over your ease and skill until Dante followed you to Pudding Lane one night and reported back to me. Why did you not come to me when Pembsy threatened you?"

"I remembered the way you stared at Nathan the night we met, and I could not abide a similar look. So, I kept his threats a secret." She thought on the situation. "Dante followed me to Pudding Lane? I remember the carriage tilting as if a footman stepped on and off. Now it makes sense. So, you knew about my other identity for ages?"

"Nay. You spoke of playing one game before Pembsy appeared, and Dante took refuge farther up the street, keeping the tavern door in sight. We knew Pembsy forced you to play but I did not realize Madame Pari and my beautiful wife were one and the same until one evening at White's. One of the men mentioned Madame Pari boasted luscious mink-black hair, and everything fell into place in my mind. No one knew much about your appearance until then."

"I kept my hood on to conceal whatever part of my face my mask did not. Nathan forced me to play, and Pembsy wanted revenge. Please understand, I never meant to deceive you or Dante. But you see, I had nightmares you would send me way if you knew about my knack for games. My skill is the one thing I hoped you would never discover about me."

"I could never send you away, my darling. I dislike Nathan for what he did to my nephew and others, not the use of cards."

She told him about Papa and the way he taught her to play.

Then she thought of her brother. "What happened to Nathan? I did not ask when you came in. Is he wounded? I remember stepping over him on the floor when I ran to rescue Gerald."

"He is dead. The king's soldiers shot him seconds after he fired at us. The second gunshot came from them. No one is allowed to hold a weapon in the king's presence, and this time there is no trick. Both the king and I were aware before we arrived of Huntington's evil plan and Nathan's presence. Your nervousness and continual monitoring of the corridor gave your brother's position away, making his downfall imminent."

"And Huntington?" A shiver shimmied down her spine as she said his name. If she never met him again for all eternity, it would be too soon.

"He is locked in a cell at Newgate awaiting trial for his crimes. He will not be free for some time, if ever. No one puts the king's life in danger and walks away. During his confession, I learned he is responsible for hiring the man who climbed to your window in the night. He wanted to abduct you then, but his man found your room empty. Afterward, when I hired extra men, he could not get close. In frustration, he set fire to our townhouse to frighten us and had a full year to think up the perfect plan for revenge on us both. Me for taking you, and you for taking Lady Sarah, coupled with Nathan's thirst for vengeance. He found the perfect partner in your brother."

"Did he send the man to shoot at us in the park?"

"Aye. The odds were, I would take you to my

country estate for safety, and there he could abduct you without all the extra eyes of the neighbors. He knew of the wild area between the estates and the movement of my guard. Dante and I have gone over the situation and come up with a new system. I am quite amazed at the amount of effort Huntington put into his plan. He and Nathan must have planned it since your brother's escape."

Amora sighed. "So much hatred for something he assumed happened. Antony would have gotten nowhere in his pursuit of Sarah if she did not wish to get caught."

"And what of you? Did you wish to be caught?" He nuzzled the side of her neck as his hands wandered her body.

"By you and no one else. Too many think they own me."

Gerald fussed from his cradle beside her bed, and she moved to the edge to gaze down at him. She ordered the babe's cradle carried to her chamber before retiring, preferring to keep the child close. Never again would she trust another to look after him the way she would.

"I would say there is another who makes a good argument about owning you."

"Gerald. Yes, he does, and I do not mind in the least. Lean close and see how he smiles in his sleep when his papa speaks. He missed you and cannot wait until morning to see his papa again."

"Gerald's papa cannot wait either and missed him and his beautiful mother more than she knows."

A new thought crossed her mind. "Did you send Antony to Watford to play against me?" She thought of the way he avoided eye contact and smiled.

"Aye. I sent him because I could not come, and I had

to know if you were alive and well. Though Olga assured me you were, I wanted proof."

"They thought I cheated, and Antony offered to search me for extra cards. He never let on he knew me."

"He could not, or they would know I knew. None of us could anticipate what they would do next, and we had to keep you as safe as we could."

Tears filled her eyes. "If I had known, my plight would not have been so grievous to bear. You will never know the torture I endured as I anticipated your and the king's response when I removed my mask. I thought my life was over, and then you touched my hand and kept me in the game. I came close to swooning for the first time in my life. If I were not so deeply in love with you, I would be all over again for your kindness for this one act alone. Thank you for sparing me the embarrassment of revealing my identity before the king and for coming to my rescue. Who needs a white knight brandishing his shiny sword when I have you?"

A chuckle rumbled beneath her ear. "Who needs a white knight when you have me brandishing my…" Turning her in his arms, he kissed her soundly.

"Will the news the king knows who you are distress you? When I made my report on Huntington before coming home, His Majesty suggested a private game with you as his secret weapon when the dauphin arrived next month. He is fascinated with the idea of a woman on his counsel and suggested I speak with you on the subject. What say you?"

"I shall think the matter over. In the meantime, what are your plans to convince me?" They clung together, touching and caressing until a tiny cry broke the silence.

Alexander lifted his head when the baby fussed

again. Smiling, he slid from beneath the covers and padded over to lift the child in his arms before returning to her side and cuddling their son between them.

"You never finished your sentence. What do you brandish?" Her heart filled with joy as she gazed upon the two most important people in her world.

Love shone from his eyes as he stroked her cheek and then the baby's. "I brandish the love of a faithful heart which beats only for you, combined with the promise of a loving husband and father to fulfill all the expectations, fantasies, and delights you can dream. All I have is yours, now and forever, my darling. I never thought I would find a woman as perfect as you, and I could not believe what my search for Hargrove delivered. I thank the gods I found you, despite the circumstances. I gambled with my heart today in Watford and won, as Olga predicted. How can I explain the terror and pain I endured during the time we were apart? You two were all I could think about. Never again will I allow either of you from my sight."

Amora gazed at her sleeping son with his downy black curls and chubby face resting on her husband's arm and sighed with contentment, for she realized, once again, she held the winning hand. Beside her lay the king and jack of her heart, and together they created the perfect hand to play the game of life with. Glancing up, she smiled. If Mama gazed from the heavens tonight, she would know she had not been accurate about gambling.

Gaming may be a trick of the devil designed to lead men astray unless it involved the Duke of Ravencroft, and then it was heaven sent. For he burst into her life in the middle of the night, providing an unexpected deliverance like an ace in the last draw or the coveted number on the last shake of the dice. But then, Amora had always been good with cards and games of chance. Papa called her a natural.

A word about the author…

I enjoy knitting, crocheting, and quilting. I love roses and the smell of gardenias. I have two large dogs who like to keep me company while I write. Beethoven is an Aussie/ Great Pyrenees mix and Mozart is a Mastiff/Collie mix.

I occasionally bake when the mood strikes me. Mostly I consider cooking and baking necessary evils.

My husband of forty years is my greatest fan/critic and I don't know what I would do without him. My family is my greatest support and I love every minute I spend with them. Life is a journey and I can't wait to see where it leads me next!